"I'll do everything in my power," Nicholas whispered, "to be the man you've always dreamed of."

You already are, Angela thought in panic. Through her heavy veil, his eyes looked as mesmerizing as they were violet...his hair whiter blond and silkier than any she'd ever seen.

In a slow, fluid movement, Nicholas lifted the veil.

She gulped.

He stared.

His bride—whoever she was—wasn't Sylvia Sinclair! The mystery spouse had dangerously dark, midnight eyes, not blue ones, and her hair curled in sensuous tendrils. Her lips, though small, were full and passionate looking. Rosebud lips.

"I'm not—" she began.

"Nearly as happy about this as I am," Nicholas finished casually. Then he bent her in a swift clinch and kissed her.

ABOUT THE AUTHOR

Coastal England has always captured Jule McBride's romantic fancy—from childhood stories where ladies trapped in turreted towers were rescued by Prince Charmings, to the magic of real-life royal weddings. So, in 1983, while waitressing in her hometown of Charleston, West Virginia, Jule saved for a vacation to England, intending to indulge those long-ago, fairy-tale fantasies in which an English nobleman swept her away. Because Jule never forgot that vacation, or her fantasy nobleman, she leapt at the chance to write about both him and the very regular woman who becomes that very special lady in her contemporary knight's romantic realm, in *The Wrong Wife?*

Books by Jule McBride

HARLEQUIN AMERICAN ROMANCE
500—WILD CARD WEDDING
519—BABY TRAP

Don't miss any of our special offers. Write to us at the following address for information on our newest releases.

Harlequin Reader Service
U.S.: 3010 Walden Ave., P.O. Box 1325, Buffalo, NY 14269
Canadian: P.O. Box 609, Fort Erie, Ont. L2A 5X3

JULE McBRIDE

THE WRONG WIFE?

Harlequin Books

TORONTO • NEW YORK • LONDON
AMSTERDAM • PARIS • SYDNEY • HAMBURG
STOCKHOLM • ATHENS • TOKYO • MILAN
MADRID • WARSAW • BUDAPEST • AUCKLAND

For Elizabeth Bass, a.k.a. Liz Ireland—
a great writer, great friend and maker of "happies"—
may all your dreams come true!

ISBN 0-373-16546-3

THE WRONG WIFE?

Copyright © 1994 by Julianne Randolph Moore.

Prologue

"Daddy, Daddy, I'm going to jump off a cliff!"

Something between a smile and a grimace twitched at Lord Nicholas Westhawke's lips. "Right, luv," he murmured gruffly. He watched Rosemunde race down the stony steps chiseled in the cliff, with their half wolf, half shepherd, Baskerville, nipping at her heels.

Then he squinted in the dusky light, his eyes roving over the letter and photo in his hand again. Sylvia Sinclair certainly looked pretty enough. She had a short, thick, dark bob and bright blue eyes. He glanced at the flourishing curves of her signature, then at her last words.

We *are* doing the right thing, Nicholas. My work requires the isolation Cornwall offers, I love children, can't have my own, and am so shy that only our letters have enabled me to open up. I'm content to be Rosemunde's mother, knowing you'll always love your past wife, but knowing you'll love me, too, since our joint professional interests will provide the basis for true companionship. So, Nicholas, this is my last letter before we are actually married....

> Soon to be yours,
> Sylvia Sinclair

"Watch me, Daddy!"

Nicholas carefully placed Sylvia's letter and photo in his back jeans pocket. When he turned toward Rosemunde, his long, white-blond hair whipped across his eyes; he brushed the unruly strands from a face that was less weathered but every bit as sculpted as the rocky cliffs themselves.

"C'mon, luv," he yelled, seeing that his daughter had made it down all the steps, to where the ocean crashed perilously against the jagged rocks. "Time to go inside."

Exactly when had Rosemunde become such a wild child? he wondered as she and Baskerville bounded toward him. She looked more like a forest creature than a little girl, and she certainly didn't look like an heiress. He leaned into a sudden rush of wind and braced a lean, well-muscled thigh against the railing, knowing his daughter wouldn't bother to stop running but would crash right into him, which she did.

Without asking, she caught the corner of Sylvia's picture and plucked it from his pocket. "She's so pretty," Rosemunde said breathlessly. "Which is why we had to go all the way to the United States to get her. Right?"

Nicholas's penetrating violet eyes narrowed. Rosemunde was almost five, but already so complex that he didn't know what she was thinking half the time. How did she really feel about Sylvia's impending arrival?

The knees of his daughter's dungarees were torn, her tangled, tawny hair was thoroughly wet from ocean spray, and different lengths, since she'd decided to cut it herself this afternoon. He couldn't see her nose for the dirt, either. Every time he mentioned such things to Mrs. O'Reilly, the older woman merely reminded him she was a housekeeper, not a nanny.

"She's going to hate the house, Daddy," Rosemunde said matter-of-factly, still staring at Sylvia's picture. "It's a bloody mess."

"Don't curse," he said. His gaze swept over the cliffs, past the forests and the untended caretaker's cottage where Mr. Magnuson lived, then took in the rounded tops of two crenellated towers. It was all he could see of Westhawke Hall, the two-hundred-room monstrosity of a castle they called home.

"It looks like the Addams Family's house," Rosemunde groused. "Except bigger and scarier."

"You shouldn't watch so much American television," he chided, even as he acknowledged that she was right.

"But it does!" she protested. "And you don't wake up until dark, Daddy, and you work all night long!" Rosemunde handed him the picture, with an unsure expression. "She'll probably think we're vampires or something! Couldn't you at least get a haircut?"

"Speaking of haircuts..." he began, with a censuring glance.

He wasn't sure, but he thought the tough, little tomboy's eyes actually teared. His heart constricted. Why did he always seem to say the wrong thing?

"I was trying to look pretty, if you must know," Rosemunde snapped.

"And you look beautiful," he assured her, attempting to gentle his voice. "Everything is going to be fine."

But was it? he wondered as Rosemunde suddenly flung her arms around his legs in a contrite, bearish hug. Sylvia Sinclair's acclaimed academic treatise, entitled *The Dracula Myth in England*, had placed him in contact with her, then the mental flights of fancy she'd taken in her letters had delighted him. But was that enough to make a marriage?

Running his fingers through his daughter's damp, messy hair, he hoped so. He just wished Sylvia had agreed to meet him first, before they were actually wed. Still, the fact that she hadn't had tweaked his curiosity. Besides, if things didn't work out, they could always annul....

Suddenly, he smiled, thinking of the very strange arrival he'd planned for Sylvia. Only she would understand it, and he knew she'd be utterly amused.

"Everything will go exactly as planned," he whispered, assuring himself as much as his daughter. Yes, tomorrow night, when the clock struck midnight, Rosemunde would have a mother again, and he—Lord Nicholas Westhawke of Cornwall—would be a married man again....

Chapter One

"I swear I don't have a gun!" Angela Lancini wailed. She tried to pass through the airport's beeping metal detector again, but the skirt of her wedding gown was so wide she had to squeeze through the arch sideways.

Once through, she obediently raised her arms, so the security official could run his hand-held device in and around the wedding dress. Unfortunately, he began at her veil and worked ever-so-slowly downward.

"Oh, please hurry," she whispered, hoping Frankie wasn't chasing her. At any second, a mammoth black Cadillac full of men wearing sunglasses and shoulder holsters would surely pull up to the curb....

"Beneath your skirt, I believe," the guard said gently.

The garter! Frankie had given her a garter, with a solid-gold stocking support attached, on which their initials and planned wedding date had been engraved.

Angela backed through the detector. Fighting a flush, she hiked her skirt, rolled the garter down her leg, then placed it in the plastic tray. She squeezed through the arch again, this time without beeping.

"Just keep it, sir," Angela called, as she heaved her heavy blue suitcase from the conveyor. "That charm's solid gold."

With that, she raced through the crowded concourse and toward the nearest ladies' room, beating back her unwieldy ten-foot train with one hand and hauling her suitcase with the other. She was wasting precious minutes, but she simply couldn't stand in the ticket line in a wedding gown. Besides, she didn't know where she was going yet...other than as far away from Frankie and the altar as she could get. She had even brought her passport, which she'd gotten for identification even though she'd never been abroad.

In the ladies' room, she slammed her suitcase on the floor and pressed the latches. The case sprang open, and she swiftly took stock of her honeymoon outfits. In under a second, she decided to wear her new beige travel suit and low-heeled brown pumps.

She whirled toward the mirror, tugged her veil, then groaned. At least a thousand hairpins were holding it in place! As she fumbled with the pins, her gaze met another woman's in the mirror.

Where Angela was petite but full figured, with a long waving mass of curly black hair, the other woman looked as if she'd just stepped from a society page. She had a chestnut bob, a square chin, bright blue eyes and an athletic figure. She also looked very curious.

Angela didn't blame her. It was undoubtedly rare to see three miles' worth of wedding gown come barreling through an airport or to see a virginal Italian-American bride holding up the line at the metal detector.

"Here," the woman finally said. "Let me give you a hand."

"I just left someone at the altar," Angela explained, as she felt the woman's deft hands work their way under her veil. She could hear the shock in her voice. A hint of raspiness, too, since it had grown hoarse after her last fight with Frankie. "I mean, he probably chased me here and I feel terrible, but I simply can't marry Frankie! I thought I could, but..."

Angela sucked in a quick breath and tried to fight her rising hysteria. "My biological clock was just ticking away," she continued, as the other woman began to dexterously unclasp the pearl buttons at the back of the dress. "And I just turned thirty." Angela's voice suddenly quavered. "And then my father died and I was alone. And I was just so sure I must be the last American virgin left. So I guess I just..."

"The veil's off and you're all unbuttoned," the stranger said.

"Oh, thank you so much." Angela leaned, and the heavy beaded basque bodice, which was supported by whalebone, fell forward as if it were made of lead. When Angela stepped out of the skirt, both women started laughing. The fabric was so wonderfully crisp that the gown remained standing even though no one was in it.

"I'm truly a vanished bride now," Angela murmured.

"And you've just convinced me to run from the altar, myself," the woman returned, when she regained her breath. "Now, I'll pack the dress, while you get into that travel suit."

"I can't thank you enough," Angela said once she was dressed.

"I proposed to a man I've never even met!" The stranger sat on the suitcase in an effort to shut it.

"You've got to be kidding!" Angela plopped down next to the woman, hoping their combined weight might help.

"No, I'm just so shy around men...." The suitcase latched, but a wayward strip of wedding lace still stuck out by the handle.

"You don't *seem* shy," Angela countered as the woman helped her lug her suitcase outside.

"Only around men," the woman said, sighing.

Looking toward the ground transportation area, Angela gasped. A big black Cadillac *had* pulled to the curb....

"That's Frankie! Where am I going to go?" Angela said in a rush.

"My plane's boarding," the woman said with a grin. "Could you use a one-way ticket to England?"

"ENGLAND!" ANGELA whispered excitedly as she left customs and stepped into the crowded deplaning areas of Heathrow airport. She was thrifty, but could she survive on the one hundred dollars she was carrying? If she found a youth hostel, maybe she wouldn't have to use her credit cards until she bought her return fare, which meant Frankie wouldn't be able to follow a paper trail.

Fortunately, no one had questioned her ticket, even though it was in the name of Sylvia Sinclair, and the stewardess—whose sympathetic gaze had caught the tuft of wedding lace by the suitcase handle—had allowed Angela to board the plane, even though her baggage was hardly carry-on size. Of course, Angela thought guiltily, the stewardess undoubtedly thought she was running *to* a wedding, not *away* from one.

Nonetheless, all she had to do now, in exchange for the ticket, was tell a man named Nicholas Westhawke that his marriage was canceled. It was an unpleasant task, but that had been the deal. Within seconds, Angela spotted the groom. He was the only blond, blue-eyed man in sight, thus the only one who answered Sylvia's vague description, and he was expectantly watching people leave customs. He was also a little homely and Angela couldn't help but think—snobbish as it was—that he was just the type who might try finding the love of his life via the postal service.

"Mr. Westhawke?" she asked as she reached his side. She lowered her already hoarse voice, hoping to prepare him for the bad news it was her duty to impart. "Sylvia Sinclair sent—"

"Wrong man," he said, just as a strong grip closed around her upper arm from behind.

"Miss Sinclair, I presume?"

When she turned, she gasped. He couldn't be Nicholas Westhawke! Black bangs curled from beneath his squarish, narrow-brimmed hat and he had small black eyes. He also had an unnaturally erect posture and even though it was warm, he was wearing an overcoat.

"I'm supposed to meet Nicholas West—"

"Hawke," he finished curtly, with a pronounced English accent. He wrestled her bag from her. "Follow me."

The man didn't even wait! He strode swiftly toward the doors without a backward glance. Fortunately, he was tall, and his hat bobbed above the heads of other travelers...right up until it disappeared. Angela ran after him, not about to lose her luggage.

She found him standing beside a long, black stretch limousine. With one hand, he held a back door open for her. With the other, he held up a small oblong white sign that said SYLVIA SINCLAIR.

"Where's my bag?" she exclaimed, hoping the man didn't expect her to actually get in the car with him. Her voice broke at midsentence and ended on a croak.

"In the trunk," he said evenly, though something in his tone indicated she was asking the obvious.

"Look," Angela said. "I just need to speak with Nicholas Westhawke. I mean—er—he did send you here?"

"I am taking you to the earl."

"Earl?" Was Nicholas Westhawke an English earl? Or was "the earl" a place?

"Lord Nicholas Westhawke," he said, not bothering to hide his exasperation.

And were earls called lords? Angela wondered now. As tough as she liked to think she was, the man was intimidating, and she didn't particularly want to argue with him. Furthermore, this was a free—not to mention nicely appointed—ride into town. Besides, Nicholas Westhawke was truly beginning to tweak her curiosity. After all, he'd sent a limousine.

In the most carefree move of her life, she hopped inside, slamming the door shut before the tall fellow could do it for her. She squinted through the tinted windows as he circled the car and got in. Then he began to maneuver them through the crowded parking lot.

She leaned back in the plush, leather-upholstered seat, glancing around just long enough to see that the English countryside by Heathrow looked pretty much like New Jersey. When she felt a moment's panic, she forced herself to relax. The man was clearly Nicholas Westhawke's driver. But why would Mr. Westhawke employ someone so lacking in people skills? And was Nicholas Westhawke really an English nobleman?

With her luck, she thought, suddenly toying with a strand of her mussed hair, he probably *was* a nobleman. After all, Sylvia Sinclair—with her perfect square chin and teeth—had looked like the type meant for royalty. And Sylvia *had* assured her the man was charming. Still, anyone who was willing to marry based on a mail correspondence alone had to be a loser.

Angela suddenly wished she wasn't quite so grimy and tired from traveling. She'd never flown before today, so she hadn't slept on the plane. And going overseas had meant a long flight, with time changes. She hadn't slept the previous night, either, since she'd been in such a quandary about her own wedding. Then her early morning fight with Frankie and her later decision to flee the altar had been stressful. And now, she was sure calling off Sylvia's Sinclair's marriage was going to be more difficult than she'd anticipated. Did English nobility behead the bearers of bad tidings? she thought wryly. Or was that the Greeks?

"What have I gotten myself into?" she whispered, shutting her eyes. For one short minute, she decided, she would think of how a fabulous free ticket to England had so fatefully fallen into her hands, and pretend that none of the rest of this was happening. If she concentrated on the ticket and the limo, it seemed almost like a fairy tale....

It was hard not to think about Lord Nicholas Westhawke, too. The man was looking for a wife. Or he would be soon. Perhaps he lived in a light, airy mansion, with Grecian-style columns and rose gardens. Nicholas, himself—Lord Nicholas, she thought dreamily—would be positively breathtaking....

And slipping into a dream about the enigmatic stranger, Angela accidentally fell asleep.

LORD NICHOLAS WESTHAWKE was leaning against a marble column, cradling her in his arms.

"Come along," someone said.

Angela's smile faded when she realized the speaker had a dangerously firm hold on her elbow.

By the time the man's grip convinced her it was Lord Nicholas Westhawke's driver, not her dream version of Lord Nicholas, himself, she'd already been marshaled from the car and left beside her suitcase in the road.

"Wait!" The tiny croak of her voice infuriated her. One iota of stress, and she was reduced to talking in whispers. She shook her head and blinked. It was true! The driver had gotten back in the car and slammed his door. He was driving away!

"Wait!" Angela tried to yell. She began running after the car, then realized she wouldn't catch it. Besides, she couldn't

leave her belongings untended. She headed back toward her
suitcase, wishing she was still asleep and dreaming....

She wasn't. Not a soul stirred on the narrow, dusty cobbled road. The place was overhung with shadowy trees, and
it was dark and getting chilly, which meant they'd driven for
some time.

When she reached her suitcase, she saw that it was sitting
in front of an old forked road sign that said, Westhawke
Hall. Unfortunately, she couldn't walk in the direction of
the arrow, not with the heavy suitcase. She seated herself on
top of it and toyed nervously with the tuft of wedding lace
by the handle.

For an instant, she felt like Rip van Winkle. Had she
slept ... only to wake up in another world? Another time?
She glanced both ways down the road again. Nothing. With
her luck, cars didn't even use this back road. Angela wasn't
sure, but she figured that Sylvia Sinclair had changed her
mind, called off her marriage over the phone, and that an
angry, inconsiderate Lord Westhawke had then called his
driver on a car phone. Ergo, she'd been left here to rot.

At least the man took swift actions when things bothered
him, she thought wryly.

Then she cocked her head. Was it her imagination or did
she really hear a soft, rumbling roar? It was waves! She was
at the ocean. If she weren't so tired, she would probably
have smelled the salt in the air before.

But beneath that sound, there was something else ... a
thundering. In the shadowy dark, England sure looked
stormy, just like in all the books and movies. But how could
Lord Westhawke have left her here? Was the man as stormy
as the country he inhabited?

"Horses?" Angela jumped up from her suitcase and
peered down the road. Her jaw dropped, her heart pounded
double-time, and she told herself it simply could not

be . . . but a team of horses *were* thundering around a curve. And they were galloping straight toward her!

"Ya!" the driver yelled, as his whip stung the air with a snap.

Angela had intended to flag down the first driver she saw, but now she stepped behind her suitcase, hoping to hide until he passed. Heaven knew, she'd craved adventures beyond those offered by New York's Little Italy, but this was simply too much!

Unfortunately, the man's loud commands suddenly shifted from "ya's" to "whoa there's." The team of horses stopped—rearing on their hindquarters and tossing their heads—not five feet away from her.

She watched in horror as the driver hopped down from the fancy carriage, grabbed her suitcase and tossed it up, all in one swift motion. Then he took his post in the driver's seat again. He was cloaked from head to toe, but something about his manner—or lack of manners, Angela thought—made her sure it was the limo driver again. That meant Nicholas Westhawke might not have heard from Sylvia. Just what was the man up to?

With all her being, Angela wished she wasn't losing her voice. She wanted to say that she was a normal person. She was practical, sensible and had just completed her master's degree in education. Every overwrought nerve in her body quivered, wanting to demand that Nicholas Westhawke step forward and explain himself.

She circled the carriage, trying not to get too close to the horses, and stared up at the man's face. It was the same driver, all right. Was *he* really Lord Westhawke, but in disguise?

"Where *is* Nicholas Westhawke?" Angela croaked.

"The earl awaits thee," the driver said simply.

"Awaits *thee?*" she whispered. Something in the man's formal tone sent a chill down her spine, but perhaps that was because it was fully dark now, on a shadowy, tree-lined road in the hinterlands of England.

On a spooky road where I do not intend to spend the night, Angela suddenly thought. She quickly finished circling the carriage and hoisted herself inside. Then, with a mock flourish of her arm that seemed to fit the unusual circumstances, she mustered her most commanding croak and said, "Drive on!"

The sooner he moved, the sooner she'd meet Nicholas Westhawke. She'd imagined him as hopelessly homely. But, then, in her dreams, he'd been gorgeous. Now, she felt compelled to find out what kind of man hired a carriage and team of four to meet a bride he didn't know.

"Ya!" the driver yelled again.

As the horses lunged forward, she was thrown back against a padded velvet seat. Her fingers flew over the sensuously soft fabric, groping for a handhold, but it was no use. Nicholas Westhawke had already unbalanced her more than any carriage ever could, and she hadn't even met him yet.

Not five minutes later, they rounded a curve. Stark cliffs rose in front of them. Glancing up the rocky mountain, she realized the man she sought lived at the very top of it. When the driver began ascending a winding circular road, a combined thrill of fear, anticipation and romantic fantasy coursed through her. Just who *was* this guy?

As the strong-limbed horses drew the carriage ever upward, her heart thundered beneath her ribs. When they rounded the final bend, she was sure it would stop beating altogether.

Westhawke *Hall* was a misnomer. A stone *castle* with two round, crenellated towers sat perched on the edge of the cliffs, silhouetted against the moon. Crazed vines twisted around the dark upper turrets. Taking it all in, Angela felt her little adventure spinning out of control. Because she knew exactly where she'd seen that castle before. In the movies. It was where Count Dracula had lived.

"And where Lord Westhawke lives now," she whispered.

ONE OF THE MASSIVE double front doors swung open, but it hardly seemed an invitation. The driver breezed through it and past Angela, carrying her suitcase as if it were feather light. Which it was not, she thought with a chill.

Lights flickered in the cavernous entrance hall, barely touching the wide stone steps that lay in front of her. To her right were columned archways and more stone steps, this time going downward. Stair banisters stretched forever in the darkness, and newel posts ended in carved faces that looked like they belonged on the mastheads of ships. Angela was in such shock that she barely noticed when the driver and her luggage began vanishing up the stairs.

"I demand to see Nicholas Westhawke immediately!" Angela squinted into the darkness, then ran after the driver. Upstairs, the twisting corridor walls were lined with panels. Weren't there any doors in this place? she wondered.

She caught up to the driver in a dimly lit room. Her suitcase was safe and sound, placed by the door. At least she hadn't lost that.... Even if she was beginning to feel as if she were losing her mind.

She found two lamps before she located the overhead switch. Just as she hit it, she turned to get a good look at the man who'd brought her here, but the door was creaking shut.

"How hospitable," she whispered tightly. And then she heard the rattle of a key and the lock slide into place.

Do not panic, she thought, staring openmouthed at the door. Frankie was a locksmith, and he'd taught her how to pick locks on their oh-so-unromantic dates. She glanced around the room where she'd just been entrapped, and her eyes widened until she found herself blinking as if the room might disappear. She told herself to hate it every bit as much as she should have been hating Nicholas Westhawke, but the place was fantastic....

In a corner was a deep, turreted recess with tall diamond-paned windows. There was a fireplace, and a lovely, long-stemmed red rose lay on the sumptuous, canopied, Empire-style bed; the bed was ancient, with carved, clawed feet, and two bolster pillows were placed at either end. For a second, Angela forgot that she was locked in and murmured, "How romantic!"

The walls were hung with creamy fabric that looked to be silk, and old portraits in gilded frames hung on the fabric. Whoever Nicholas Westhawke was, he was obviously rich as sin and truly outside her experience. She understood buying wall units and using floral cardboard boxes for under-the-bed storage—not rooms like this.

"Sure beats a youth hostel," she finally whispered.

The suite had its own bathroom, too, which looked modern enough, in spite of the claw-footed tub. And a covered silver tray sat on a table, apparently bearing what smelled like a real meal!

"Might as well not have my stomach rumble when I meet him," she conceded after another long moment.

When she lifted the cover from the serving dish, she thought she was looking at a kidney pie. Just glancing at it almost cured her appetite.

"Westhawke," she muttered as she forced herself to dig in. "You just dropped a notch in my book. You, too, Sylvia." How could the woman have gotten her into this mess?

Nonetheless, she polished off her plate, then stripped to her slip and headed for the bathroom, willing herself to ignore the perfect fragrant rose. She told herself that cleaning up just a bit before she met Nicholas Westhawke wouldn't hurt matters. She'd feel much more rational after a bath. Much more prepared. Much more *pretty*. She immediately squelched that thought.

Within minutes she was ensconced in the big, old tub, and scrubbed to perfection. The room and bath were pure heaven. So was the profusion of thick terry towels that had been left for her.

But the man had brought her here in a very strange manner, his house looked like Dracula's mansion and she was locked in a room, she suddenly reminded herself. It was almost as if the sheer luxuriousness of the place were seducing her!

She hadn't slept for two whole days now.

She was running on nothing more than adrenaline and fear.

And she was clearly going crazy.

She rose swiftly and wrapped a towel tightly around herself. Nicholas Westhawke might be some rich eccentric, he might even be a real vampire, but she wasn't about to be seduced by the sumptuousness of a room! Or by thoughts of a man she'd never even met....

She'd march through every cold, windy room in this castle until she found him. She'd discover why she couldn't have just driven here in a car, like a normal person, and then she'd tell him Sylvia had ditched him. She'd even add that she didn't blame Sylvia one bit. And then she would demand immediate transport out of this strange place!

Angela nudged open the bathroom door and glanced out. What she saw made her whole body freeze. Her suitcase had vanished! Only one outfit remained. It was laid out on the bed and smoothed to perfection. She was going to meet Lord Nicholas Westhawke, all right.

The only question was whether she'd be stark naked... or wearing her wedding dress.

ANGELA HALF WISHED she'd just married Frankie that morning, because now she was picking a lock with one of the very hairpins that was supposed to hold her veil in place.

"Good," she whispered raspily when the lock turned over.

Now, I can escape. But where? As she inched down the dark corridor, she lowered her veil. After all, she meant to get a darn good look at Nicholas Westhawke, before *he* saw *her.*

If she'd arrived with her voice intact, she'd simply lean against the paneled walls and scream for the man at the top of her lungs, she decided as she took a number of promising-looking turns. Suddenly, she cocked her head. A shiver shot straight down her spinal column. Was it her imagination or was that really a child giggling? The sound came right through the walls! *The walls that had no doors...*

She clasped her hands in front of her, took a deep breath, and continued walking. *I'm tired and it's just my imagination. The events of this day are understandably making me hysterical.*

Blowing out a shaky breath, she spotted the vague outline of a door. She ran forward so quickly that she nearly tripped over her train. A real door! She shoved it repeatedly, then realized it was secured with a heavy padlock.

"That's off-limits and you'll get in big trouble," a voice said. Then a child—the same one she'd heard before—broke into giggles again. "Your *husband* keeps his things there."

Husband! Angela whirled around. She opened her mouth to scream, but no sound came out. A wild-looking little girl in a white gown seemed to waver in the dark shadows. Grinning wickedly, she looked exactly the way Angela always imagined ghosts might look. Angela managed to take an uncertain step backward. And then, with a wave, the little girl receded right into the wall!

I have seen a ghost. I have really, truly, honestly seen a ghost. No wonder no one would marry Nicholas West-hawke! Angela gulped. She had no intention of looking for Nicholas Westhawke now. She meant to find the front door... *her suitcase be damned! She tried to remind herself that there was a rational, concrete explanation for everything. Except for love,* she suddenly thought illogically.

Somewhere, far off, she heard the chimes of an old clock strike. She began following the sound, counting each of the strokes. *Eight, nine, ten.* Her heart and steps sped with each climbing chime. "Twelve midnight," she croaked, just before the clock fell silent. When she heard the sound that followed, she began to run.

Because from the same general direction, an organ had begun to play.

And it was playing the wedding march.

Chapter Two

Angela skidded to a dead halt when she reached a small candlelit chapel on the ground floor. From sheer momentum, the long train of her wedding gown kept moving until it hit her slippers and bunched around her ankles. Her mouth dropped open and she started shaking like a leaf.

It had to be him.

Lord Nicholas Westhawke.

And the man was every bit as incredible as his castle. It wasn't so much that he was tall and broad shouldered, or even that he wore an elegant, romantic black wedding tux with tails, which indicated he was still expecting Sylvia Sinclair.

It wasn't that his hair was white blond and silkier looking than any she had ever seen, either, or that it hung midway down his back. What amazed Angela was that he was so self-contained. She could feel a subtle, charismatic magnetism *radiate* from the man, as if all his innate energies were conspiring to compel her silently forward.

When he turned around, her throat constricted, shutting as tightly as a trap. His eyes were as mesmerizing as they were violet and the pair of them was enough to convince her that he simply couldn't be real. She tried to run forward, knowing she had to tell him—right here, right now—that she wasn't Sylvia Sinclair, but her knees felt so weak she could barely walk.

"Hello, my love," he said simply. His English-accented voice was soft but it carried.

Nicholas Westhawke smiled, unable to believe his good fortune. Sylvia Sinclair was an absolute vision. *An amazing, heaven-sent angel.* It was hard to believe a woman that gorgeous would be satisfied with a career as a reclusive academic. Or that in mere minutes she would truly be his wife.

For heart-stopping seconds, he hadn't even been able to turn around. At first, he'd only seen her reflection in the shining metallic front of the table in Westhawke Hall's tiny chapel. Because theirs was a candlelit ceremony, that reflection had seemed to waver, almost surreally, as if to point up the fact that Sylvia Sinclair was just too perfect to be true.

She'd only sent a head shot, and though Nicholas couldn't see her face since it was covered by the veil, he never would have guessed that her body would be so lusciously curved. No, he'd imagined Sylvia would have a squarish, muscular, tennis-playing build. But here she was, her figure a perfect hourglass that reminded him he hadn't touched a woman for three years.

Her posture was so erect that she could have balanced an apple on her head, and her slender hands were gracefully quavering at her sides. The slow, almost cautious way she began walking down the aisle made his heart go out to her.

His smile was faltering just as much as her steps. He could only stare, with his mouth dry and his lips parted and his heart pounding. As Sylvia reached his side, a thoroughly unexpected pang of longing—the kind he hadn't felt since his wife's death—twisted in his lower body. He knew exactly how she felt—just as nervous and as excited and as overwrought with anticipation as he was, he thought.

"You're so beautiful, Sylvia," he murmured. The lacy sleeve of her gown was rough between his fingers, and when he took a deep breath he realized she smelled of the same soap he used. "Far more beautiful than I ever expected or imagined."

Tell him you're not Sylvia Sinclair, Angela thought. But she couldn't move; she certainly couldn't speak. Wild thoughts raced crazily through her head...that she was broke and had nowhere to stay. That Frankie would never find her here. That Sylvia Sinclair hadn't possessed a picture of Nicholas Westhawke, which meant he probably didn't have one of her. In turn, that meant Angela could pretend to be Sylvia.... *But why?* she wondered in shock. And yet the answer was close enough to touch...near enough to hold...right before her eyes. The man was gorgeous.

Nicholas dropped his fingers from her sleeve in a near caress, taking in how Sylvia's breath made her chest rise and fall in quick, seductive movements that took away his own breath. He knew she was excruciatingly shy with men, but he wished she'd say something. Would her voice be high-pitched? Low? Sexy? As if she'd read his mind, a small gasp met his ears.

"You don't need to say a thing, luv," he reassured, a bit guiltily. No matter how painfully shy she was with men, she would have to talk to him eventually. He'd only worried, since passion seemed lacking in their correspondence. But now, any such reservation had been laid to rest.

It was as if he'd just entered a room packed with people and his romantic radar had picked her out of the sizable crowd. He felt that kind of undeniable attraction. Strong and inexplicable. And one in a million.

Nicholas nodded at the magistrate, who promptly began speaking in hushed Old English. Then Nicholas faced Sylvia again. The Old English ceremony had been her doing.

She'd written a paper on it once, and had said she'd always been intrigued by it because it was traditional.

Nicholas took another deep breath, feeling his heart begin to race. They had so much in common. He was attracted to her. She wanted to be a mother to Rosemunde. And now all he had to do was penetrate the wall of this lovely woman's shyness with men.

The lulling lilt of the magistrate's voice made Angela start. A ceremony was underway! And worse—it was like none she'd ever witnessed! She could only hope it wasn't some pagan ritual. Thus far, all she'd done was stare deeply into Nicholas Westhawke's eyes, keeping her own conveniently hidden by her veil.

"I—" She meant to tell him who she was, but her voice was barely audible. Nicholas only touched her sleeve sweetly again, as if in emotional support. She had to put an end to this! She couldn't believe she'd been considering pretending to be Sylvia! Only a man who looked like Nicholas Westhawke could have made her entertain such dangerous, devious notions!

But what about the man who was marrying them? she suddenly wondered. Certainly, someone of Lord Nicholas Westhawke's status would be embarrassed by her announcement that she wasn't Sylvia Sinclair. He'd be further mortified if she announced that Sylvia hadn't even come to ditch him in person. Shouldn't she convey the information privately?

Wait it out, Angela. Tell him when it's over. The least you can do is help the man save a little face. Still, a face like his hardly needed saving. It was over-the-top handsome.

Nicholas glanced away from his bride when the magistrate's words ended. The man presented Nicholas with a wreath of roses, which—once placed on Sylvia's head— would signify their union. Very slowly, Nicholas rested the wreath on top of her veil.

She reached for the lacy bottom, seemingly meaning to uncover her own face. Her eagerness touched him, but just as quickly, he grasped her wrist. Her skin was dry and soft against his own and the pulse point of her wrist was beating wildly out of control. Tingling pricks of awareness skated along his arm.

He reached around her delicate waist and pulled her against his chest, then slowly began to lift the veil. When he'd raised it to her chin, he stopped and swallowed. *Could a marriage like this really work?*

"I'll do everything in my power," he whispered, "to be the kind of man you always dreamed of."

You already are, Angela caught herself thinking in panic.

In a slow, fluid motion, Nicholas folded the veil over the wreath on her head.

She gulped.

He stared.

His bride—whoever she was—was not Sylvia Sinclair.

The woman had dangerously dark, flashing midnight eyes, not blue ones. Her hair was not only longer than Sylvia's, but now he realized it curled in a thick, wavy, sensual mass. Her face wasn't square, either, but heart shaped, and her lips, though small, were full and passionate looking. Rosebud lips.

"I'm not—" she began in a low, hoarse voice that was so sexily raspy that a shiver ran right down his back.

"Nearly as happy about this as I am," he finished casually. And then he bent her in a swift clinch and kissed her.

THE WOMAN TRIED TO leap away, but her silk slipper caught in her train. When she hopped to break her fall, his arms tightened around her back. He left her no choice but to arch against him while his tongue plunged between her lips. The long length of his body towered over hers as he bent her backward—so far that the wreath spun to the floor and rolled away like a wheel. Her veil followed, drifting down-ward in a puff of lace. After a long moment, he lifted her right off the floor and into his cradling embrace.

"Wait!" she managed to say, as he carried her out of the chapel and into the foreboding darkness. Her voice was a mere whispery rasp. "Wait . . . just wait. . . ."

"I can't wait either, my love," Nicholas said smoothly. He headed down a pitch-black corridor and ascended a set of stairs, feeling pure fury. The second he'd lifted the veil, the second right after he'd seen how pretty her face was, he'd decided that Sylvia's ideas, which had once seemed so whimsical, were pretty bloody strange.

The woman began to twist and writhe in his arms. "Stop," she gasped. "You have to . . ."

"Stop at nothing to make this the finest night of our lives," Nicholas continued in a mocking tone, wishing her voice wasn't so spine-tinglingly raspy. Sylvia Sinclair—with her passionless letters and insistence on marriage before they actually met, and on Old English services, had suddenly turned on him. Sending another bride in her place was def-initely the last straw.

"Put me down!" The woman punched him, but her small, clenched fists only met the hard muscles of his chest.

When he glanced down, he saw that a hank of his long hair had literally fallen into her cleavage. Undoubtedly, it was tickling her bare skin. "Oh, I'm going to, my love," Nicholas assured, thinking he'd put her down, all right, with a bloody thud. Why would Sylvia send someone in her place? And yet, she had. This particular bride had come packing a wedding gown.

"Could we please talk?" She wailed the words as an-other fisted assault rained down around his shoulders. When that didn't get her what she wanted, she started squirming again.

"Why, certainly," he returned with deathly calm. He could see perfectly well in the dark—it was a special talent of his—and he wished she weren't quite so attractive. And a lot more honest. "We're talking now, and we'll continue to do so until death do us part. Right, Sylvia?"

Feeling how his hands molded perfectly around her back and beneath her knees wasn't helping matters at all. He assured himself he'd only kissed her in order to buy time...until he could find out what kind of game Sylvia was playing. As worried as he'd been, this prank rankled. So did the involvement of the woman who was now in his arms. What was he going to tell Rosemunde?

The woman didn't bother to answer him, but only wrenched in his arms again. "It's no use struggling, Sylvia." His words were delivered in such a gruff tone that he was surprised at how positively mean he sounded. And it wasn't her fault alone, he thought. Ever since his wife's death, he'd been as prickly as a porcupine.

"You've got this all wrong!" the woman squealed.

"Oh, do I?" he asked flatly, wending his way through yet another corridor.

"Yes!"

He tried to ignore what her incredibly throaty voice was doing to his insides. "Now, what could be wrong with carrying my new bride across a threshold?" he asked, attempting to sound reasonable.

"I've about reached *my* threshold," she croaked. She flailed her feet with the fury of a professional kick boxer. They merely whooshed in the air, making him tighten his grip around her knees. "What are you doing to me?"

"Carrying you, luv," he said with deceptive softness.

"Well, I'm begging you to stop," she returned in that hoarse-sounding voice. It was so low and raspy that goose bumps rose on his arms. In another swift move, she tried to jump out of his grasp. He tightened his hold again, so her face wound up pressing against his starchy white shirtfront.

"I know you're so anxious you'd rather run, my dearest Sylvia," he murmured, in a voice laced with irony. "But I insist on carrying you. It's so romantic and bloody traditional and all."

"Thank you so much," she whispered tightly. "But I am not Syl—"

"Silly?" he asked quickly, not about to let her come clean until he'd been able to torture her a bit for her dishonesty. "Of course, you're not silly. I'd hardly marry a silly woman. Now would I?"

At that, the fool woman reached up, caught a lock of his hair, then yanked it with all her might. He grunted gently in pain as he rounded another curve in the corridor.

He wasn't sure, but he thought the sound made her shiver. For a long moment, his hair remained between her fingers. And then, as if she realized her movement had only served to bring his face closer to her own, she dropped her hand as if the white blond strands had sizzled with sparks. He suddenly felt a little breathless, but assured himself it was merely from the exertion of carrying her.

"Please listen to me," the woman whispered. "Syl—"

"Silver for your anniversary? Isn't it a little early for that?" he asked, attempting to sound conversational.

She gasped. "Look. Syl—"

"Silk sheets," he interrupted. "Don't worry, luv. My linen cabinets are full of them."

"I'm not Syl—"

"I know you're no sylvan-wood nymph," he said, drowning her out. "You're a flesh-and-blood woman. But madam, you're every bit as tempting as the mythical maidens of the forest, I do assure you."

"If you don't stop..." A pleading sound crept into her voice.

He stopped walking. "You'll do just what, exactly, luv?" he asked. When she didn't respond, he continued in a taunting tone. "So what are you going to do, Sylvia? I knew you were shy, luv, but this is rather ridiculous."

"I'll belt you," she returned meanly.

He merely chuckled. "Right, luv."

"I will," she whispered. "I really will."

Her weak voice didn't sound too convincing. His chuckle tempered to a soft, throaty hum. "I suppose we could stop long enough for me to seduce you into compliance," he found himself saying. When her mouth dropped open in shock, his tongue dipped quickly between her parted lips. He began walking again, even though he was kissing her. Even while she flailed against him, kicking and waving her arms, he kept kissing her. And all the while, he told himself he was merely doing it to shut her up.

And yet, after a moment, she seemed to experience complete meltdown in his embrace. She began relaxing against his chest. Her knees were buckling over his arms, even though she wasn't standing. It had been so long since he'd felt a woman responding to him....

This is absolutely insane! he thought, but with each touch of their exploring lips, his own arms seemed to weaken. By the time he'd reached his room, she was sliding down the length of him. He leaned against a wall, holding her in the absolute, utter darkness. His hands cupped her neck and his thumbs just brushed the contours of her chin.

Then he reached above her, hit a light switch and stepped back—all in one dangerously swift motion. The light was so bright, she instinctively covered her eyes and peeked through her fingers.

He stared back at her. His lips were slightly parted and his breath was as uneven as hers. She flushed, every bit as brightly as the light in the room. "So, luv," he asked, after a long moment. "How does it feel to be a married woman?"

ANGELA COULD DO NOTHING more than stare at him. She couldn't believe he'd just kissed her as she had never been kissed before, or that she'd let him, or that he was so remarkable to look at.

The color of the man's eyes didn't exist in the natural world. The irises weren't marred with specs of other colors or striations, the way most eyes were. They were a solid, piercing, penetrating deep, deep blue violet. Even though he was markedly rude, especially considering the fact he thought she was his bride, those eyes had made her usually logical mind cease to function!

She had spent the past fifteen minutes quaking and trembling in his arms, and now she was sure she'd faint. Those eyes truly belonged in the movies. They belonged to Svengali in the close-up shot, right before virginal maidens all over town started rising from their beds and heading for their windows in trances!

She gulped, ripped her gaze away from his, then glanced over one of his muscular shoulders and gasped. The room was far more impressive than her own quarters. It was only the beginning of a series of rooms, too. Far off was the vague outline of a canopied bed.

Her fingers crawled over the paneled wall behind her, seeking escape. As if by magic, they found a small knob in the panel. She tugged, and the panel behind her opened.

"Don't tell me you mean to hide in a closet on our wedding night," Nicholas said sweetly.

"A closet?" she echoed after a long moment.

"Don't you have closets in America?" he asked, as if it were a real question. "I'd hate to think of Lady West-hawke as having been so deprived."

Angela tried to glare at him but couldn't. One look into his eyes and her expression softened. She felt spellbound and completely powerless to move. *Angela. This is the ef-*

fect of all-too-human hormones, and Nicholas Westhawke is not Svengali! Don't romanticize this!

She narrowed her gaze to a squint she hoped would pass for a glare, then whirled and stared through the crack in the paneled doorway. Sure enough, it was a regular human-style closet, full of polo shirts and jeans. The paneled door might explain how the ghost-child she'd seen had disappeared, too. All the panels in all those walls probably opened into rooms. Suddenly, Angela felt like an idiot. Was it possible that wild-looking little girl had been a real child, not a ghost? *But she'd wavered in the shadows and disappeared!*

"Well," Nicholas finally said in a gruff, forced voice. "You're quite the talker, aren't you?"

Angela slammed the closet door shut. The man was truly obnoxious, which was obviously the reason he'd tried to get a bride via the mail. He was undoubtedly nothing more than a spoiled, rich polo player. She'd never met anyone like that, but it was a type she was sure she'd hate. She slowly turned around, to give him a piece of her mind.

Again, his violet gaze rendered her speechless. She'd heard of jet black, and if there was such a thing, his eyes could only be called jet blue. They were the vivid color of purple flames. And her skin caught fire everywhere he looked.

She'd saved him face by not publicly announcing her identity, but now she had to tell him the truth. His eyes suddenly made her want to find a way to soften the blow. She sighed. The recent events in her usually so ordinary life were just too much. And this house was too much. And above all else, the man with the softest lips she'd ever felt and the entrancing eyes was too much.

The way he was staring at her was so marvelous that she could barely be angry at him for stepping right up and kissing her. And yet she couldn't mistake the way this place had set her nerves on edge with an uncharacteristic and yet overwhelming desire for a complete stranger! When he blinked, she jumped, as if she'd just been burned.

"Lights a little bright for you?" he prodded.

"At least you *do* have lights in this mausoleum," she found herself saying, as if in defense against what his eyes did to her.

He turned abruptly, walked a few paces and seated himself on a chaise lounge. It was antique—very antique—and so dainty that its delicately carved wood and damask upholstery actually seemed to shrink beneath him. His elegant slacks pulled as he sat, accentuating his powerful thighs. With his physique, it was no wonder he'd been able to carry her for what felt like a full fifteen minutes.

"So, you don't like your new house, Lady Westhawke?"

His mocking smile erased her resolve to deliver the news kindly. In a spirit of one-upmanship, Angela forced herself to glance around, as if considering. The objects in the room weren't even expensive-looking. They were bona-fide priceless. The phrase *rich eccentric* did not apply. No, the man was multibillion-style crazy. Like Howard Hughes. Except a lot better looking. She suddenly sighed in relief. As much money as this man obviously had, he was very clearly anchored to the dog-eat-dog material world.

"I've seen worse on Wall Street," she finally snapped, hoping her weak voice could communicate pure disdain.

"Can't hear you, luv," he said.

"Maybe that's because you keep interrupting me," she returned.

His eyes turned a shade more purple. "You sounded so much nicer in your letters...." He idly shifted in the chaise and clasped his hands by the waistband of his pants, as if intentionally calling her attention to his lower body. Then, he fixed those eyes on her again.

"Excuse me for being testy," she said raspily. She winced, knowing that using her voice would only weaken it, but everything about him—the strange transport he'd arranged from the airport, his scary, old castle, the way he'd kissed her and how he lounged so idly and looked so comfortably at home in such absolute splendor—made her edgy. In fact, it made her want to kill him.

At least she was getting used to him, which was a plus. *Yeah, now you can both look at him and talk at the same time. Pure genius, Angela.*

He merely stared at her calmly, as if he could do so all night long, maybe even for eternity…and without ever even blinking again. He was sitting so incredibly still that it was hard to remember how nimbly lithe he looked when he moved.

"Well, I don't suppose friendly conversation is absolutely essential to a marriage." Nicholas looked her over again. "But since your letters are far more entertaining than your person, perhaps we should continue to correspond via post, even though you now live here."

"I can be very entertaining," Angela snapped defensively. "But I have lost my voice. And I don't live—"

"Well, you kiss well," he interrupted. "And I suppose that's what matters."

Her jaw dropped. "Excuse me?"

His smile only widened. "You blush quite well, too."

"What kind of man would say such a thing?" she asked in horror.

He merely shrugged. "Don't pretend to be such an innocent."

"Are you always given to such torrid discussion?" Her voice broke, and she ended up mouthing most of the sentence.

"Always," he returned. "For instance, there's nothing I love more than how a woman sounds when a sore throat transforms her voice into that low, sensuous rasp." His smile broadened. "Perhaps, my dear, we should keep you out on the terrace . . . in the cold night air."

"I'd most definitely prefer it to your company," she said, not missing a beat. Angela was beginning to think he was baiting her. And yet, it was as if his eyes—those devastatingly handsome, deep, dark violet eyes—were lulling her into her trance again. They just looked so expressive and so strangely haunting in his pale face. And with all that soft, silky, oh so remarkably light hair . . .

"Look," she finally managed to say. "We need to talk."

He was off the chaise in a flash. He moved so quickly that she was suddenly sure, once again, that the man couldn't be human. She tried to retreat, but she was still hugging the wall. There was no place to go, unless she really did hide in his closet.

Before she knew it, he was standing right in front of her again, so close that she could feel his breath against her cheek. He placed his hands on either side of her, then cocked his head and gazed at her. "Go ahead," he said. "Talk. Or croak like a frog," he added with a dangerous-looking smile. "After all, that does seem to be your way, Lady Westhawke."

"Your little pagan service hardly makes us married," she managed to say.

"If I recall correctly," he countered, "you were the one who insisted on the Old English ceremony. Now weren't you, Sylvia?"

Angela nearly sagged against him in relief. She hadn't been married in a pagan ritual, after all. She wasn't some kind of virgin sacrifice, either. "Would you mind kindly explaining the strange transport I received here?" she whispered, knowing it would be her only opportunity to ask. Once she said she wasn't Sylvia Sinclair, she wasn't going to get any answers out of him.

"Your idea, too," he said.

His patronizing look said she was the forgetful type, but that he didn't mind humoring her. If she wished she had her own voice, she also wished his wasn't quite so musical. It was soft and lilting, with that cultured English accent that made everyone who had it sound so incredibly smart.

"Oh, yes," she said, fighting to keep the irony from her voice. "Now I remember requesting that carriage ride. What could be more entertaining than bouncing along the cliffs in a cart?" She flashed him a quick smile. "But did you have to lock me in my room?"

"Oh, I suppose I didn't have to," he returned amicably.

"And you did fail to mention your resident ghost," she continued throatily.

At that, she was relieved to see that he looked a little concerned. His light eyebrows raised ever so slightly above those unnaturally violet eyes. Then, suddenly, he smiled again. "You mean the one who's about four? Unkept tawny hair, less than one meter tall?"

She could only nod. After a moment, she found the voice she barely had. "Just how many ghosts do you *have*, Mr. Westhawke?"

"Lord Westhawke," he corrected. "Since we're married, you should at least try and get my name straight."

"How many?" she demanded, unable to believe Sylvia Sinclair had actually agreed to marry this man. He was great to look at, but a real loser in the personality department. What in the world had made Sylvia decide he was charming? "How many?" she repeated.

"All in good time, my pretty," he said. And, then, the man actually laughed. Suddenly, his shoulders began to shake and he simply cracked up. In that moment, he looked as absolutely normal as any man she'd ever seen. If about a thousand times more gorgeous.

"Honestly," he said, "I wouldn't let that one scare you overly much."

Angela reminded herself that if the ghost-child were an actual girl, she could conceivably have gone through a paneled door. But what was she doing up so late? "She disappeared!" she said, determined to get to the bottom of the matter.

Suddenly, Nicholas Westhawke's face seemed masked. He sobered, and dark, haunted emotion seemed to touch his eyes. "People do that sometimes," he said softly.

Angela hardly wanted to ponder the meaning of that. Suddenly, with his breath so close, his eyes now roving over her face, she wondered just exactly what this man was going to do when he found out she wasn't Sylvia Sinclair. And how was she going to explain why she hadn't told him immediately? How could she explain that his eyes had mesmerized her?

"Perhaps we should just talk tomorrow," he said in a gruff voice, lifting one of his hands and running it beneath her hair, against her neck. At his touch, goose bumps rose on her arms.

"I don't feel a chill," he continued, seeing them. "So perhaps we should . . ." He nodded over his shoulder, in the general direction of the bed in the distance. He leaned forward, seemingly to kiss her again.

She jerked back so quickly that her head nearly hit the wall. Before it actually connected, his palm swiftly curled around her head, softening the blow. Heavens, was he quick!

"Why would my own wife be in such a hurry to escape me?" he asked, as if it were merely a rhetorical question. Everything in his eyes said it wasn't.

"I'm not your wife," she croaked. Unfortunately, the words didn't pack nearly the punch she'd thought they would.

"Not a half hour ago, we got married," he said. "You were there, I was there, a magistrate was there. . . ."

"I'm not Sylvia Sinclair," she wailed. In midsentence, her voice broke again and at least one of her syllables came through with flying colors. Overly loud and bossily New York. Like Angela herself.

The gorgeous man remained nonplussed. "Well, luv—"

"And do not call me 'luv,'" she managed to mouth. "I find it rude."

He only lifted one of his shoulders slightly, as if to say the discussion wasn't worth much more of his effort. "Well, I'm sure you—whoever you are—must have poor habits with which I'll have to learn to contend."

"None," she whispered forcefully, unable to believe that the man was acting as if they were going to live together. Why was he doing this to her?

"What about . . . lying, for instance?" he asked silkily.

"You knew I wasn't Sylvia Sinclair!" she swiftly accused, suddenly realizing that had to be the case. He must have been furious when he'd seen her; that was why he'd acted so obnoxiously. "And you kissed me!" she continued, hoping to put him on the defensive. "Strung me along!"

His mouth dropped open in astonishment. "Strung *you* along? I mean, if you aren't my wife, then, I'd think you might want to introduce yourself."

"I didn't want to embarrass you in the chapel!" Angela protested.

"Or by divulging your identity to my driver?"

"Yes!"

"Oh," he said, his voice heavy with irony. "How very thoughtful of you." His lips curled in a terse smile. "Well, given that I hardly knew Sylvia, I do suppose that one wife might be quite as good as another."

"Sylvia asked me to come here and call off your marriage," she continued, ignoring his mocking tone and the humiliation of knowing he'd kissed her just to toy with her.

"Ah," he said softly. "So you do know Sylvia."

The effort of speaking was making her throat burn so much that she felt like a woman who swallowed flaming swords at a circus for a living. She merely shook her head.

"You're in the habit of doing such large favors for people you don't even know?" His lips twisted into an increasingly cynical smile.

"I met her at the airport!" The man looked furious now, if also unnervingly self-contained.

He merely shrugged again. "I suppose that propensity for kindness to strangers explains why you'd agree to come here for her . . . and become my wife. That must have been your intention, since you brought a wedding gown."

Even she wasn't so nice that she'd play stand-in bride! Or was she? It sure looked like she was well on her way. Still, she wasn't about to let Nicholas Westhawke know she, too, had left a man at the altar.

For a moment, Angela was so lost in thought that she didn't realize Nicholas Westhawke was leaning extremely close to her again. Then her whole body went white-hot, like she'd just been hit by lightning, and her knees turned as rubbery as a string band. They buckled as in a wind, and she just knew a storm inside her was about to be set loose on the world . . . or on him. If anything, she'd imagined spending the night comforting a weeping, ditched groom! Defending her own honor had hardly entered the picture.

She shoved his shoulders with both her palms, as hard as she could. "Don't you dare come near me!" *Angela, you have to get out of here!*

He merely gazed at her, with those powerful eyes, as if to say he did what he pleased.

Angela knew it was time for her best non sequitur. Her best tactic in every come-on situation. Men—without exception—fled in terror when she dropped this line. She cleared her throat.

"I—I'm a virgin." She smiled sweetly, knowing Nicholas Westhawke was now wondering what was wrong with her. The odds were exactly four-to-ten that he would ask her how old she was, after a polite pause.

True to her expectations, he took a quick step backward. His beautiful eyes widened and his lips twisted in a way that almost made him look cute...if such a man could ever look cute.

Good. She was back on her own turf. The poor man was staring at her as if she were from another planet. *And whatever planet it is, it's sure not Venus,* she thought a little sadly.

"You're really serious," he said after a long moment. "Aren't you?"

"I'll tell you," she croaked, "when you tell me why that damn metal door where you keep your things has a padlock on it." She let her gaze slowly drop from his eyes down the length of his body, as if it didn't affect her in the least. And then she glanced around at the luxurious room, just as casually as you please.

"I'd say your torture chamber was in there," she added, raising her arm, to indicate their current surroundings. "But now, I've already visited it."

He stared at her as if she'd gone crazy, right in front of his eyes. She straightened her shoulders, pointed her chin in the air, then daintily raised her wedding gown above her ankles.

She knew good and well that his eyes could stop her in her tracks. She managed to ignore them, brush past him and step over the threshold, hoping with all her heart that for the last brief heroic moment, she'd looked nowhere near as lost as she felt.

When she turned, her gaze settled on his shoes, which was a far safer choice than his eyes. "And Nicholas? Your name *is* Nicholas, isn't it?"

"Something else for you today, Lady Westhawke?" he asked, sounding shocked.

"I like my breakfast at six," she said coolly. "And I would prefer never to see another kidney pie."

Chapter Three

Nicholas very calmly unknotted his tie while he watched her retreating back. His mood felt nearly as stormy as the kiss he'd shared with ... he still didn't even know her name!

The woman—whoever she was—had begun this game of confused identities and he'd almost enjoyed playing it out. She'd made her bed, probably at Sylvia Sinclair's urging, and he'd let her lie in it awhile. Or rather, he thought wryly, he'd let her squirm in it until he tracked down Sylvia and demanded an explanation. This time, one he could believe. In the meantime, he could only hope the grand arrival he'd planned for Sylvia had put her on edge, which was what she deserved.

"And there's more to come," he murmured, as her white-clad figure continued to recede down the unlit paneled hallway. In spite of her duplicity, he had to fight the urge to chase her down. A part of him even wanted to divest the rest of his suit before he did.

His measured breaths fell rhythmically with each of her steps, and the very air seemed to say, *Don't be a fool, Nicholas. Follow and conquer.* He could still taste her lips, still feel the way her knees had buckled and still see the startled wonder in her dark eyes when she'd looked into his.

"What's going on here?" he muttered. And why, for the first time in three long years, did he feel so completely alive?

Why didn't he feel coldhearted fury? After all, the one sure fact was that Sylvia Sinclair had called off their marriage. Which, he now knew, was definitely for the best.

When the woman was good and gone, Nicholas shrugged from his jacket. It landed half on the chaise lounge and half on the oriental rug; one sleeve draped over a heaping stack of New York and London newspapers. With an arching sweep of his long, sinuous arm, he retrieved the jacket and tossed it toward the closet.

He glanced quickly through all the apartments that led to his bedroom. The mystery woman—with her rosebud lips and pale, flushed, very full pink breasts—hadn't even been able to see through all the rooms, to that level of sumptuousness. Nonetheless, Nicholas knew the outer salon had overwhelmed her. Its walls and doorways, which were gilded with fleur-de-lis and heavenly cherubs, and the brocade furniture, and prismed chandelier might have proved a little daunting.

Had the woman actually met Sylvia Sinclair in an airport, as she'd said? *No, she was lying.*

As he began walking toward his innermost room, he deftly released the pearl stud buttons from his shirt and pocketed them. By the time he'd reached the long rail that lay in front of his bed, he was stepping from his trousers. "Baskerville," he said in greeting when he heard a low half yip under the bed.

The dog's wet nose lifted the bed's dust ruffle, and Nicholas chuckled. He tossed his trousers over the rail, then headed for the closet that contained his work clothes and found his hospital greens and lab coat.

"I'd be a bloody fool to lose a night's work over her, Baskerville," he muttered, shrugging into the clothes.

Thoughtfully, he pressed an intercom button. "Mrs. O'Reilly?"

"Sir?"

He was relieved to hear his housekeeper sound so awake. "I believe you'll find a bride wandering the halls. She likes breakfast at six, detests kidney pie and is probably lost." *Which is all I know about her.*

"I'll be glad to find her."

"Good," Nicholas said, fishing in his night-table drawer for the key to his padlocked workshop. "And when you do..."

"Yes, sir?"

"Please lock her in."

"Sir, I didn't have time to inform you that she picked the lock last time."

Nicholas's mouth went dry. The lock hadn't been a particularly secure one; he was merely indulging Sylvia, since she'd said she wanted to feel like a woman locked in a tower who was about to be swept away by an English knight. "Use both locks this time," he finally said, then released the intercom button.

If his mystery spouse could pick locks, she could be a criminal, he realized. Was she a fortune hunter? Had she done something horrid to Sylvia Sinclair, in order to take her place... and make a killing? Should he call the police?

Still, if this were some prank, then he'd look ridiculous, especially since he'd been left at the altar. He didn't want bobbies charging up to Westhawke Hall in the middle of the night, either. It was the only time he could work and his deadlines were tight. Besides, they might wake Rosemunde. Of course, the fact that the stranger was beautiful had nothing to do with his decision not to call.

But she *was* beautiful....

And possibly dangerous.

Nicholas found and pocketed his workshop key as he picked up the phone. He'd never actually spoken to Sylvia, but it was high time he did. Either she had played a nasty prank by sending another bride in her place, which should make him furious. Or there was the other possibility, the one he didn't want to think about.

Was the woman a hardened criminal with a money scheme? Or was his mind—which was so accustomed to the realm of ghouls and goblins—merely working overtime? She'd hardly looked like a criminal, but then he assumed most women didn't while wearing a wedding gown.

It was early evening in Connecticut, and Nicholas knew he wouldn't be able to work until he knew Sylvia Sinclair was safe. As much as he hated her horrendous prank—if that was what it was—he had to know she hadn't been harmed. He glanced in his little black book, then punched in the United States country code and Sylvia's number.

As the phone rang, he decided his best defense would be to thank Sylvia Sinclair. After all, the woman she'd sent had felt better in his arms than any other woman ever had. Including, he thought, with a shock that suddenly shook his whole body, his late wife.

NOT TEN SECONDS after Angela fled inside her room, she heard the lock cylinders turn, and then the bolts—two this time—slid home with definite, resounding clanks.

She felt so rattled she didn't even mind. In fact, she thought, as she rummaged through her returned suitcase, she was glad she was trapped. The way the man's kiss had made her feel, she could probably use a lock or two...to keep her from falling into his arms again.

"Of course, I can always pick them," she muttered throatily. She wished Nicholas's oddly intense eyes would quit haunting her, and that she had something other than her honeymoon peignoir set to wear. She slipped into the gown.

It was floor length, with tiny, delicate straps and layers of sheer, wispy white illusion lace. The robe was nothing more than a long-sleeved layer of transparent film that made her appear every inch the gothic heroine.

Every inch the virginal woman locked in a tower, too, she thought sadly as she flicked off the bedside lamp. She told herself she had to move the rose on her bed if she was going to sleep, and yet once she'd touched it, she couldn't quite force herself to lay it aside again. It hadn't fully bloomed; the simple bud, so thoughtfully placed, was just about to flower. She could almost see the petals unfolding before her eyes, slowly releasing all the romantic promise in the world....

If the man had known she wasn't Sylvia Sinclair, why had he kissed her anyway? Had he been as instantly attracted to her as she had been to him? After all, that had a great deal to do with why she hadn't confronted him immediately. She blew out a sigh, wondering if the wild, little girl she'd seen was actually his daughter and, if so, what had happened to his wife.

She carried the rose toward the recess in the room and unlatched one of the tall, rectangular windows, telling herself she needed some air, to clear her mind. As stressed as she was, it was understandable that a day such as this one would leave her feeling restless.

The double windows suddenly blew inward. Her skin chilled, since she couldn't help but remember all the horror films she'd seen where virginal women slept peacefully, until such windows opened of their own accord—for Dracula, Nosferatu, Svengali—or some such man with mesmerizing eyes and charismatic powers. A man such as Nicholas Westhawke.

She leaned far out, bending over the sill, the sleeves of her white gown billowing with the coastal breeze, her fingers gently touching the contours of the rose. Looking down, she realized just how foolish a window escape would be. About thirty feet below her, adjacent to the second floor of the castle, was a stone terrace. On either side of the east and west wings were the two rounded, crenellated towers.

Her gaze roved over an unused fountain beyond the terrace and the many overgrown shrubs that looked as if they'd once comprised grand landscaped gardens. Suddenly, she gasped. A wolflike creature was running toward the eerie cliffs. It *was* a wolf.

And Nicholas Westhawke. He was moving swift footedly over the rugged terrain, following the wolf. His hair was so white that the full moon seemed to catch in it. Shining strands feathered across his face with the breeze, and the tails of a long white coat flapped against his sides.

The man looked so otherworldly that Angela couldn't force herself to move, even though she knew she was in danger of being seen. He knelt periodically, and with something she couldn't see, began drawing shapes on the ground. Glow-in-the-dark spray paint? she wondered. At least, she hoped that was what it was.

How could someone so fantastic-looking be so strange? After a moment, she decided it made sense. It was like when people didn't hear very well but could taste twice as well. Nicholas Westhawke had clearly paid for his looks by being severely lacking in the sanity department. But was he always as hard to handle as he'd been this evening?

When he stepped back, silvery, dustlike shapes glowed in the dark—circles and X's and arrows that glimmered in the moonlight. Gazing at him, Angela felt her mouth go dry. Something strange was going on here, and yet Sylvia Sinclair had seemed too normal to involve herself with someone crazy. Nicholas Westhawke—at choice moments, of course, like when he smiled—looked truly normal.

As if sensing her presence all along, Nicholas turned slowly and stared at her. Angela's heart thudded dully in her ears and her cheeks began to burn. He looked every bit the mythic man—his broad shoulders thrown back, his chin held a little haughtily in the air, his white blond hair blowing. *Why move?* she thought a little dreamily. *The man's already caught me watching him.*

She was a good thirty feet up, and he was the equivalent of a football field away... and yet those reference points—football fields and measurements in footage—hardly fit this strange place or these strange circumstances. He began to walk stealthily toward the castle and she clutched the rose so tightly that a thorn pricked her finger. Not that it brought her back to reality, of course.

Don't do it, Angela. The urge to call out to him was so compelling that she couldn't fight it. Even from this distance, she could feel the heat in those marvelous eyes. And it was her wedding night, she thought. Or, it was supposed to be. He reached the fountain in no time, and then he lithely floated up the steps to the terrace.

Don't do it, Angela! But he cut such a romantic figure that she quickly tossed the rose over the windowsill. "Now, I bet you're really wondering about me, Nicholas Westhawke," she whispered with a smile.

His stride was even, and his long, lean, well-muscled legs carried him toward her as if he were moving on the wind. The nearing touch of his midnight blue eyes was as tactile as if his lips were searing hers. He leaned agilely and lifted the rose from the terrace.

And then the spell was broken. Angela even found herself laughing. The enigmatic Lord Westhawke stuck the rose between his teeth, stared up at her and waved. In a heartbeat, he disappeared inside. She stood there for long moments, still smiling. He'd given the kind of playful, flirtatious gesture that said he was a regular guy. Sweet, even. As soon as he cooled off about being left at the altar, he'd undoubtedly drive her back to London, himself.

All at once, the wind picked up perceptibly and the wolf, who had been standing on the cliffs, howled and bolted for cover. Wings flapped madly in the treetops and a flock of birds arrowed toward the sky. Angela clutched the windowsill. Something was about to happen.

A thick, white mist seemed to roll up from the sea and buffet the edge of the cliffs. When it dissipated, three women were left standing right on top of the strange, dustlike shapes Nicholas had drawn. For all the world, the women looked like the brides of Dracula. She was not imagining them, no more than she'd imagined Nicholas Westhawke's bewitching eyes.

Yes, three women in long, white gowns and with flowing dark hair were wavering on the cliffs. They were transparent, and through their bodies Angela could see the cliffs and the stars and the moon. She couldn't move, no more than if Nicholas's arms held her captive. She couldn't even move when they began walking toward the terrace. . . .

The wolf shot from the cover of a stand of trees, lunged at them, then ran right through their bodies. Angela's mouth dropped as, one by one, each of the brides vanished—just the way Frankie Mancini probably thought she had today—into thin air.

In their wake, Angela recalled how Nicholas had said people disappeared sometimes. There was no doubt in her mind that Nicholas had made those brides do so, somehow. But was it because his own wife had vanished?

"FEELING RIGHT AT HOME?" Nicholas forced himself to ask the next evening. The woman had completely opened the house. *His house.* The summer breeze filtered through windows and doors and hazy beams of sunlight streamed into long-forgotten corners. The scent of garlic and peppers had led him right to her.

It was six in the evening, he'd just risen from bed and his eyes still felt heavy with sleep. She'd caught him off guard the previous night by looking so lovely, all dressed in white and framed in the window. But now he hoped his brides had thrown her off kilter, since that was where he intended to keep her during her stay. Which, he assured himself, would be short-lived.

"You call this place a home?" the woman finally returned, without even looking at him.

Her voice was back, even if it occasionally caught sexily in her throat. He didn't know whether it was because of her comment about his ancestral castle or because her knee-length skirt allowed him to see her legs for the first time, but he advanced on her in the large modernized kitchen. He didn't stop until he was leaning idly against the counter next to her.

"If it's not a home, then what would you call it, luv?"

She whirled around to face him. Her hair, which had lain over her shoulder, whipped right against his black T-shirt with such force it almost stung. When she realized they were only inches apart, her dark, flashing eyes widened. Why did they have to look so fiery and intense and . . . wonderfully alive? Every time she looked at him, he was reminded of what a hermit he'd become. And that he'd been as celibate as a monk.

"So what would you call it?" he finally repeated.

"Monstrosity?" she asked, keeping her voice level. "I spent all morning trying to get some air into it. It's nothing more than a stuffy, old, creaky—"

"Chamber of horrors" he prodded, with a mocking smile. "Or did you really believe it was haunted?"

"If you understand the effect the place has on people, I'd think you'd spruce it up." She nearly snarled the words. "I'd get rid of the wolves, too. Not to mention the vanishing brides. It might also be nice not to lock in your guests."

The darker depths of her eyes looked so brightly alert that he nearly smiled. "So you liked my brides?" he asked softly, feeling almost sorry he'd scared her. He glanced pointedly away, down the long, wide kitchen counter. His usually pristine Formica was flour coated and strewn with mixing bowls. Chopped vegetables lay in piles on cutting boards and globs of dough-dotted waxed paper covered all the remaining surfaces. He tried to ignore that the place smelled like heaven.

"Well, my monstrosity *was* clean." His gaze returned to hers.

"Look," she said. "I wouldn't be here at all, if I could figure out a way to carry my suitcase back to London without a ride! It's hardly my fault that Sylvia ditched you!" She threw up a hand, as if he were being entirely unreasonable, and half grunted a quick "Ha!" She also stepped away from him. He quickly moved forward, figuring if his presence made her uncomfortable, it might be something he could use for leverage.

"Even if you don't have a name, you must be Italian-American," he said. His gaze dropped from her sparkling eyes, to her petite, saucily rounded figure, then to her slender legs.

She heaved a heavy mixing bowl into her arms and began to stir some meat concoction, as if to save her life. The amount of culinary activity in his kitchen superseded the ordinary, so he could only guess that cooking was something his mystery wife did when she was upset.

"And what exactly do you mean by that remark?" she finally burst out.

A wry smile touched at his lips and he leaned closer. He shoved his hands in the back pockets of his well-worn black jeans, hoping he looked far more in control than he felt. "Well, luv, your coloring, combined with your penchant for garlic, peppers and olive oil, not to mention the way you throw your hands in the air and say 'ha' and 'ah'..." He could tell that rankled, by the way she slammed down mixing bowl number one.

"I did not say 'ah,'" she snapped. She brushed past him, now hauling away mixing bowl number two. Her shoulder and hip grazed him as she passed. Not that she seemed to notice. She slammed down bowl two, which contained dough, and started rolling it out on the opposite counter-top.

"So, you little fireball," he continued, half glad he'd just found out how to unnerve her. "Your name must be—" He paused, staring at her no-nonsense blouse, which was hardly criminal wear. Her equally practical skirt was suitcase rumpled, but she still looked as fabulous as she had in her wedding gown. "Christina Marie," he continued softly, wondering what her name really was. "Or maybe just Mary..."

She turned around so fast that her hair caught in the flour and a tiny ray of powdery dust sprinkled over the floor. "It's Angela."

"Knew I'd get it out of you, somehow," he said, trying to keep his tone gruff.

"Why, aren't you full of tricks!" she exclaimed, without masking her irony. "But it hardly bothers me that you're so dense as to stereotype Italians," she continued. "Just don't forget that all English aristocrats—"

"So you *do* know I'm an aristocrat?" he interrupted, suddenly feeling sure she was a fortune hunter.

She looked him up and down and her estimation clearly wasn't good. "Oh, please," she snapped. "Who could miss it?"

Once again, Nicholas had to remind himself not to smile. He now understood why he hadn't immediately called the bobbies. In his entire life, no one—absolutely not one single person—had ever talked to him the way she did. It was a bit shocking, but for the briefest instant, he felt like a regular Joe. Like someone people weren't afraid to get mad at.

"As I was saying before I was so rudely interrupted," she continued huffily, "don't forget that English aristocrats look like death warmed over, by which I mean unaccountably pale, and live in decadent, spooky castles on cliffs. They're always in need of nannies, since they're unmarried, too." She glanced quickly around the kitchen, and then glared straight into his eyes. "And for very good reason."

Does she know I'm a widower? "Well, my marital status is the question, isn't it?" he managed to say. He crossed the room again, very much doubting that she thought he looked like death warmed over, since no woman ever had. He brushed past her, so close the hairs on their arms touched. In just a breath, his arms could have snaked around her waist and pulled her next to him. He leaned against the counter.

"Your marital status is hardly my concern," she said loftily.

At that, he crossed his hands over his chest and simply stared. "Oh, no?"

She smiled tightly. "Oh, no."

"So far, this is a complete repeat performance of last night, luv," he said, feeling his temper surfacing. "Except that I now know your name." He caught her elbow and turned her to face him. "Angela," he said softly, thinking, even as he said it, that it suited her. "Do you mind telling me just who the hell you are?"

She merely stared into his eyes for long moments, looking like she was drowning. Suddenly, she blinked and attempted to shrug off his grasp. He tightened his hold. She was so round and soft against his hardened muscles that he drew in a quick breath and braced himself against the counter. "Who are you?" he repeated, his voice lowering and becoming silkily persuasive.

"I told you that my name's Angela. Lancini," she added as if that could explain everything, including the sparks that were igniting between them.

Has it really been three years since I've been so near a woman? Three long, hard years since I've kissed one's lips the way I've kissed hers? Suddenly, his mouth felt as dry as brittle paper. "Lancini," he echoed, sounding as hoarse as she had the previous night.

Involuntarily, he tugged and drew her a half step closer. "Well, Angela Lancini..." Her wonderfully lively eyes were mere inches from his own. "I may be an English aristocrat in a spooky house, but then, that's hardly a mystery now, is it?"

"May be an English aristocrat?" she burst out, her gaze flying from his and fidgeting around the room. "We already established that you are. And besides, all the rococo and baroque decor in this castle would easily speak for itself."

"So, I see you know your architectural styles," he said with a lightness he didn't feel. Not when this fiery woman was so close. Not when those rosebud lips were pursed just inches from his own. Not when she was berating him for a life-style he had hardly chosen.

"Rococo," she snapped. "Wall panels, too much gold, not to mention gilded bronze and lots of ridiculous curlicues. Introduced into Europe in the mid-eighteenth century. Just what do you think I am, Westhawke? An idiot?"

She wrenched out of his grasp with a movement so lithe and quick that his jaw dropped. He watched her charge toward the other side of the kitchen again, with her chin jutting out into the air.

"And you think *I'm* regal?" he muttered. The way she dominated his kitchen, she might well have been the Queen Mother, herself, snapping at hired help.

"I most certainly do," she said in a singsong voice that particularly annoyed him.

"Am I supposed to graciously accept this situation?" he continued. "A strange woman popping up on my doorstep, cooking in my kitchen, sleeping in my—"

She whirled around. "Need I remind you," she said pointedly, "I was locked in. And you hardly seem inclined to offer transport out of this nightmare."

"So, which part's the nightmare?" he found himself asking. "Me or the house?"

"Both, Mr. Westhawke."

"Lord," he corrected. "Remember?"

"Oh, pardon me," she said, suddenly gentling her voice and bending into a pretty, nicely done mock curtsy. "My lord." She smiled coyly. "Far be it from me to complain about your locking me in."

"Luv," he said flatly, "for all I know, you're an ax murderer."

"Murderess, my lord," she countered, gracefully rising from her curtsy.

"Is that an admission that you're a criminal?" he managed to ask.

"I'm not—"

"Judging from the way you're so well versed concerning architectural styles, could it be you've researched my humble abode?"

"Researched you?" She sounded genuinely puzzled.

"You're a con artist," he bit out. "A fortune hunter."

"Oh, please!" she exclaimed. "I take it you're supposed to be my good fortune?" Her gaze dropped boldly over him, as if to say that not one single inch of him had fortune written on it.

He advanced on her again.

"Would you please quit pursuing me?" she snapped.

When she glanced over her shoulder, he shot her a smile. "Why, luv," he said softly. "As near as I can tell, I may be the one who's being pursued. In which case, you're the hunter."

"Huntress." She tossed her head and turned back to her rolling pin.

"Whatever," he muttered.

Just as he came up behind her, she whirled around again. The rolling pin was in her hand, and for a second, he was sure she meant to slug him with it. Even he hadn't meant to get quite this close. But since he was, he rested his hands on the counter on either side of her. "I don't intend to quit pursuing you until you tell me who you are."

"I have told you—"

"I want more than your name."

"I'm sure you do," she snapped, meeting his gaze dead on.

"Do what?" he asked, unable to hide his teasing tone. *What's she doing to me? Am I actually flirting?*

Her face turned beet red, and he was oddly disappointed when she didn't take up the innuendo. He definitely wanted to hear phrases like "want more" come from between those lovely lips. Instead, she nearly screamed, "Rosemunde!"

His whole body froze. The woman had met his daughter! Of course, while he'd been sleeping, Mrs. O'Reilly had fed her breakfast and brought her downstairs. She'd probably told Angela that he was a widower, too. He glanced over his shoulder, then stepped quickly back. Through two sets of doors, he could see Rosemunde setting the formal dining table!

"Yes, Mum!" Rosemunde appeared in the doorway and waved.

Mum? Rosemunde had seen Sylvia Sinclair's photo and knew Angela wasn't her! That his daughter was referring to their strange guest as her mother was even more disconcerting than Angela Lancini's proximity.

"Have you finished setting the table?" Angela called, as if it were the most reasonable question in the world.

"Just another minute," Rosemunde yelled. Nicholas watched his daughter vanish from the doorway, presumably to complete her domestic chore. She'd never set a table in her life!

"Ingratiating yourself with my little girl?" he asked in shock. This whole game, whatever it was, had gone too far. Worry wasn't even the word for what he was feeling.

Angela observed him coolly. "So sorry," she shot back. "But your daughter wants to call me Mum, even though I explained that I am not, by any stretch of the imagination, her mother. She also looks a little lonely. Besides which, she clearly hasn't had a decent meal in years."

For the briefest moment, Nicholas's concern for his daughter overrode his worries about Angela. "She eats quite well. Why, she . . ." He wanted to say that Rosemunde was merely at the bottomless-pit tomboy age. She ate all day, every day, and was still as skinny as a reed. "I mean, Rosemunde . . ."

"Has clearly eaten far too many kidney pies," she finished.

"I like kid—"

"You would," she said dryly. "But don't you think *she* deserves real food? Not to mention playmates?"

Clearly, once they were off the subject of who she was, the woman regained her footing. She was making him feel guilty as sin, too. Since his wife's death, he'd felt like half the father he used to be.

"I mean, ghost brides and wolves and carriage rides on the cliffs are fine," Angela continued, "but don't you think she's still a bit young? Couldn't we save those amusements until her preteens, at least, dear? Perhaps, for this year, we should just get her an ordinary bicycle?'' A wide, very false smile suddenly lit up her face. ''Or what about a nice crawling hand!''

Nicholas stared at her, slack jawed. Was she just baiting him, or did she *know* Rosemunde had an upcoming birthday? The only way to throw Angela off balance, and the only way he was going to get any solid information out of her, was to use his physical presence. That much, he'd discovered.

He glanced toward the dining room, making sure Rosemunde wasn't present, then swiftly curled his hand around her neck, his long fingers deftly fisting into the tangle of silky black hair at her nape. He kissed her, quick and hard, telling himself it was an unfortunate necessity. It lasted less than a millisecond, but he could tell he'd acted swiftly and effectively enough to shock her into silence.

''I told you!'' she squeaked.

''Yes?'' he prodded.

''I met Sylvia Sinclair in Kennedy airport yesterday.''

She sucked in a quick, quavering breath. He'd meant to continue with his interrogation. Instead, he found himself asking, ''Do you always react to kisses as if they contain truth-telling Pentothal, luv?''

''I—I—just . . . stand back!'' she said, gasping.

He casually stepped back a pace, but never took his eyes from hers.

''I was in a wedding dress,'' she continued. ''And I guess she saw me . . . and since weddings were on her mind, she followed me into the ladies' room, where I went to change clothes. I was looking for somewhere to go, and she had apparently decided to call off her marriage to you. . . .''

Nicholas's eyes narrowed with every word. Angela might not be a criminal, but she was clearly a little strange. Of course, she probably wasn't nearly as strange as she *thought* he was.

"And so I took her ticket and said I'd tell you your marriage was . . . well, canceled . . . and—" She stopped talking and gulped.

He decided she looked a little vulnerable. She definitely looked honest. Still, it was the craziest story he'd ever heard. "You were running through Kennedy airport in a wedding dress?" he finally asked, wondering why.

She heaved a relieved sigh. "Yes!"

She looked so trustworthy that it was hard not to believe her. But she was potentially dangerous, he reminded himself. "So where's Sylvia?" he asked after a pregnant pause, wishing he'd spoken to Sylvia, rather than to her mother.

Her face went ashen. "Why, at home, I suppose."

He shook his head slowly. "Guess again, luv."

"Why don't you try to call—" Her dark eyebrows crinkled in seeming concern.

"I did," he said, more curtly than he'd intended.

"And?"

And I should have confronted you again last night, but got sidetracked when you donned that white gown and tossed me a rose. For the first time since they'd encountered one another, the woman—Angela Lancini, he reminded himself—looked as if she were barely aware of him at all.

"And Sylvia Sinclair," he said, scrutinizing her, "has vanished." When Angela didn't respond, he continued. "Disappeared. Poof. Gone. I was on the phone half the night, and as near as I can tell, no one's seen her since she picked up her ticket at the British Airways counter."

"Maybe she decided to take a vacation," Angela said weakly.

"Maybe," he countered noncommittally. "And maybe not. Either way, Missing Persons won't get involved for another week." Nicholas turned on his heel and headed for the door. "Meantime—"

"There's no meantime," she said flatly. "I need a ride out of here! According to Mrs. O'Reilly, we're in the middle of nowhere!"

"In the meantime," he continued smoothly, "I'll be in the dining room, waiting for my dinner." He paused at the doorway and turned to look at her again. For all the worry she'd caused him, he was half pleased to see her collapse against the counter, as if she needed support. "And luv?"

Seconds stretched to full minutes, during which they simply stared at one another. Somehow, she just looked too sweet to have been involved with Sylvia's disappearance.

"What?" At midword, her voice cracked with tension.

"Until my intended bride shows—" He shot her a tight smile. "You can consider yourself—" *Effectively kidnapped.* "My...house guest." He turned away and was still congratulating himself on his decent parting line when he heard the kitchen door open.

Behind him, Angela yelled, "Baskerville! C'mon, boy!"

Nicholas stopped in his tracks. It was bad enough that the woman's kisses had revived his long-suppressed desires. But she'd conned his daughter, begun cleaning his house and was befriending his dog, too! He was going to be in dire straits if he didn't locate Sylvia soon. Because Angela Lancini couldn't have sounded more confident if she really were the new Lady Westhawke.

Chapter Four

"If I find you, Angela, I'll kill you," Frankie muttered. He turned down the air-conditioning as he headed for the living room. How could she have gotten him into this bind? It was afternoon, but Sylvia Sinclair was still pacing in her cute, little, fuzzy, sock-style slippers. Frankie had to admit it was a step up from the previous night—his supposed wedding night—when Sylvia had actually cried. Seeing women cry broke Frankie's heart. It was like seeing lost kittens, or kids with bad parents.

Frankie cleared his throat. "Ms. Sinclair?"

The damnably adorable Sylvia turned around but remained mum. Frankie tried to look relaxed, but the woman was making him feel like a klutzy construction worker lumbering through a room full of china. That was pretty much his situation, he thought. Except, he was a locksmith.

Sylvia's rumpled blue blouse was buttoned to her chin for self-protection and her pretty hands peeked beneath the longish cotton sleeves. Behind her, through the window, was the wide expanse of Central Park West.

"Or may I please call you Sylvia?" Frankie finally continued. He tried to forget that the only way he'd gotten her name was by rifling through her pocketbook and that he'd wrestled her bodily into his car at the airport. When she said nothing, he quickly added, "With all due respect."

Sylvia crossed her arms, sniffed mournfully, then sat down, perching daintily on the edge of a white sofa. She clasped her hands tightly in her lap.

Frankie couldn't figure out why he suddenly felt so...well, responsible for her. Sylvia was the only living link he knew of between himself and the woman who was to have been his wife, and yet he kept wondering if she was comfortable. He'd seen the women together and was positive Sylvia knew Angela's whereabouts.

His buddies Eddie and Paulie, who were now playing poker in the next room, had agreed to help him find Angela, and his cousin Tony had lent Frankie his swanky Upper West Side apartment, which was now headquarters for operations. Frankie could hardly have taken Sylvia to his place; he lived with his mother. The apartment he'd rented for himself and Angela was out of the question, too. What if Angela returned and found him with Sylvia? He shuddered to think of it, since Angela had a temper.

Sylvia Sinclair's lower lip started to tremble, so Frankie lumbered toward the sofa, determined to stop her from crying again. "Mind if I sit down?" He took her silence for a "yes" and plopped down next to her. Then, before he knew what was happening, he rested his hands on hers. She gasped and her cheeks flushed bright pink.

"Ms. Sinclair? I mean—er—Sylvia?"

Her bright blue eyes skated across his face before she lowered her lids and stared down at the large hands that covered hers.

Not knowing what to do, Frankie squeezed her fingers, hoping to comfort her. The way her blush deepened in direct response to his touch somehow reminded him of mood rings from the 1970s. He decided that Sylvia wasn't scared to death, which was what he'd previously thought, but rather impossibly shy.

"Are you sure you don't need to call anyone and tell them you're all right? Or maybe you didn't sleep last night. Are you afraid of the dark, Sylvia? Do you want a night-light or something?"

"Hey, keep it down, would ya? Some people are trying to play cards here."

Frankie glanced toward the doorway. Eddie was leaning against the jamb. He was shirtless and his jeans were unsnapped. Sylvia Sinclair suddenly squeezed Frankie's hand, so hard it hurt.

"Hey, Eddie, why don't you make yourself decent?" Frankie said quickly. "There's a lady present, if you hadn't noticed."

Sylvia really was some lady, Frankie thought as Eddie disappeared. She was both athletic and regal looking, with a perfect, freckled ski-jump nose, a thick brown bob and a blush that reminded a man that innocence still existed in the world.

"Thank you," Sylvia said after a long moment. Her voice sounded tremulous.

"Yes!" Frankie exclaimed, feeling his heart soar. "The lady speaks!" Suddenly, Frankie almost blushed himself, embarrassed by his own enthusiasm. "Sorry," he said swiftly. "Guess I'm used to people who talk a lot." When she didn't respond, he weakly added, "Maybe because I'm Italian." He swallowed. "Look, why don't you just tell me where Angela is and then I can take you home?"

"I swore—I—I wouldn't tell," she said. Her lips shut in a determined little line.

Frankie's mouth dropped open in astonishment. "Angela is hiding from me? All this time, I thought something horrible happened! Where is she?"

No answer. Sylvia Sinclair's warm hands remained folded tightly beneath his, as if she were afraid to move a muscle.

"Could I have something hot to drink, to help me sleep?" she finally asked. "I want to take a nap."

They were the first complete sentences she'd managed without stammering, and Frankie felt somehow relieved. Sylvia was the shyest woman he'd ever met, but he was suddenly sure she'd tell him where Angela was. He'd get the information out of her, one way or another. "How about steamed milk with Orzata?" he offered in the gentlest voice he could muster.

ANGELA WISHED NICHOLAS wasn't seating her for dinner with such gallant aplomb, while Rosemunde squirmed into her own chair. He smelled of woodsy heather, salty rain and the great outdoors. She could still feel his hard, quick kiss on her lips. Not that she had any illusions about that. The man was merely trying to shock her.

But where could Sylvia Sinclair have gone?

"Thank you so much," she managed to say, as Nicholas scooted an overstuffed high-backed chair beneath her behind.

"My pleasure." His tone turned gruff, as if to say he was only doing his duty. Angela guessed he opened doors and walked on the outside of road curbs with the same habitual air. If it had occurred to him to let her seat herself, he would have.

Only three chairs were positioned around the formal dining table, which was elegant, polished and so long the New York Giants could play ball on it. Sterling service plates gleamed up at her, empty and waiting for the food plates, which would undoubtedly be of antique china.

Everything seemed so overdone that Angela had an absurd impulse to wrench the meal she'd cooked from Mrs. O'Reilly's hands and serve it on paper plates with plastic silverware. She'd bring a squeeze bottle of catsup for good measure. Now, that would shake up little Mr. Aristocrat, she thought, with a smile. And if not, it would at least make their stiff dinner more homey.

He couldn't really mean to keep her in this dusty, old castle until Sylvia Sinclair reappeared, could he? She inadvertently drew in a sharp breath, when Nicholas finally turned and headed toward the opposite end of the table.

"This is sort of like eating in front of a mirror," Angela said sarcastically, in an effort to deflect what his presence did to her. She stared down, able to see each nuance of her own reflection in both the gleaming wood and the sterling service plate.

She glanced up at Nicholas, who was still ambling toward the head of the table. He'd pulled his long hair into a ponytail that hung between his shoulder blades. Against his taut, dark T-shirt, his hair looked as white as snow. Snug black jeans hugged his hips.

"Well," she continued with forced brightness, staring at her own reflection again, "at least I can keep myself company, seeing as everyone else has been seated *miles* away."

She shot her sassiest smile at Nicholas's back, but it faltered when he turned around. His lean, well-formed body lithely slid into a chair, so she faced him over the table's shining expanse, with only the centerpiece—a bowl of floating roses—between them.

Rosemunde sat calmly at midtable, facing the roses. And she looked much better, Angela thought. As soon as she'd met the little girl, she'd taken a comb and pair of scissors to her hair. The result wasn't exactly professional, but at least the tawny mass was even and brushed. Angela simply couldn't believe that Nicholas hadn't seen to it.

"Have a problem with Westhawke Hall's dining accommodations, Lady Westhawke?" Nicholas asked, in a tone that was as caustic as it was playfully innocent.

"Sorry," Angela called coyly, "I can't quite hear you." If he intended to keep her here against her will, the least she could do was make him miserable, she thought. "Perhaps you're too far away." She cleared her throat and added, "My lord."

"I could always come closer, luv."

"That's not necessary," she said quickly.

"Then, perhaps we should install telephones, one for each diner at the table," he said. A false smile twitched at his bewitching lips, making him look both cynical and irresistible.

"By the time poor Mrs. O'Reilly walks around this table in order to serve us, she'll be fit enough for an Olympic marathon," Angela continued. The smile she'd plastered on her face was beginning to make her cheeks ache.

"It will take her so long that our food will be cold, I'm sure," Nicholas returned with mock gravity.

"Or we'll all starve," Angela put in hastily. She noticed that Rosemunde's head was moving from side to side. The little girl was taking in the interchanges like a referee at Wimbledon.

When Mrs. O'Reilly entered the room, they fell silent, and when the food was served, father and daughter began to eat with a vengeance. Mrs. O'Reilly had insisted Angela "take tea" not an hour ago, and she'd stuffed herself with numerous tiny sandwiches. Since she cooked when she was upset, and always sampled as she went, she'd lost her appetite entirely.

Nicholas was now seemingly ignoring her. He kept his fork in one hand, his knife in the other, barely glancing up while he dug into his veal and her favorite tortellini-and-olive salad. Did he really think he could keep her against her will? Between the house and him, she'd go out of her mind. Right now, the silence, punctuated only by the grandfather clock ticking in the hallway, was making her want to do something... well, loud.

Suddenly, against her will, she felt a little sorry for Nicholas and the motherless girl she now knew was his daughter. Why did widowers always pull at her heartstrings? Yes, the two definitely needed someone to put a little life into the old homestead. She clanked a heavy silver fork against her plate noisily, but no one even looked up.

At one point, midmeal, Nicholas did look at her, making her wonder how long she'd been staring at him. She tried not to blush. He gazed back levelly, his fork and knife suspended above his plate, as if he meant to quit eating altogether.

"Don't worry," she finally snapped, feeling defensive because she'd been caught scrutinizing him. "The veal's not poisoned."

"Well, if it is, it hasn't affected the flavor," Nicholas said almost amicably, with a smile that was clearly meant to unnerve her.

It was the most backhanded compliment Angela had ever received. "Thank you, I think," she returned.

"You're welcome, I'm sure," he said. Then, he fell to eating again.

Angela blew out a sigh, defiantly placed her elbows on the table and listened to the occasional, accidental clink of the heavy silver cutlery against the plates and the ticktock of the clock. It felt like Chinese water torture.

When Mrs. O'Reilly removed the dinner plates, Angela finally said, "Do you all always eat like this?"

Both Nicholas and Rosemunde looked at her with blank expressions. "No, usually we have kidney pie," Nicholas said with a quick, ironic grin.

"And you're in my chair," Rosemunde added. "Not that I mind," she continued quickly, flashing Angela a smile. "Mum."

Angela squinted at the youngster, wondering how long she meant to keep pretending Angela was her mother. She didn't dare glance in Nicholas's direction to see how he'd reacted. "I mean, in complete silence, at a table that could seat thirty people," she finally said.

"Twenty-six," Nicholas corrected.

"Well, do you?"

"Do I what?" he asked, as if he'd forgotten the topic. For a second, Angela was sure he was attempting to flirt with her.

"Oh, forget it," she returned, watching Mrs O'Reilly serve slices of a fruit tart Angela had baked. "But would you mind telling me where I am?" Mrs. O'Reilly had said she was "far west, near Saint Ives," which had told Angela nothing. Not that she was necessarily anxious to leave. The more she thought about her meager finances, the more workable the situation seemed.

"I should think your whereabouts would be obvious," Nicholas said.

"How's that?" Angela asked, not even bothering to keep up the pretense of a smile.

"You're in your dining room, Lady Westhawke," Nicholas returned, seemingly enjoying her discomfort.

Rosemunde giggled. "Quit teasing her, Dad," she said. "You're in Cornwall."

Cornwall! That was miles from London! Nicholas was right about one thing. She should have guessed. After all, Cornwall was reputed to be rainy, creepy and full of old, tumbledown stone castles on cliffs. It was supposed to have lots of ghost residents, too, she thought with a shudder. *Like those vanishing brides on the cliffs.* Exactly what had Nicholas been doing out there? And why couldn't she have gotten a free ticket to someplace else—like Hawaii?

"Great," she finally said, as the grandfather clock began to strike.

Mrs. O'Reilly bustled in at the last chime of seven and removed Nicholas's dessert plate. "You may take Rosemunde up to bed," Nicholas said to her. "I'm sure Lady Westhawke will be glad to serve my coffee in the drawing room."

Angela's eyes bugged. That he kept calling her Lady Westhawke was bad enough. But now he was referring to her as if she weren't even in the room! Did he really expect her to serve him coffee under the circumstances? *Coffee, tea or me,* she thought illogically.

Her gaze narrowed. "It may be obvious that I'm in Cornwall," she said. "But something else is equally apparent."

"Which is?" he asked lightly.

"That men expect women to wait on them, hand and foot, the whole world over," she snapped.

Nicholas merely chuckled. He rose gracefully, tossed his linen napkin beside his serving plate, turned and headed out the door. "You'll find me through the second door on the left," he called over one of his perfectly rounded shoulders.

"DID YOU BRING my coffee, wife?" he asked in an unreadable tone. He sounded half-angry and half as if he were attempting to tease.

Angela was too exasperated to really notice the room. Like every other, it was tastefully oppressive, so large you could get lost in it, and held a faint musty scent of old books and overstuffed furniture. She'd been impressed for the first twenty-four hours, but now her patience was wearing dangerously thin.

"Well?" he finally prodded.

"No," she said coolly. "I didn't bring your coffee. And I didn't forget, either. It was intentional."

"Ah." He flashed a quick insincere smile her way. "So you just came for the company?"

"Hardly," she returned. His kissable lips started to twitch, as if he found her amusing.

"Well, then . . ." he said.

Angela stared into his piercing blue violet eyes wondering how a fool English accent could make a phrase as silly as "well, then" sound so brilliant. She mustered her best mock-British tone and said, "Wall, than, whoot?"

In response, he threw his head back and laughed. He had a wonderful, resounding bass laugh that showed off two rows of perfect teeth. His laugh was so deep that Angela half expected it to echo in the cavernous room.

"Now, you knew I was English when you married me," he chided, his laughter tempering to a lopsided smile. "So would ya like some coffee?" he continued, in something meant to approximate an American accent.

Angela giggled, in spite of herself. He sounded like a cross between Peter O'Toole and Elvis. Just as quickly, her smile vanished. "I'd prefer not to have anything that might prolong my wakefulness," she said levelly, still feeling at war with herself about being here. If she weren't so broke, she'd fight harder to leave, she assured herself.

"Brandy, then?"

While Nicholas headed for a makeshift bar, she plopped down on an overstuffed sofa with all the lack of grace she could muster. The cushion beneath her sank until she could feel springs; the other half of the sofa raised simultaneously, with a puff of dust. Nicholas peered at her over the top of a crystal decanter, looking a little embarrassed.

"The place isn't quite as neat as it used to be," he said gruffly, as he poured two deep amber brandies into bowl-shaped glasses. "I let a lot of people go." His voice became lower still. "A few years ago."

Angela glanced around at the room's many treasures. The base of the marble-topped table beside her was so tarnished that it had to be made of pure silver. Tiny, ornate gold frames held countless old photographs. "How difficult for you," she crooned with irony. "Money troubles?"

He moved across the room so quickly that she almost gasped. "No," he said tersely, bending close as he placed her brandy on the end table. "I tired of having so many people around."

"Maybe they *tired* of being here," she returned. "I mean, no offense, but I'd sure rather be in London." *Even if this old castle is a bit hard to resist.*

"Oh, I'm sure you would," he said, sounding agreeable again.

She wondered just what it would take for this man to lose his calm, cool composure.

She wasn't a drinker, but she took a sip of brandy, anyway. A great ball of pure, flaming heat hit the back of her throat. She leaned forward so fast that the liquor nearly splashed out of her glass, then she started choking.

Nicholas was on the sofa in an instant. When he sat, the plump cushions readjusted again. She was buoyed back up in another puff of dust, and her chokes turned into sneezes. Even worse was the fact that he began rubbing her back. His palm drew circles over the area where her bra fastened. Thinking of his hand and her bra in the same context only deepened her blush.

"I'm just fine," she sputtered. She leaned back, slammed down her brandy glass and crossed her arms tightly over her chest.

"Are you sure, luv?"

He looked genuinely concerned, and she decided she would be fine if the man moved to the other end of the sofa. He remained on the middle cushion, so close his thigh touched hers, and took a sip of the infernal brandy. His went down as smooth as water.

Realizing she was staring at his moistened lips, she primly averted her gaze and took in the frames on the table. They looked priceless but held mere snapshots. All were of Nicholas and the woman who had undoubtedly been his wife. She was tall, willowy and blond. If people had compared her to any actress, it would have been Michelle Pfeiffer, Angela thought.

He'd been happily married, too. Although he looked his current age in the pictures, he'd seemed to lack the edgy, self-contained air that now clung to him like a second skin. Angela had seen glimpses of his sense of humor, but it seemed tinged with bitterness. He and his wife—whether they'd been sailing or bicycling or simply grinning for the camera—had clearly been inseparable.

She glanced beside her. One look at Nicholas's eyes and her chest constricted. She swallowed her own breath in an audible gulp and held it for a heartbeat. Those eyes had turned as hard as stones and his lips were stretched into a thin, bloodless line. He looked like he hated her.

Angela felt as if she'd been caught going through one of his more private drawers. "You're the one who suggested we come in here," she managed to say, knowing he couldn't argue with that. If he hadn't wanted her to see pictures of his wife, he should have thought of it before now, she thought defensively.

"That I did."

She watched him tilt back his head. His brandy glass followed, and he downed the remaining contents in one long draft. The liquor was so potent, Angela flinched just watching him.

"Strong stuff," she said weakly, hoping to steer the conversation clear of his wife.

"Come on," he said curtly. He rose from the sofa and shoved his hands in the front pockets of his jeans impatiently, as if he'd been waiting for a long time.

She'd expected a continued interrogation about Sylvia Sinclair, not for him to take her somewhere. Her heart soared. Maybe he felt his privacy had been invaded, since she'd been staring at pictures of his wife, and so he'd changed his mind and was taking her to London!

As much as she liked her new room, she simply couldn't stand to be stared at so coldly. "Where?" she asked hopefully.

"I'm locking you in for the night."

She wanted to say she was sorry for looking at the stupid snapshots, sorry they depicted the obviously perfect marriage he had lost, but she didn't. "It's not even eight o'clock," she protested.

His arm swept across the room. "Feel free to take a book," he said flatly.

The books were so big she could read titles from where she was sitting. "The *Aeneid* by Virgil, Pliny's *Histories, The Philosophy of History* by Hegel." She scowled at him. "I'm afraid they'd put me to sleep."

He stared right back. "As I said, feel free to take a book."

"I'm not staying here!" she nearly shouted. At times, the man seemed as if he were actually flirting with her, then he turned around and shot her truly murderous glances. It was driving her crazy.

"Well, then, luv," he said in a bored tone. "You're free to walk back to America."

Not knowing what else to do, she rose daintily from the sofa. For a full minute, she made a show of dusting off her skirt and picking imaginary lint from it. Then she literally skipped toward the bookshelves. She lugged down the largest book she could find—a leather-bound, gilt-lettered volume of the complete history of England—and staggered with it to the door. The tome, she decided, had to weigh at least fifty pounds.

She leaned against the doorjamb, then tapped her foot. "Coming?"

He raised his arm in a mock flourish. "Only after you, darling."

Angela nodded and headed down the hallway. He followed right behind her, his eyes boring into her back. If dinner had made her feel sorry for him, seeing the pictures of his wife made her heart ache. He must have grieved deeply, to shoot her such a terrifying look.

Thoughts of all the nice things she could do to improve his life ran through her mind. Oh, why did she have to be such a sucker for people she felt sorry for? She'd spent her whole life playing caregiver to people on Mott Street . . . and now she was contemplating saving a mean, bitter, widowed aristocrat.

If only he and his daughter had seemed just a little happier, she thought. If only the house had been a little smaller and the dining table a little shorter . . . and if he hadn't kissed her. Then, she wouldn't need to save him. But she did.

There was only one solution. Escape.

Chapter Five

"Bon voyage," Angela whispered, wishing that the second lock had been as easy to pick as the first, so she could have escaped via the door. "Chips ahoy," she added. She shoved her heavy suitcase through the diamond-paned window with a grunt, hoping the latches held.

They didn't. Her luggage hit bottom first, with a thud. Then, the latches popped and the case sprang open, reminding Angela of the snappy way in which Mary Poppins had opened her umbrellas. *Except Mary Poppins was the nanny who fixed everything,* she thought guiltily, while her wedding gown unfolded, as if it were ready for her to wear. Her lovely honeymoon peignoir tumbled across the terrace during impact.

"Great escape plan, Angela," she muttered, hoping no one had heard the noise. She tossed her makeshift rope, which was really sheets knotted together, over the windowsill, then stared down at the two windows directly below her own. If she could just manage to reach one, open it, then crawl inside...

She took a deep breath, half sure it would be her last, then hauled leg number one over the sill. As if protesting her foolhardy plan, a beige pump jumped from her foot and spun, toe over heel, into darkness.

Just don't look down. She swallowed and threw leg number two over the ledge. *It's a mere thirty, maybe forty-foot drop, and you were athletic in high school.* "Which was ten years ago," she croaked.

It's now or never.

She grasped her rope with tightly fisted hands, twined her ankles around the cotton, squeezed her eyes shut and swung outward, refusing to think about the fact that her whole life now depended on a floral-print bed sheet. Her best silk blouse snagged and ripped on the crumbling stone ledge of the castle windowsill. Her out-of-shape arms already ached and she hadn't even gone anywhere. Why hadn't she changed into jeans and a jacket? She was cold and her knee-length skirt was hiking high on her thighs.

When she opened her eyes, she was facing what had previously been her room. Suddenly, it didn't look so bad, she thought wistfully, staring at the Empire-style bed and cozy little fireplace. Then she remembered the way Nicholas had kissed her, and how she felt compelled to save his miserable, isolated, oppressive life. No, there was no turning back.

Inching downward, feeling her skirt rise an inch higher with every movement, she hazarded a quick glance at the cliffs. They were her only hope. The perimeters of the property were surrounded by high wrought-iron fences and the front gate, which she'd cased that afternoon, was every bit as impenetrable as Nicholas's cool countenance.

There simply had to be some pathway down from the cliffs. And if not, she would at least have a high vantage point from which she could see the lights of Saint Ives. *Wherever that was.*

She took another deep breath, while her trembling, fisted hands negotiated one of her knots. She'd traversed the floral sheet! The next was printed with sailing ships. Perhaps Nicholas had bought it for his tomboy of a daughter. She felt a twinge of guilt, but forced herself not to dwell on how desperately Rosemunde needed female guidance.

She'd covered less than five feet, but hazarded another glance at the cliffs. Looking toward the sea seemed better than looking up. Definitely better than looking down.

She forced herself to keep shimmying, even though the chilly summer night seemed to close in all around her... so dark and cool and damp. Eerie, phosphorescent blue-green sea mists rose over the cliffs and rolled landward. Far behind and below her, she could feel the gnarled, ancient, moss-hung trees in the dense woods. Even though she was suspended in space, she could imagine their clawlike roots snatching at her ankles.

A vibrating tingle raced up her spine, so quickly she nearly let go of the sailboat sheet. She nearly screamed. A shadowy disembodied face swung back and forth, not inches from her own! Someone was staring at her! Someone who looked exactly like her!

"Oh," she whispered weakly, realizing she'd reached the window below hers and was staring at her own reflection. She looked scared to death.

"I *am* scared to death," she whispered mournfully. "Marrying Frankie would have been so much easier."

She shook her head to clear it of confusion. All she had to do now was reach forward, unlatch the window, tumble inside, and then creep down to the front door. She'd circle the house and retrieve her ruined suitcase. She had no idea how she'd keep her clothes in it, or where she was going, but she decided she could cross those bridges when she came to them. Or traverse those sheets, she mentally amended.

She rocked her weight, swung toward the ledge and reached for the windowsill. Just as she found a hold in the crumbling stone, a light snapped on. Her hand flew back to the sheet, and she gripped it as if to save her life. She held her breath so long she thought she'd faint.

And, then, the worst imaginable thing happened. Nicholas ambled into the frame of the window, with that lazy, long-legged gait of his. If she wasn't about to die bodily, she thought, she'd surely die from mortification, when he saw her hanging outside his window. She squeezed her eyes shut and waited.

Nothing happened.

Angela's eyes flew open ... only to see Nicholas standing in front of an open closet, with his back to her. He tugged off his taut black T-shirt, clearly unaware he had an audience.

Angela told herself to shut her eyes again. She told herself to keep moving. But she was frozen in place, swinging in front of his window by the fool sheet, with her mouth hanging wide open. His skin was so smooth and pale and muscular that all she could think of was Greek gods. He had long, sinuous arms, strong, rounded shoulders and muscles that kept flexing on either side of the perfect ridge of his spine.

If someone had told Angela he'd been carved out of marble by Michelangelo, she would have believed it. And yet he was hardly a statue. He was pure flesh and blood. And as if to prove it, he started unzipping his jeans.

With all her heart, Angela wanted to rap on the window or call out, just so he'd stop. But if she did, he'd see what a ridiculous position *she* was in and worse—he'd know she was escaping! She merely gulped, as he stepped out of his jeans. He did it so fast that she couldn't have averted her gaze, not even if she'd wanted to. At least, that was what she told herself.

When she took in his backside and legs, Angela was sure she'd lose her grip and land right on top of her wedding gown. She tried to pretend he was wearing bathing trunks. But it was impossible. His waistband was twisted and she could read the word "Jockey" from where she hung. Besides, the white cotton briefs clung the way trunks never could. She blew out a shaky breath of relief when he tugged a pair of green lab pants over them.

Still facing his closet, he put his hands on his hips and stared inside, as if he couldn't decide which shirt to wear. "None would be good," Angela managed to mouth at his back, feeling her own confidence returning, at least until she glanced down and realized her stockings were ripped to shreds and her skirt hem hugged her waist.

When she heard a loud, resounding yowl, her head jerked up. Sure enough, Baskerville had trotted into the landscape of Nicholas's bedroom. Nicholas might not have noticed her, but the half wolf, half hound sure did. He parked himself right in front of the window, cocked his head, twitched his pointy ears to full attention, then started wagging his bushy brown tail like the devil. He barked gleefully.

That got her moving. *Forget going back into the castle,* she thought, as she quickly slid down the sheets. After another few minutes, she drew up short. The absurdity of her situation hit her full force, and her shoulders began to shake with a hint of hysteria. "I've really reached the end of my rope," she whispered weakly. Unfortunately, the end of her rope was still a good five feet above the ground.

She sighed, stared down at the suitcase beneath her and said "Bombs away." Then, she simply let go.

She landed feetfirst, staggered a pace, then plopped into her open suitcase. Her rear end landed squarely on the wedding dress and the chiffon poofed around her, like a cushion.

"At least you're good for something," she muttered in the general direction of the gown. She stood and retrieved her peignoir. Unfortunately, she couldn't find her missing beige pump, but a navy one nearly like it was within easy reach. She shoved it on her foot, telling herself she'd worry about matching later. Then, she quickly reassembled the contents of the case and shut it. In lieu of the broken latches, she thriftily wrapped her veil repeatedly around the case then knotted it on top. Not knowing what to do with the long loose ends, she secured them in a giant bow. Finally, she lifted the suitcase with both hands and stumbled breathlessly toward the end of the terrace and the stairs.

She'd passed the fountain and an overgrown rose garden and was halfway to the cliffs when she realized Baskerville was on her tail. Undoubtedly, the dog had continued to bark and Nicholas had let him out. Angela whirled around, stomped her foot and said, "Go home, boy." Then, she put her hands on her hips and took a couple quick breaths. *Why did her suitcase have to be so darn heavy?*

Baskerville merely sat on his haunches. Angela pointed at him and snapped, "Home!" She spun back around and lumbered toward the cliffs again.

"Steps!" she whispered breathlessly, only moments later. The underside of the cliffs was nothing like she'd imagined . . . and stone steps—complete with a rail and punctuated by landings—led all the way down to the crashing Atlantic. The underside of this particular cliff was lush and green. High winds, forceful tides and rainy weather had eroded the rock face, hollowing out deep, cavernous indentations that the wind howled through.

In the distance, she could see hundreds of twinkling little lights. It had to be Saint Ives . . . and freedom.

She got beneath her mammoth suitcase and lugged it down, onto the first step. Glancing up, to get a better sense of the angles, she caught her panting breath. "I said, go home," she burst out.

Baskerville gingerly stepped onto the top stair and shot her a pitiful look. Then he thumped his tail once on the landing above him.

"Home! Bad dog!"

Baskerville merely cocked his head and whimpered.

Angela felt those fingers plucking at her heartstrings again. The same ones that played whole symphonies when she thought of Nicholas being a lonely, isolated widower. "Just go home," she whispered, a pleading tone creeping into her voice.

For the next few moments, she ran between Baskerville and her luggage. Finally, she managed to haul the case down to the second landing, even if Baskerville was far less easy to control. She kept her arms tightly wrapped around the suitcase, ready to tackle the next set of stairs, and glared at the dog.

"You're every bit as ornery as your master," she finally huffed.

"Well, luv," a velvety voice said from the darkness, "it *is* damnably difficult to teach old dogs new tricks."

NICHOLAS LEANED AGAINST the stair rail and crossed his arms over his broad chest, thinking she was the strangest woman he'd ever met. His throaty chuckle tempered to a wry smile only when he saw her furious expression. "Sorry," he muttered.

"Just what do *you* have to be sorry about?" she snapped, staring up at him breathlessly. She sounded embarrassed and he could tell her face was beet red, in spite of the darkness.

He wasn't quite sure. It was just that she looked rather ridiculous, with both her arms wrapped round her big, broken suitcase, complete with its lace-veil bow.

"Well?" she demanded.

"Well, your stockings look like you just ran them through a paper shredder," he finally managed to point out. "And you *are* wearing mismatched shoes." Nicholas gave her a moment to turn a shade redder, then added, "I didn't exactly miss the bed sheets hanging from the side of my house, either." Thinking of what she must have looked like shimmying down them, he chuckled again.

"I'd hardly call the castle you live in *a house*," she said curtly. "And if you're so sorry, then please do me a favor and quit laughing." She stared down self-consciously, as if to see just how bad she looked. For long moments, her eyes remained glued to her mismatched shoes.

"Do you intend to ever look up again?" he asked.

She slowly raised her gaze. When her eyes met his, an impish smile stole over her lips. She looked like a kid who'd just got caught doing something naughty. At least until she crossed her arms defensively over her chest. "How could you do this to me?" she finally asked, in an accusing tone.

His breath caught in his throat. She was panting slightly, from exertion, and moonlight danced in the dark locks that fell over her dew-damp, blush-stained cheeks. She looked beautiful. "I didn't do anything to you, luv," he said. He'd felt terribly uncomfortable when she'd seen the pictures of him and his wife, but now he ambled down the stairs, moving toward her like a moth drawn to flame.

He sat on the stone step nearest her. From that lower vantage point, his eyes could feast on the curves of her hips and legs. They were every bit as lush and full and awe inspiring as the myriad plants growing in the cliffside.

"Why don't you sit down?" he asked, trying to sound reasonable. Perhaps, he told himself, it was time he played the friend, rather than the captor, in order to get information out of her. Since she was escaping, he could safely assume his other tactics weren't working.

"Oh, I suppose I could use a breather," she finally returned, in an almost bored tone that was undoubtedly meant to mask her embarrassment.

As she sashayed across the landing, the businesslike skirt she'd worn at dinner swept the tops of her delectably rounded knees. It was so good to watch that he barely noticed the skirt, itself, which was rumpled beyond repair. The heel of one shoe was higher than the other, so her hips twitched, probably more than she meant them to. Her soft-looking skin and lacy bra strap peeked through a tear in her blouse.

She turned around regally, right in front of him, and for a moment, he actually thought she might curtsy again. Instead, she sat beside him and tugged the hem of her skirt toward her knees primly. Goose bumps were visible on her arms. Why hadn't she worn a jacket? *Must have been in a real rush to get out of here,* he thought, suddenly wondering just how uncivil he'd been.

"Where were you going?" He'd meant to sound angry—after all, she *was* his captive guest—but his voice sounded velvety soft, almost gentle.

She shot him a glare, then pointed to the lights in the distance as he shrugged out of his lab coat. "To Saint Ives." Her eyes narrowed until they became dark slits, but they glinted with playfulness; her lips curved into a smile. "And to freedom!" she pronounced loftily.

He fought back another chuckle, glad she was capable of laughing at herself. There was nothing he disliked more than people who took themselves too seriously. "I do hate to tell you this, luv," he said, "but those are the docks at Saint Mary's." He gestured in the opposite direction. "That's Saint Ives."

"Oh," she said weakly.

He draped his lab coat over her, briefly brushing her soft, rounded shoulders. When he saw her grateful glance, he was more sure than ever that feigning friendship was the way to go. "Here, you look rather chilly."

"What are you, anyway?" she asked, pulling the white cotton coat tightly around herself. "A mad scientist?"

He tried to remind himself that she was possibly a criminal who'd done something to Sylvia Sinclair, but he simply couldn't believe that when he looked at her. Her eyes could never lie.

"Why couldn't I be some great doctor?" The flirtatious tone of his own voice shocked him. It had been years since he'd talked to a woman like that. "Perhaps I'm up there—" he nodded back toward his castle "—researching cures for—"

"I very much doubt it." She smiled wryly.

He smiled back, noticing how the salty sea mists made her skin glow. "So, which were you tired of this time? My haunted house or me?" He was fighting to maintain an appropriately harsh attitude toward her, but each time he spoke his voice became ten times too soft. *I'm merely befriending her, in order to find out whether or not she knows where Sylvia is.*

"Your house isn't haunted," she said in a reproving tone, then glanced upward as a gull circled above them.

Nicholas sighed. "Oh, but it is." He could feel the heat of her gaze on his face now, how her eyes rested on his own. Had he caught her staring at him that way at dinner, as if she could do so forever, or was it just his imagination?

She cleared her throat and blinked. "And how's your house supposed to be haunted?"

He shrugged, staring past her at the cliff. "This is my favorite spot," he said, this time more gruffly than he'd intended.

"Nothing like having a conversation in complete non sequiturs," she quipped.

"Well, it *is* my favorite." He didn't feel particularly inclined to discuss the many things that haunted his house and his life, even though it might make her divulge more about herself.

"This very step?" she prodded, clearly giving up on the conversation she'd initiated.

Her voice rose and fell in a soft cadence, almost as if she were flirting with him. Maybe being caught in such an awkward position had thrown her off guard, he thought. "Actually, yes."

"Oh, rubbish," she returned in her best mock British.

"It really is," he said, with feigned exasperation.

Her glance followed his, back to the dark underside of the cliff. "It's not at all like I'd imagined out here."

"No?" he asked.

"I expected a sheer drop, straight down to the water."

"So, what did you intend to do when you got here, luv? Jump into the bloody ocean?" Looking at her, he decided she probably would have. No woman he'd ever met would've had the guts to scale so dangerous a drop, hanging by sheets.

"Guess so," she said sheepishly. She quickly added, "But there *were* steps."

"My great-uncle built them." His eyes roved over her face. Locks of her disheveled hair cast shadows beneath her eyes, making them look even darker and more mysterious. Every time he looked at her, he nearly forgot their strange situation. Suddenly, he wasn't sure whether he was being amicable because he wanted information, or because he wanted her to like him.

"I've always loved sitting here," he continued after a moment, feeling like an idiot for repeating himself. *Who are you?* was what he really wanted to ask. And yet, he knew that no explanation she might give would completely satisfy him. Somehow, what he wanted to know about her right now seemed beyond words.

"It *is* beautiful. I've never been anywhere like this before."

He nodded, their surroundings working their magic on him, just the way her presence was. Behind and above him, he could feel the lush, deep green woods. And here, the ocean mists touched his skin...and hers. The sea itself turned luminously green and blue and purple when reflecting off the ancient jagged rocks.

The underside of the cliff was phosphorescent green and like a steep, lush meadow. Grasses that were longer than his arms hung in the nooks and crannies, growing around ivy vines, brightly colored wildflowers, brambles and gorse. Gulls circled overhead, while other birds—rooks and pigeons—busily flew to and from their nests in the cliff wall.

Nicholas sucked in a deep breath of salty air, tinged with the stinging, biting scent of wild garlic. Beyond those scents, he could smell her... the lavender soap she'd used and the indefinable, heady scent of a woman. *It's been so long.* He exhaled quickly, fighting an illogical impulse to kiss her.

"So, why do you think your house is haunted?" she asked again.

He placed his elbows on the stair above him, leaned back and stretched his long legs over the landing. "I don't mean literally."

"Just what *do* you mean?" she asked a little huffily. "You're a very difficult person to talk to, do you know that?"

"Sorry," he murmured.

"And you apologize an awful lot," she added.

"And you're pretty critical," he returned. Her lips parted, and she looked a little hurt by his remark. He started to say "sorry" but stopped himself. "Well, you are," he said.

"Sorry."

He chuckled. "And you apologize an awful lot."

That got a giggle out of her. She looked so much prettier when she smiled. She had a small mouth and tiny, very square teeth. For just the next few moments, he told himself, he'd completely forget why they were here... that Sylvia had vanished, that Angela had come in her place and that she'd been trying to walk to Saint Ives.

If he could open up a bit, she'd tell him her real purpose in coming here, he thought. He just wished he could fight the attraction that coursed between them. Was it because she was so unlike any woman he'd met? Or because she looked on his belongings with such disdain? After all, most women were determined to like him—whether they actually did or not—simply because he was rich.

"I was saying the house was haunted because of my wife," he finally said. "She died a few years ago...."

"Of what?" she asked softly.

He shrugged. "An aneurysm," he said gruffly. "When she died," he quickly continued, "I closed up our house in London and came here. Well," he amended, "not immediately."

She was looking at him with rapt attention. Or was that just his wishful imagination again? He gazed long and hard into her eyes, as if the answers to those questions were there.

"So what did you do first?" She sounded honestly curious.

"First, I holed up in London for a year. And then, the following year, everyone I know..." His voice trailed off. Why was he telling her this?

"Which is probably a lot of people..." she prodded.

"Yes, a lot—" He chuckled. "A lot of prying do-gooders crawled out of the woodwork. And each came bearing the woman of my dreams."

She laughed in disbelief. "Everybody was trying to fix you up?"

"What's so funny about that?" He both felt and sounded offended. "Believe it or not, a fair number of women actually find me rather appealing."

"Oh," she said quickly. "I mean, you're very—" Her mouth snapped shut and her face went dead white before it turned scarlet again.

He inched closer and lowered his voice. "So you find me attractive?" he couldn't help but tease.

She jerked away so quickly that she nearly moved to the step above. "Well—well—attraction isn't—well, it's not everything," she stammered. "And I'm sure some of those women who crawled out of the *woodwork* were nice," she added in a censuring tone.

He leaned his head back and smiled, gazing deeply into Angela's eyes. *The woman of my dreams,* he thought, and immediately squelched the thought. "I'm sure they *were* nice women," he managed to say.

"Maybe you just weren't ready," she said levelly.

He shook his head. "No, I didn't like them," he said, his voice becoming tense. "They reminded me too much of my wife. All old school chums, friends of friends..."

"That's how it was with Frankie!"

Nicholas held his breath. Apparently talking about himself *was* the way to get to the bottom of where she'd come from. "Hmm?" he hummed, trying to sound noncommittal.

She shrugged. "Frankie and I grew up together. The same neighborhood. His family knows my family." She pulled the lab coat more tightly around her shoulders. "Everything was just so..."

"Familiar?"

"Easy."

"So it seemed everything would work out wonderfully well?"

Her quick sigh sounded forced. "Well, it *seemed* that way," she burst out. She gazed into his eyes for so long that Nicholas wondered whether or not she meant to continue. Then she blinked.

"My father was ill for a long time. I cared for him while I was in school, and Frankie would always come around, bringing dinners his mother had made, fixing small things that were broken. You know, like the toaster."

Nicholas nodded, even though he had no clue. He'd never even made his own toast.

"He *was* really good to us...."

"But not nice enough to marry?"

"No," she said, sighing. "He *was* too nice, and that was the problem."

"So you're attracted to mean men?" he teased.

She looked thoroughly shocked. "Of course not!"

How could a woman as clearly innocent as this one do something as daring as scale the walls of a castle? "I'm joking," he said.

"Oh," she said weakly. "Well, Frankie just seemed so sweet and like the ideal husband, but I wasn't...well..."

A telltale flush stained her cheeks again, making Nicholas wonder if she really was a virgin. Not that he was about to ask. "In love with him?" he offered.

For a moment, their glances met and held. She shook her head. "No, he's just a friend. And I wanted something..."

"Different?"

She nodded.

He sighed. "I'll never forget the year I was running about, to parties where people were attempting to—as you say—fix me up. Everyone expected me to merely resume my life, just as it had been before, with a woman who resembled my previous wife in terms of class, background and family connections. Even looks," he added suddenly. "They were all very blond, blue eyed and—" His gaze shot to Angela's dark eyes and hair. His mouth went dry and he swallowed. "And English."

"But none of them captured you?" she asked with a smile.

Suddenly, he laughed—a deep belly laugh, the kind he hadn't felt in years. "My saving grace was my great-aunt."

Angela shifted her weight on the step, tugging her feet nearly beneath her. "What did she do?"

"What *didn't* she do," he returned, smiling. "Lady Anne Bromley grilled every girl who came my way. She even made some cry." Nicholas sat up, crossed his arms sternly across his chest, then pursed his lips in a way that made Angela giggle. "Now young lady, I see you have designs upon my nephew. And what—" he arched his brows, wondering again if Angela really did have designs on him "—do you intend to bring to the marriage?"

A gale of laughter escaped her lips. "You sound like Margaret Thatcher!"

"Oh, no." Nicholas reclined against the stairs again. "Margaret Thatcher sounds like my great-aunt. After all, Lady Anne must be first in absolutely everything."

"So how did you get married in the first place?"

"My great-aunt had been abroad for nearly two years. By the time she returned, I'd announced my engagement."

"She sounds kind of awful," Angela ventured.

"She is," he returned with a smile. "Nonetheless, she doesn't think anyone's good enough for me." He shrugged. "Perhaps she's right."

Angela rolled her beautiful eyes. "My, aren't you cheeky?"

He shrugged. "People always think couples should be together for ridiculous reasons."

She laughed. "Frankie used to say our love was fated because our last names rhymed."

"How bloody awful!" Nicholas exclaimed, trying to run down the alphabet. *Lancini. Bancini. Cancini...*

"At the time, I thought it was kind of cute," Angela said, defensiveness creeping into her voice.

"No passion in that, luv," he said after a long moment.

"Guess not."

"You don't know?"

She didn't answer. She probably is a virgin, Nicholas thought. How could a woman who looked like she did manage to save herself so long? Perhaps his wasn't the first castle wall she'd descended, after all, he thought, trying not to grin.

"Well, when one's in love, one always knows," he found himself saying gently, hoping the words didn't sound trite.

She gulped. "So true." She tugged his lab coat again, as if in self-protection.

"Cold?" he asked. He started to add "Shall we go in?" but then he remembered their circumstances. Angela had been escaping to Saint Ives.

"Just a little."

Looking at her sparkling eyes and how her silky, dark hair framed her heart-shaped face, he suddenly wished they'd met in some other way. And that no one connected with her appearance had vanished. "Angela?"

She turned her shoulders, so that she nearly faced him.

"I really would appreciate it if you'd stay...." His voice trailed off when he saw her jaw begin to drop. "Only for a few days," he added quickly. "Just until I can reach Sylvia. I'm worried about her." Angela's expression softened at that.

"How's my being here going to make her call?" she asked.

"It won't," he admitted. "But it would make me feel better. You're probably the last person to have spoken with her. Maybe you'll even remember something...." A thought suddenly occurred to him. "Do you have a job or something that—"

"No. I haven't even started sending out résumés." A look of horror crossed her features, as if she wished she hadn't said that.

"So there's no real difficulty with your staying," he continued smoothly.

"I suppose not." Her voice was so low he could barely hear it.

"So you'll stay," he said briskly, as if it were all decided.

"Well," she said. "Okay."

This time, Nicholas's mouth dropped. He'd expected protests, sighs and a lot more argument. Was he wrong about her honesty? Did she have an ulterior motive? Had she manipulated things this way, so he'd think having her stay was his own idea?

"I'll stay, Nicholas, but only if you'll carry my suitcase back to the house. It's heavy."

She'd not only regained her footing but was now delivering ultimatums. He decided to worry about the broader implications of that later and was on his feet in a flash. "I think you'll find I'm always the gentleman, luv," he said simply.

He reached down, caught her hand and pulled her to her feet. Her palm was warm and dry, and he held her hand just a second longer than he had to.

As if realizing he was thinking about their physical contact, she slid her hand deftly from his, then turned and marched up the stairs, leaving him to retrieve her luggage.

By the time he'd hauled the suitcase up the steps, she'd managed to run halfway to the house. She stooped every time she stepped on the mismatched shoe with the shorter heel, and a strip of her torn stocking actually blew in the breeze. Watching her, he grinned. They might be able to share a few laughs, but the woman was still as prickly as a porcupine. *As prickly as I am.*

"Match made in heaven," he muttered wryly, assuring himself he'd call Sylvia's mother again soon.

"WHAT IN THE WORLD is that man doing?" Angela whispered. She glanced at her travel alarm. It was four in the morning, and Nicholas was once again drawing those odd *X*'s on the cliffs.

"And what am I doing?" She stepped away from the window a pace when he headed inside. Nicholas could be frighteningly self-contained and then more flirtatiously romantic than any man she'd ever met. Hours ago, he'd flustered her so much she'd fled indoors. When he'd delivered her suitcase, he'd merely set it by the door and said a quick, gruff good-night; then he'd left, this time without locking her in.

She'd rinsed her soiled veil, then gone straight to bed, only to be awakened by an eerie, howling sound. Had she really agreed to stay here? For how long? She stepped toward the window again and leaned on the sill, waiting. She was absolutely sure that within fifteen minutes those fool brides would appear. *Maybe they have nothing to do with his wife's death,* she suddenly thought. *Maybe they're some kind of strange message for me! Impossible.*

"Well, hurry up," she said sleepily. This time, she meant to stare the brides down until she figured out what they were made of. They simply couldn't be ghosts, no more than Rosemunde had turned out to be one.

"Here come the brides," she suddenly whispered. Sure enough, they magically appeared on the edge of the dark cliffs, but this time, their transparent gowns seemed to flow and their arms waved gracefully.

After a moment, they began to dance in a circle. The fluidity of their movements captivated Angela. They separated, came back together, floated upward and then descended. They disappeared, reappeared and then turned in the wind like ballerinas. Angela felt somehow awed by the unexpected beauty of it. They mesmerized her as surely as Nicholas's eyes did.

"Who are you, Nicholas?" she whispered much later. "A magician?" As if in answer to her question, the brides vanished one by one. And Angela realized it was dawn.

Chapter Six

Sylvia drew her feet under her on the comfy white sofa and tried to keep her eyes glued on her book, but ever since Frankie had entered the room, it had become impossible. She glanced up surreptitiously. Frankie was setting the dinner table . . . for two. With a linen tablecloth and candles!

She stared down at her book again. Where were Eddie and Paulie? Was she dining alone with Frankie? She'd been here for days, and she could barely even look at the man! *Damn my infernal shyness,* she thought.

It wouldn't be half so bad if Frankie Mancini were truly holding her prisoner. But he was just about the kindest, sweetest, most thoughtful man she'd ever laid eyes on. It was taking him a full hour to set the table, for instance. Now, he was rearranging the plates, resituating the candles and polishing the silverware for the umpteenth time.

She felt a little dizzy. Had she been holding her breath? Was it possible that Frankie was beginning to have feelings for her? She felt a warm hand on her shoulder and nearly jumped out of her own skin.

"Sylvia, honey?"

Frankie's voice was soft and concerned. He'd clearly guessed she was impossibly shy and was being extremely patient about it. The color drained from her face.

"Hmm?" she managed.

...kie colored a little, himself. "Well, I don't ...to tell you this...but did you know your book ...pside down, Sylvia?"

Color poured back into her cheeks. Lots of it. She quickly turned the book around and gulped while Frankie patted her shoulder.

"I made you some chicken cacciatore," he said, still looking at her from kind, dark eyes. "My mother's recipe, so it ought to be good. It's a little spicy." Worry crossed his features. "Do you like spicy?"

She nodded. Then, she gulped again. "You're just being nice to me because you want me to tell you where Angela is," she said weakly. Had she sounded too accusatory?

For a long moment, he only stared in protest. Then he put his hands on his hips. "That's not true," he said in a shocked voice.

She clutched her book. Why had she mentioned Angela?

"You're a very nice woman," Frankie said. "And you're smart," he added quickly. "And you're pretty. And you're so shy...so I just thought..." Frankie sighed, threw his arms in the air and, then, as if not knowing what to do with them, shoved them in his trouser pockets.

"C'mon," he finally said. "You gotta try some of this chicken cacciatore."

"Sorry," Sylvia said contritely. She got up and headed for the table, feeling Frankie's eyes on her back. Her own self-consciousness made her knees wobble. What was coming over her?

First, she hadn't called home when she could have. Then, she hadn't escaped, even though she'd had ample opportunity. And, now, she was spending her days staring at books she could no longer see because the words swam before her very eyes. She could think of nothing other than Frankie, who, she'd decided, looked quite a bit like Robert DeNiro.

She was halfway across the room, when his hand slid beneath her elbow. *It's just a man, seating me for dinner! For heaven's sake, don't faint, Sylvia!*

"Thank you," she murmured, as Frankie scooted her chair beneath her. Surely, she told herself, she was developing a crush on Frankie simply because she'd never spent so much time in such proximity with a man. She was a totally reclusive academic, with a real shyness problem.

Perhaps she should just tell him where Angela was, she suddenly thought. That would be a surefire way of ending her growing one-sided relationship.

She realized Frankie was still standing behind her chair. "Thank you," she repeated in a strangled voice.

He leaned forward. "You're very welcome," he whispered in her ear. Warm tingles raced down her back. She turned her head, just slightly, meaning to tell him he should sit down, but when she did, she realized his face was just inches from her own and she couldn't say a word.

Then he kissed her. It was a chaste kiss, nothing more than the soft pressure of his lips against hers. "I really do like you, Sylvia," he said. Then he circled the table, sat down opposite her and began to serve her dinner as if nothing had happened.

But something *had* happened. She was seeing stars! And somehow, she felt suddenly sure her whole life had changed. "I—I'm really glad—glad you like me, Frankie!" she managed to stammer in a rush.

"ONCE THE WOMAN DECIDES to stay, she certainly moves in," Nicholas muttered. He always woke grumpy, but this morning he felt somewhere closer to furious. He wished Angela would let him sleep, but all her happy household projects were noisy and her luscious curves very definitely inspired insomnia.

"Sunlight." He groaned aloud, tossing his covers off with a sweep of his arm. He rested a hand on his naked chest, absently twined his fingers in his chest hairs, then glanced at his bedside clock. "It can't be noon," he murmured. "Oh, please, not noon." He hadn't seen noon for years. And what was that infernal whirring noise?

He got up and headed for a window, realizing that Angela had been at Westhawke Hall for six days and that he'd awakened exactly one hour earlier every day since her unusual arrival. If she stayed, he'd soon be getting up at the bloody crack of dawn, which was when she got up.

He squinted through the window and grunted. Outside, old Mr. Magnuson was riding a power mower, and the knee-high grass was actually starting to resemble a lawn. When Nicholas's wife had died, he'd told Magnuson to retire to the caretaker's cottage. All he'd asked him to do over the past three years was pick up Angela at the airport. Now, of course, she'd found the missing man and put him back to work.

Might as well shave. Not that he'd go downstairs. He hardly wanted her to know that she'd completely rearranged his life-style. He wasn't reading his newspapers regularly, as he generally did, and if his sleeplessness continued, he wouldn't be able to work nights. His brides were barely visible in daylight.

He reached over, picked up the phone and dialed Sylvia's mother. It was early morning in Connecticut. There was no answer, only the machine. "This is Nicholas Westhawke," he said at the beep. "I wanted to see if the police are willing to become involved tomorrow. That's all, thank you." He hung up, wondering how he really felt about Sylvia's disappearance. He hadn't loved her, of course, but she'd seemed kind in her letters, even if Angela had nearly made him forget them.

He headed for his bathroom, stepping over the latest stack of collected newspapers. Every day, it was something, he thought, leaning against the sink and lathering his face. A floor was polished, another unused room opened and cleaned, a tarnish covering removed from a chandelier... What the hell did she think she was doing?

Still, her dinners *were* heavenly, he thought, raking the razor over his cheek. He now hoped *he'd* never eat another kidney pie. She cooked every night, but only on the condition that they ate outside on the terrace, at a small, round, intimate table, which she let Rosemunde set with mismatched flatware. Twice, the woman even used paper plates. Paper plates on a four-hundred-year-old mosaic table!

The worst thing was that she was both the prettiest and the most skittish woman he'd ever met. At least, skittish when it came to him flirting with her. Or at least he *thought* he was flirting. It had been so long, it was hard to tell.

He tossed his razor on his toiletry table, then rinsed his face and patted it dry. Towel still in hand, he suddenly leaned forward and squinted in the mirror, thinking that maybe she was right. He was awfully bloody pale. He groaned. Why couldn't he quit wondering what she thought of him?

He slapped the towel against the side of the sink and let it rest there. The only new information she'd offered lately was that she was jobless, between apartments and had supposedly transferred what little money she had into her husband-to-be's account, which meant Nicholas couldn't call a bank to verify her story. Was Angela her real name? Well, if the police interviewed her, they'd question her more effectively than he had.

If Angela was her name, it really did suit her, he thought. She looked like an angel. Nonetheless, she was causing mounting problems. Rosemunde had taken to her and would be hurt when she left. He'd only recently found out that it was Angela who had cut his daughter's hair. Lately, it seemed to stay brushed, too, which was good.

But, then, there was the fact that he was going out of his mind. His own home no longer belonged to him! Angela pursued domestic endeavors and the care of his daughter as if she really were his wife. He'd simply have to tell her to occupy herself with something other than bringing tumbledown Westhawke Hall back to life.

Yet he felt equally inclined to let her do as she pleased. He hadn't wanted a woman in a long time, not the way he wanted her. And each day, he became more certain that he wouldn't let her leave Cornwall without having her.

THE SCENT OF THE budding roses, with their fresh green leaves, was all around her. Angela sighed, leaning back on her haunches in a row of the old rose garden. She'd served lunch at noon—well over four hours ago—and she was already starved. She wished she hadn't promised Rosemunde a real American meal—which meant hot dogs—for dinner. She could definitely use something a little more substantial.

She'd also found out that Nicholas's daughter's birthday was tomorrow and that no party had been planned. Of course, she'd spent half the morning correcting that oversight. What kind of father was he? Rosemunde loved him, there was no doubt about that, but the man clearly forgot the kinds of things wives always remembered.

Must be hungry because I'm working so hard, she thought, listening to her stomach rumble. Oh, how could Nicholas have done so much damage to his own property? Fortunately, the *X*'s and circles he'd drawn on the lawn were only of chalk.

Undoubtedly, he'd let the place go to rack and ruin because of his grieving. And, Angela thought with renewed

determination, while she was here she could do him the favor of fixing up the place. Westhawke Hall was fit for a
king, but it really did look like Dracula lived in it.

"Maybe he does," she muttered. After all, the man had
still never appeared before dusk; the nights remained full of
strange noises and odd apparitions. She hazarded a glance
toward the upper reaches of the castle, as if Nicholas might
appear. Nicholas...whose kisses she couldn't forget, no
matter how hard she tried.

"The old fountain's all cleaned up, it is," Mrs. O'Reilly
called. Angela turned toward the voice. The wiry, red-
headed housekeeper waved, then headed toward a toolshed,
tugging off her rubber gloves.

Far off, on a side lawn opposite from where Mr. Magnuson drove the rider mower, Rosemunde ran through the
grass, picking up sticks and stones. Angela glanced over the
rose garden again. Once, it must have been beautiful.

At the back of the castle, the two rounded towers marked
the east and west wings. The second floor opened onto the
wide stone terrace; a stone rail ran its length. Curving stone
steps led down to the first-floor portico which also faced the
unused three-tier fountain. Mrs. O'Reilly had spent all
morning removing leaves from it, then she'd scrubbed it
clean.

According to both Mrs. O'Reilly and some pictures Angela had found, the roses had had prominence. Ten perfect
rows had flanked either side of the fountain. Beyond that,
sculpted bushes—now wild and overgrown—had been en-
closed by stone beds. Angela smiled wryly. Yes, it had truly
been fit for royalty.

You ought to quit daydreaming and get back to work.

Angela leaned forward on her knees, tugging up weeds by
the handful and shoving them into a plastic trash bag. She
was so engrossed that she barely noticed when a cool
shadow fell over both her and one of the rosebushes.

Because she was kneeling, her eyes fell right at the apex of Nicholas's jeans-clad thighs when she glanced up. She quickly craned her neck further skyward. The waning afternoon sun was behind one of his shoulders and light streamed into her eyes, throwing his face into seeming silhouette. He looked like a hero in a western movie who was about to ride off into the sunset.

Except that he wore no cowboy hat. His face was too aristocratic and his hair too long and blond. He was wearing another of his overly tight T-shirts; this one was pristine white and showed off every contour of his chest. Angela could even see the outline of the curling hairs that flattened against his pectorals. Just looking caused a breathy sigh to escape her lips.

"Who are all those people in my house?" he finally growled. When he tossed his head, a lock of white blond hair fell across his high cheekbone and down the plane of his cheek to his jaw.

"Good morning to you, too," she said, forcing a sweet smile. Was it her imagination or was Nicholas furious? What could she have done wrong? When he shoved his hands deep in his pockets, her eyes were drawn to his thighs again. She gulped. *Staying in England is a definite mistake.*

"Nice to see you before nightfall," she managed to continue. She looked at his face, determined to keep her gaze there, even if the man's eyes still mesmerized her and he looked mad as the devil.

"Well," he returned, "the only reason you're seeing me before nightfall is because all your infernal racket awakened me." He glared down pointedly, placing his wide, perfectly formed hands on his hips. His fingers trailed over his thin black leather belt.

She shifted her weight on her haunches, to get a better look at him. "You can hardly expect the world to run on your own private schedule," she said, trying to keep the sheepishness from her voice. She hadn't considered that the noise might wake him.

"Oh, can't I?" His tone made clear that was exactly what he was accustomed to doing.

"Not while I'm here," she said lightly. He was still towering over her and showing no signs of going elsewhere, so she decided she'd better stand. Not that it would help. He was a full two heads taller.

As soon as she moved, his hand circled her wrist and he pulled her up. The next thing she knew, she'd stumbled against him, and her nose nearly nuzzled against his chest. She leaned away from the heady scent of his clean shirt.

"So do you mind telling me who those people are?" he asked, without dropping her wrist.

"It should be obvious," she said, this time taking a small step backward. The soft warmth of his hand tightened its hold. "I mean, are they putting up curtains?"

"And oiling and waxing the floors. And airing out furniture." His voice lowered, and his breath was so close that it lifted a lock of hair off her cheek. "As near as I can tell, half my sofas are on my front lawn."

She shot him another overly innocent smile, both wishing he'd let go of her wrist and wishing he wouldn't. "Well, airing them is less expensive than complete reupholstering."

"You're paying these people?"

At that, she found herself trying to swallow around the guilty lump in her throat. She tried to step back another pace, but his hold tightened again, so much so that she stepped forward instead. His shirt smelled as clean as the summer air, and his own scent—which was woodsy and undeniably male—mingled with that of the freshly cut grass and musky, sweet unkept roses all around them. "Not exactly," she finally managed to say.

"Someone *must* be paying them," he said, as if the thought had just occurred to him.

"Well," she ventured after a long moment, "you're rich, right?"

His eyes narrowed, turning a deeper shade of violet blue. Everything about his glance said he suspected he wouldn't like what he was about to hear. "Quite," he said softly. "So?"

"So—er—"

He tugged her wrist, pulling her a fraction closer. "Yes, luv?"

She cleared her throat loudly, trying to tell herself she'd done the right thing and wishing she could ignore the softness of his skin. "I—er—told them to bill you."

"You what?" he asked in a low, lethal voice.

This time, he did drop her wrist. And she really wished he hadn't. His skin was so warm and his hands and arms were so strong. She could still remember the feel of them around her when he'd carried her through the castle. Of course, that was back when she'd thought he was Svengali, not some cantankerous, mean widower, she assured herself.

But he wasn't mean the night he caught you escaping his castle.

"Sorry," she finally said defensively, "but your place is a wreck." Her voice gained resolve. "And it clearly used to be so beautiful. And I was so bored and I just thought—"

"You're merely to stay here until Sylvia Sinclair turns up," he said gruffly, staring deeply into her eyes. "Can't you find some other way to occupy your time?"

His closeness was driving her crazy! "Excuse me," she fumed. "I guess I'm not nearly as good as you are at being idly rich."

"I'm hardly idle," he returned.

Was it her imagination or had he really come just a little closer? His midnight eyes were starting to have their effect

on her again. Her knees were wobbling and her breath was
growing short and her lips were beginning to part invitingly
and... She had to quit thinking like this!

"Well, you seem pretty idle to me," she managed to say.
"Since you're the only one up at night, I assume you have
something to do with those brides who keep vanishing beneath my window in the wee hours, now don't you? I mean,
are *you* sorry for keeping *me* awake? And do you call making weird, howling noises that reverberate over the cliffs an
occupation?"

His lips started to twitch, genuinely infuriating her. She'd
worked really hard on the place, and all she got in thanks
was his bad attitude. Now, he was laughing at her!

"Actually, yes," he said. "It's an occupation, of sorts."

"Of sorts," she echoed in a knowing tone. "How so?"
She held her breath, hoping he'd tell her what in the world
he was doing at night.

He said nothing, merely gazed into her eyes, while his own
twinkled. With the speed of light, he grasped her wrist again
and pulled her right into his arms, crushing her against his
chest. Her gasp was lost against his shirt.

"All I know," he said, leaning to whisper into her ear, "is
that with you around, I keep wanting to give up my current—er—occupation."

One of his arms dropped to her waist and circled it. He
was so close she could barely breathe. "What do you think
you're doing!"

"Holding you," he returned softly, completely nonplussed by her tone.

Unable to think of a comeback, she simply sighed. "And
why does knowing me make you want to give up your job?"
She wished her voice didn't sound so darn fluttery. He was
smiling down at her, his earlier anger seemingly gone. "You
sure blow hot and cold," she muttered.

That only made him grin, even if he ignored the comment. "I want to quit my job, so I can take up those other occupations traditionally favored by the idle rich," he teased, cocking his head slightly.

"Like what?" she croaked. If he got any closer, she was sure she'd quit breathing altogether. Still, she couldn't quite bring herself to push him away. His nearness just felt too good. But how could he act like this when he'd been furious just moments before?

"Like womanizing," he whispered. He chuckled.

Womanizing! Before she knew what was happening, one of his hands slid up her back, under her hair and against her neck, until his fingers twined in her thick curls.

"Womanizing! You can't just—"

Her protest was lost as his lips claimed hers, in a kiss that delivered an all-out assault to her senses. His heady scent overwhelmed her. His tongue flicked inside her mouth like a spark that had just burst into flame. Her eyes squeezed shut in a natural response. And she found herself reclining in his arms while he leaned into the kiss. His fingers tightened against her scalp, pulling softly at fistfuls of her luxurious hair.

It was the kind of kiss that led to lovemaking, she thought. The kind of kiss that you saw in the movies, right before the lovers began to fumble with each other's buttons! Right before they...but she'd never gotten that far! She gasped against his lips, but he only deepened the pressure of his kiss. *He's crazy,* she thought vaguely. They barely knew each other!

He stepped closer still, something she hadn't even thought possible, wedging his thigh between her legs. An arm tightened around her and his free hand massaged her scalp. He moaned against her lips, then swiftly turned, pressing her fully against him. She froze. The man was thoroughly aroused!

She pushed against his chest. Not that she got far. He caught and held her close, so she could still feel the most intimate part of him against her. She wrenched her hips away, but only wedged herself further between his rock-hard thighs. Such things were happening and he was merely staring down at her face!

"You're so beautiful," he said after a long moment.

Beautiful? She was stunned. She couldn't think of a word to say. "Look," she finally managed to say. "If womanizing is what you're interested in, then I suggest you better—" She stopped midsentence, wishing Nicholas's eyes weren't narrowing again in an expression of fury. But what was she supposed to do? Let him think she was that kind of woman? Besides, she hated him for being furious one minute, then amorous the next.

"Better what?" He let go of her.

She stumbled backward, trying not to blush. With all her might, she forced herself to not look down. "Find yourself another woman. I'd hate to think of myself as a full-time occupation for an idle-rich English lord." Her voice rose a haughty notch. "Or given what you're suggesting, I suppose I'd be a sort of employee." *That would get him to back off.*

For a moment, he merely squinted at her, his pale brows drawn together above his violet eyes. "You think I want you to be my mistress?" he scoffed.

"I don't know what you want," she said, the scalding flush now rising to her cheeks, unchecked. He blew hot and cold so fast she felt her head was spinning. Her whole body definitely was.

"Well, luv," he said softly. "All my employees have apartments, bank accounts and ID cards. I wouldn't hire anyone unless I knew who they were."

"One thing sure isn't a mystery," she snapped. "And that's that I'm not staying here long!"

"Good," he ground out. He turned on his heel and stalked toward the woodshed. Why was she so skittish? she suddenly wondered, feeling confused. After all, she'd wanted him to kiss her again, hadn't she? *But not so hard that she was sure he meant to make love to her!*

She blew out a shaky sigh, thinking she was every bit as standoffish as he was. Maybe even more so. But she was here under strange circumstances and felt far too unsure to let him pursue her, especially since he was so unreadable.

Besides, she'd been saving herself for the right man. "But where is he?" she muttered. He'd never come along. She'd almost given up, which was why she was going to marry Frankie. She'd even considered just sleeping with someone. She was getting too darn old not to know what it was like.

And here she was, with the sexiest man on earth. When he tried to kiss her, she always sent him packing. He was standing by the woodshed door now. He glanced up and returned her stare.

"Dinner's in an hour!" she yelled brightly, on impulse. And then, feeling like a complete idiot, she waved.

Not that he waved back.

After a few moments, she caught another glimpse of him and chuckled. The man was loping toward the front lawn, with a pair of hedge clippers in his hand!

Apparently, kisses of that caliber, even if she broke them off by nearly knocking him to the ground, worked wonders with the man.

"DINNER READY?" Nicholas asked tersely, not about to let her know that the taste of her lips still had his heart singing. Or that she was the reason he'd changed into slacks and a sport coat.

She descended the stairs, smelling of roses and lavender soap. Her hair was still wet and she'd changed into sweatpants and a T-shirt. Somehow, she didn't look half as cute as she had kneeling in the garden, with her defenses down and a dirt smudge across her nose.

"It should be ready by now," she said when she reached the bottom stair. He suspected her clipped tone had more to do with confusion over his kisses than with her actually being angry. Watching her fight to maintain a scowl, he grinned. A kiss like that would confuse anyone. Had she really never been with a man? he wondered. And what would it be like to initiate a woman into the art of lovemaking? He'd never done so before.

Suddenly, her eyes widened. "It looks like we've got company," she said slowly.

He glanced through the window just as two toots from a car horn sounded, and he bit back an audible groan. An impressive gray Rolls limo had stopped in the drive, which could only mean one thing. He glanced at Angela. She'd gone from slack jawed to fully openmouthed.

"Who is that?" she asked in a stunned, little voice.

The worst possible guest, he realized, inwardly cringing. What a day! He'd been mad at Angela for acting as if she were his wife, and he'd taken his temper out on her, but then he'd turned right back around and kissed her like the devil. Now this.

"Who?"

Before Nicholas could find his voice, the driver swung open the car's back door...and out she stepped. Buxom, bossy and wearing a black crepe dress adorned with a single strand of pearls. She shot the driver a purse-lipped stare rather than thanking him, then charged up the many front steps, wielding her thick black cane like a mountaineer's walking stick. Nicholas swore she was the only woman who could make having two chins look dignified.

True to form, his great-aunt flung open the front door, then merely stood on the threshold, with an impossibly erect posture, waiting to be announced.

"Angela—" Nicholas placed his arm beneath her elbow, both to keep her from running and to offer support. She felt frozen solid and wasn't about to protest his touch, not even if he had kissed her senseless just two hours ago. He pulled her next to him.

"Yes, Nicholas?" she croaked.

"I'd like to present my great-aunt," he said. "Lady Anne Bromley. You may call her Lady Anne."

I MAY, MAY I? Angela thought, feeling disconcerted by how formal Nicholas had become. She might have forgotten it at times, but the man was an aristocrat, through and through. Right now, excessive breeding oozed from his every pore. Lady Anne was just as formidable.

"I—I've heard so much about you," Angela finally managed to say. *One, that you're a nightmare! Two, that you interrogate all women who come within ten feet of your nephew and make them cry.*

"I'm very sure you have," Lady Anne said in a booming voice, as if she knew exactly what Angela had been thinking. "And *do* be *quite* assured I have heard equally as much about you."

What could the woman have heard? Everything in Lady Anne's tone made clear that whatever she'd heard wasn't good. Angela stepped forward, politely extended her hand and did her best to smile.

The woman was every inch the veritable gray-haired iron maiden. Worse—she wasn't shaking Angela's hand! Lady Anne's metal gray eyes were scrutinizing her and clearly despising every single thing she saw. She was apparently well aware that Angela was standing there with her hand idiotically outstretched and a painful grin on her face!

Long moments passed.

Finally, not knowing what else to do, Angela slapped her dangling hand on her hip. How rude of the woman! "Sorry if I'm not up on court manners," she said tightly, her pride getting the best of her. "Am I supposed to curtsy, or what?"

Nicholas looked appalled. *Good.* She wasn't his wife. She wasn't his girlfriend, either...even if he had had the audacity to kiss her as if she were. Given the circumstances, she shouldn't have to contend with his most impossible relative!

"Oh," said Lady Anne, with such long vowel sounds that it seemed to take a full minute for her to say that simple, one syllable word. She pursed her lips again. "American?"

She said "American" with the same intonation she might have used for "criminal." Angela felt her temper rise another notch. "Good guess," she returned in a clipped tone. She glanced at Nicholas, whose enchanting eyes had grown wide, and smiled sweetly. "You didn't tell me your aunt was so...perceptive."

"And you're quite the fast worker!" Lady Anne exclaimed. It wasn't a compliment.

Fast worker? What did the woman mean by that? Nicholas's hand tightened on her elbow. She tried to shrug it off but couldn't. "The only fast work I've done is on your nephew's wreck of a house," Angela said. She glanced around in disdain, as if being a houseguest in the castle were beneath her.

As if sensing things were about to get truly out of hand, Nicholas tugged Angela nearly into his arms. "And it looks wonderful."

Angela glanced at him. Was that for her benefit or his aunt's? she wondered, trying not to notice how perfectly her shoulder fit in the crook of his. Did he really mean to take up for her?

"I was referring to the work on my nephew," Lady Anne continued pointedly, as if Angela were an idiot. "Or have you had designs on him for a long time?"

"Oh, years," Angela returned flippantly. The fear she'd felt on first seeing the woman was nothing next to the anger that was quickly replacing it.

After a long moment, Lady Anne mustered a sound that was something like "Humph."

"Don't worry. If I've had designs, I assure you they've come to nothing." Angela shot Nicholas a level look.

"Nothing!" Lady Anne boomed. "Nothing! A marriage—or should I say elopement!—to a member of the English peerage is nothing to you, young lady! Why, it's the talk of all of Cornwall. Everyone's heard about it, beginning with the people you hired to work on the house. Need I remind you two that gossip travels fast?" Lady Anne glared straight at Nicholas. "Especially when a gentleman marries beneath himself."

Angela gasped. Did Lady Anne actually think they were married? *Impossible!* And worse, for brief seconds while Nicholas had kissed her today, Angela had actually dreamed they were.

"Excuse me?" she finally asked, hoping she'd misunderstood.

"You heard me well enough," Lady Anne said.

"And now you hear me," Angela found herself saying. "I'm good enough for your nephew any day of the week." Her voice lowered. "If not better." She stared at Lady Anne, wishing she'd denied the marriage instead of defending her pride.

"All's not what it seems," Nicholas said in a calm voice. "Dinner's waiting, so let's sit and discuss things, shall we?"

Lady Anne's eyes were shooting daggers. "Of course, let's be civilized. And, dear, I'm sure you were just about to change." Her gaze dropped over Angela's sweatpants and she winced. "When Edward and I were newly married and in India, we dined regularly with the maharaja. We always dressed quite formally. And, of course, it's still the style in London, today." She cleared her throat and added, "Well, only in the better houses."

Angela watched Nicholas's expression go completely blank. Why was the man so enigmatic, so mysterious and so hard to read? Why didn't he tell his aunt they weren't married? She had an impulse to reach out and smack him into action.

"It's inarguable that the Seymours and Channing-Downes have the best laid, most tasteful tables in London," Lady Anne continued. "Catherine Seymour—I believe you dated that lovely girl, once, Nicholas—was wearing the most remarkable—"

"While you two catch up," Angela interrupted, "I do believe I *will* run up and change into something a bit more formal." She'd wear her fool wedding dress, that's what she'd do! She whirled out of Nicholas's grasp and charged up the stairs, taking them two at a time.

"Nicholas, I'm not quite sure I like her," Angela heard Lady Anne say before she was out of earshot.

Now, there's an understatement! Angela thought. Just who did these people think they were?

"Don't worry, lady," Angela muttered under her breath. "When I'm through with you, there'll be no doubt in your mind."

Chapter Seven

Not her wedding dress! At first, all Nicholas caught were snatches of glowing skin and pearl-encrusted lace, as Angela whirled around in the drawing-room doorway. He nearly choked on his predinner cocktail.

Then she swept into the room, with grace befitting a queen. Her shoulders were drawn back, her head was held high, and her chin jutted out at a sharp angle. Everything about her said, "Off with their heads!" Everything except her thick, dark hair. It fell in waves over her shoulders and said, "Touch me, Lord Nicholas."

After a full moment, he realized it wasn't *exactly* her wedding dress, and that she looked so good it was taking away his breath. She'd modified the gown by ripping out the hoop-style underskirts, then cutting the hem to calf length. A thick band of lace hung below the new hem and hid the rough edges. The sleeves were gone, leaving her delectable shoulders fully bare. Somehow, she'd crisscrossed her veil over them, as if it were a filmy shawl.

It was the perfect garden dress for dining on the terrace on a summer's evening. Nicholas could barely believe his great-aunt was nodding Angela's way, with something resembling genuine approval.

"You look lovely," he said softly. Of course, he knew her well enough to know that she'd headed upstairs with every intention of donning the dress, just as it had been. Her feistiness and pride drew him to her. And yet, the fact that she hadn't gone through with her plan touched him even more. Had she decided to try to impress his formidable great-aunt, for his sake? *Good luck,* he thought.

"I'll have dinner ready in another five minutes," she announced in a lofty tone.

"You're serving!" Lady Anne exclaimed in an appalled voice, when Angela turned to go.

Angela shot her a long, level look. "I gave Mrs. O'Reilly the night off."

"Oh," his great-aunt said. She was still drawing out the long vowels of the short word when he followed Angela.

He found her in the kitchen. Her hands were riffling over the items on the counter: paper plates, plastic straws, foam cups, an empty box that had contained instant macaroni and cheese, and some empty cans of sweet potatoes. Something from the oven smelled unusual . . . if sweet and heavenly.

For a long moment, he merely watched how the glowing skin of her shoulders shone through the filmy veil. Tendrils of her black hair coiled against her long, slender neck. He fought the impulse to head for the safe where he kept some of the family jewelry. A neck like that, as far as he was concerned, should be encircled by a delicate strand of diamonds . . . or was that rubies? Emeralds even? He was still trying to decide, when she whirled around and gasped.

A hand shot to her heart. He couldn't take his eyes from the spot where her palm pressed against her breast. She drew another quick breath. "You scared me!" she accused. "How long have you been lurking there?"

"I wasn't lurking," he said softly, almost regretting that he'd kissed her today, since it had made her so prickly.

"No? Then what exactly were you doing?"

He lithely moved toward her and leaned against the counter next to her. Up close, he caught a whiff of mixed scents that were purely feminine. "Just watching you," he said, unable to believe how husky his own voice sounded.

"Hope you got an eyeful," she said tartly.

He couldn't help but grin. Her dark eyes were flashing with temper. "Oh, I certainly did," he said, his voice still sounding low and throaty to his own ears. Was Angela really attempting to impress Lady Anne?

She ignored him and opened a cabinet above her. When she did so, straining upward on her tiptoes, he decided she very definitely had the most luscious body he'd ever encountered. She pulled down some china.

"No paper plates tonight?" he teased.

"Never for Miss Lady Bromley," she returned, her voice laced with irony. She continued, as if talking to herself. "I just can't believe I promised Rosemunde hot dogs." She shot a mean look in his direction. "And I'm not changing the menu, just to appease your damn aunt."

"We're having hot dogs?" he managed to ask after a long moment.

"Don't worry," she said, looking a little mortified, herself. "We're eating on real plates."

He chuckled. "Well, there's a comfort." *Maybe she's a fortune hunter, after all, and that's why she's trying to impress my relatives.*

"Glad you're so comforted," she fumed, shoving a stack of china and silver service plates in his hands. "You can set the table. The one outside."

His jaw dropped as he stared down at the plates. When he looked up, her eyes were daring him to refuse.

"You've seen what a table looks like once it's set?" she asked lightly.

He cocked his head and met her eyes, dead on. "Of course, my dear," he said dryly.

"Well, just act as if you've done it before," she said, clearly losing patience. With every word, she seemed to be saying that he was the kind of man who was used to being waited on hand and foot. Which he was.

"Just do me a favor and help me out," she said, a little more softly.

"Only if you'll answer two questions," he teased.

She sighed. "And what might those be?"

"Well," he said. "I know you headed upstairs, determined to wear your wedding gown—"

"How do you know that?" she interrupted.

"Oh," he said, shooting her a teasing, knowing glance. "I'm beginning to know you well. Quite well. I mean, it is true, isn't it, luv?"

Her dark brows drew upward, as if answering that question was beneath her. "Maybe," she said.

"So my question is, 'Why did you change your mind?'"

"Far be it from me to stoop to *her* level," she answered without hesitation.

"Ah," he said smiling. "And my second question is, 'Why are you suddenly intent on impressing my great-aunt?'" He waited, wondering what he wanted her to say... that she had feelings for him?

Her face lit up in a remarkable smile that made her cheeks turn pink and glow. She looked so radiantly beautiful that he wanted to drop the fool plates and make love to her. A lightning-quick fantasy shot through his mind. He'd drop the plates, lift her in his arms and make love to her, right here, right now, on the kitchen floor.

Instead, he said, "So what's the answer, luv?"

"Sorry," she said in a light, teasing tone that sent a thrill right through his body. "But that's actually your third question. You said I had to answer two." She wiggled her brows. "And I have."

With that, she turned around and began to fill serving dishes in earnest. After a moment, she glanced over her shoulder at him. "Are you going to set the table or not?"

"You win," he said smiling.

"As always," she quipped.

"No, luv," he said sweetly, heading for the door. "You may have won the battle, but I'll win the war."

"Oh?" she called lightly. "And which exact war was that?"

"Why, madam," he returned, just as playfully, "the one for your undying love."

"You turned it on!"

Nicholas nodded, listening to the excited breathlessness of Angela's voice. He glanced behind him at the three-tier fountain beneath the terrace. The floodlights worked, even if they looked dim in the dusky evening light, and he'd forgotten how impressive it was to see the arcing jets of water stream from tier to tier, with the cliffs looming in the background.

"Edward installed that fountain, you know," Lady Anne said. What she meant was that Nicholas had long been in the doghouse for letting her deceased husband's contribution to Westhawke Hall go untended. "Humph," his great-aunt added, now staring down at her plate.

"Mummy promised me a real American meal today," Rosemunde said, grinning at her elderly aunt and digging in.

Nicholas sighed and glanced at Angela to gauge her reaction, but she was placing a linen napkin in her lap. He'd explained the situation to Rosemunde countless times, but his daughter made a show of ignoring him. As long as Angela was here, Rosemunde meant to act as if she were Angela's daughter.

If Lady Anne had a soft spot in her heart, it was for Rosemunde. "I'm sure that was quite nice of—er—your mother, Rosemunde," Lady Anne finally said, still staring down at her plate as if she had no idea what to do.

Actually, the table looked as impressive as it could, given the cuisine. Nicholas had found a lace tablecloth and candles, and Angela had brought out silver chafing dishes. They contained sweet potatoes, which were topped with an unhealthy amount of gooey marshmallow, baked beans, hot dogs, buns and boxed macaroni and cheese. Every time he glanced at the homey offerings, served with such pomp and circumstance, he had to fight not to laugh. The dishes had seen food as varied as caviar, crustless vegetable sandwiches and pâté. But they'd surely never held hot dogs.

After a long moment, Angela pushed an antique glass serving dish in his great-aunt's direction. "I think they're best with chili and onions," she said, with an amused smile.

Lady Anne pursed her lips, but obediently dished chili onto her hot dog with a delicate silver pearl-handled spoon. She ignored the onions, but just as dutifully picked up her heavy sterling cutlery, then began to cut her hot dog into tiny, denture-manageable pieces.

"Don't they look quite wonderful!" Rosemunde giggled, picked up another hot dog and shoved it into her mouth. "We're having hot dogs at my party, too, aren't we, Mum?" she asked, with her mouth still half-full.

Angela smiled and nodded. "Yep."

Party? Nicholas cleared his throat. "What party?"

Angela met his gaze levelly. The sparks from the candlelight seemed to catch in her dark eyes. "Tomorrow's your daughter's birthday," she said, in what he took to be a censuring tone.

"I know that," he found himself saying defensively. He glanced at Rosemunde, who grinned back. At least she knew he'd never forgotten her birthday. What kind of man—and father—did Angela think he was? For all the world, he wanted to tell her that *he'd* planned a party. But he couldn't. It was a surprise.

"I didn't forget," he finally reassured pointedly, glaring at Angela and feeling another twinge of resentment. What was this woman doing to his life? And just who had *she* invited to the party she'd planned? He prolonged his glance, hoping to let her know they were going to have a very long talk later.

As if sensing the sudden tension at the table, Lady Anne said, "Your birthday is, of course, one of the reasons for my visit." The meal was definitely growing on her. She shoveled a healthy portion of baked beans between her almost pursed lips.

"So what did you get me, Auntie?" Rosemunde teased, raking the marshmallow topping off her sweet potatoes with a fork and downing it in a bite.

"I'll never tell," Lady Anne returned, in such a teasing voice she nearly sounded human. Not that it lasted. She turned abruptly to Nicholas. "The other matter we must discuss is a bit more—well—sensitive."

Nicholas hadn't realized it, but he'd been gazing at Angela . . . and she'd been gazing back. She really did look breathtaking, with her dark eyes dancing in the candlelight and the tiny flames flickering over her skin.

"Nicholas!"

He glanced at his great-aunt, who was glaring at him, and fought back a groan. "Enjoy your hot dog?" he asked wryly. Lady Anne might have turned up her nose at the meal, but she'd eaten every last bite. Her plate was now polished as clean as one of Angela's floors.

"The marriage," Lady Anne said simply, looking first at him, then at Angela, who colored perceptibly, and finally back at him.

"As I tried to tell you in the drawing room, we're not really married," Nicholas said flatly.

Rosemunde laughed wickedly. "You'd never know it from the way they were kissing in the rose garden today, Auntie!" she exclaimed brightly.

Lady Anne made a small, strangled sound and Nicholas shot his daughter a censuring glance. Rosemunde merely smiled back innocently. How could a girl who was only five tomorrow have such a scheming mind? She'd probably had a hand in getting herself a second birthday party, too.

"And it *is* so good to finally have a mother," Rosemunde continued wistfully, her voice dropping to a pathetic croon. "Once I go to school next year, I know all my new friends will have normal families, with a father *and* a mother."

Nicholas pursed his lips. The only other creature who could do a better sad puppy-dog expression was Baskerville, he thought, prodding his daughter under the table with a light kick. If the circumstances weren't so dire, he would have been amused at her wheedling. But he wasn't. Lady Anne couldn't leave here thinking he was married! *Could she?* he suddenly wondered. He quickly shook his head, as if to clear it of confusion.

But his great-aunt's eyes were already going sappy. "A young girl does need a mother," she conceded softly.

"We aren't married!" Angela suddenly burst out. Her skin was flushed a deep rose and it made her look even more beautiful.

"Now, Mum, quit teasing Auntie!" Rosemunde exclaimed reproachfully. "You didn't invite Auntie or me to the wedding, so it's really not fair to—"

"Rosemunde," Nicholas warned softly.

Rosemunde tossed her hair defiantly, then fell silent, even if the pleased, naughty smirk didn't leave her face.

Lady Anne sighed audibly, snapped her napkin from her lap, and folded it beside her plate. "Things being what they are, I was truly at a loss about how to handle it," she said in a resigned tone.

"Things aren't—" Angela began.

"My dear, I have spoken with the very magistrate who married you!" Lady Anne nearly shrieked. "You have hired people all over Saint Ives to work on Westhawke Hall, and you have done so using the name of Lady Westhawke! Do you mean to tell me you were lying?"

"Well," Angela began, "I—I—"

Nicholas considered becoming more forceful with his great-aunt, if for no other reason than that Angela was at such a loss, but, somehow, the goings-on were just getting too intriguing. Besides, he thought now, if he'd met Angela under any other circumstances, he'd definitely have pursued her. *Hell, I'm pursuing her, anyway.*

Lady Anne cleared her throat, as if to recover from her own burst of temper, then shot Angela a withering glance. "And you will appear in society," she continued, her voice beginning to rise again with every word. "Nicholas has long shunned his peers and his position, and I simply will not have it! This ridiculous denial of your marriage is beginning to truly anger me." Abruptly, Lady Anne rose from her chair. "I have had quite enough!"

Nicholas wasn't quite sure what she was referring to. Was it the dinner? His refusal to play the Westhawke heir in London? Or just, as she claimed, the fact that they were trying to deny their marriage?

Even Angela, who Nicholas knew would stand up to anyone, had gone a little pale at Lady Anne's verbal assault and was now crossing her arms defensively over her makeshift garden-party dress.

"And now—" Lady Anne squared her shoulders, then leaned forward, placing both her palms on the table, on either side of her clean plate. She stared directly at Angela. "I want you to understand that I have condescended to accept this marriage." She sighed, as if realizing what she'd said was rude. "In fact," she added, as if to make up for it, "I say that going outside the peerage every few generations livens up the bloodline. Nicholas's great-great-great-uncle actually married a barmaid once," she finished in a rush, as if every word were killing her.

"Well, I'm pleased to hear he didn't marry her twice," Angela said wryly, without missing a beat.

"Why, you are . . ." Lady Anne gasped.

Nicholas groaned as he watched Angela leap to her feet. "And madam," Angela continued, her tone so utterly lethal that she nearly sounded English, "I'd like to inform you that I am neither a barmaid nor a horse with a bloodline!"

"So just what are you?" Lady Anne returned in a shocked voice.

"A schoolteacher," Angela replied levelly, gracefully seating herself again.

A schoolteacher? Nicholas quickly filed the information in his mental facts-about-Angela Lancini file. Somehow, it surprised him . . . if she really was. He couldn't help but feel his heart skip a beat. If she was a teacher, that probably meant she liked kids. Rosemunde certainly liked her. He couldn't believe how he'd begun to live for these moments of clarity, when new bits of information about her magically slipped out.

"Humph," Lady Anne said after a long moment. "Well, schoolteacher or no, you and your husband are expected at Lady Seymour's. The party's to announce the Honorable Catherine Seymour's engagement." Lady Anne reached in a pocket of her dress and tossed an invitation toward Angela. The heavy cream envelope landed squarely above Angela's empty plate.

"Catherine's getting married?" The question left his lips before Nicholas thought it through. After all, he'd known Catherine all his life and had even dated her casually. When he glanced up, Angela was shooting him a look so cool he actually felt a chill. And then—he just couldn't help it—he found himself smiling.

Maybe there was some truth in Italian stereotypes. Hot-blooded, possessive, great cooks, even better lovers . . . and passionately jealous. Was Angela wondering about his relation to Catherine Seymour?

"If you've been sent an engagement-party invitation, it's rather obvious that Catherine is to be married," his great-aunt was saying. "Some people do announce their engagements, you know."

"Only in the better houses," Angela put in.

"That is correct, my dear," his great-aunt said to Angela, seemingly nonplussed by her sarcasm. "And you'll do well to remember it, now that you have a position in society to maintain. And now, Nicholas," she continued, tapping her cane once against the terrace floor. "You will walk me out."

Nicholas rose and circled the table. Angela was staring haughtily out toward the fountain, with her chin raised regally in the cooling night air.

"Thank you so much for coming, Lady Anne," she said, turning her gaze on his great-aunt.

The two women stared stonily at each other for so long that Nicholas started to feel uncomfortable. Angela's eyes flashed darkly and his great-aunt's gunmetal gray gaze seemed to pierce the very air.

"I do thank you for having me on such short notice," his great-aunt said levelly. After a long moment, she added, "Lady Westhawke."

With that, she looped her cane over her wrist, leaned on Nicholas's arm and practically pulled him toward the door. He expected her to say something about Angela—what, he didn't know—but she didn't. More than any other woman,

Angela had gone at his great-aunt head-to-head and he had absolutely no idea how Lady Anne had really reacted.

He also couldn't help but feel a bit of pride... as if Angela were really his wife. He half smiled, supposing it wouldn't hurt to play out the charade, just for his aunt's benefit, of course. And, anyway, he'd love to see Angela all dressed up at one of those stuffy society parties. He was so lost in thought about how she'd look in such a place that he barely noticed they'd reached the car.

Lady Anne lifted a large, brightly wrapped package from the back seat and pushed it into Nicholas's arms. "For Rosemunde," she said, tilting her chin to indicate that she expected a kiss from her favorite nephew.

"Thank you." Nicholas leaned over, hugged her and planted a smacking kiss on her cheek.

"And this," she said, slapping a velvet box in his palm, "is for your wife."

Nicholas's jaw dropped as his fingers closed around the box. She'd brought Angela a present? He couldn't believe it. "Aunt Anne," he suddenly began, "we're not—"

"Backbone!" his great-aunt suddenly boomed.

"Excuse me?"

"The girl has backbone!" she said, pounding her cane on the driveway for emphasis. "And thrifty," she continued. "Not at all like Catherine Seymour." His great-aunt shook her head quickly back and forth.

"I thought that Catherine was *lovely*," he said, completely taken aback.

"That twit's spent a king's ransom for her wedding dress and would never think to make a lovely garden dress from the fabric." She sighed. "So much the pity. Well, I do apologize for all the girls I've sent away in tears over the years."

Nicholas shifted the gift packages in his arms. "You mean to say you actually like her?" he asked in shock.

His great-aunt gazed at him for long moments. Her piercing gray eyes actually started to twinkle. "Humph," she said and smiled.

Then, without waiting for her driver's assistance, she got in the car and slammed the door. Within seconds, the Rolls spun down the drive, leaving Nicholas laden down with packages. He turned after a moment and headed back inside, nearly colliding with his daughter in the hallway.

"I believe that's for me," Rosemunde said.

Nicholas handed the larger package to her, with a censuring glance. "You've been bad."

She giggled sheepishly. "Well, you are married!"

It was pointless to argue. "Just don't open that package, peek inside and then try to rewrap it, the way you did last year," he said gruffly.

"Okay, Dad," she said, fighting back a grin.

Nicholas ruffled her hair and headed for the kitchen. Just as he entered, Angela placed the last dish in the dishwasher, and turned around.

She, too, looked at him a little sheepishly. And then she chuckled softly. "Bet you just got an earful about me," she said.

He leaned against the counter next to her and smiled. "She positively adores you."

At that, Angela laughed. "Right."

Nicholas found himself laughing, too. He leaned against her, as if for support, but really because he wanted to touch her. "But it's true," he said. "She admires your backbone."

Angela squinted at him, her dark eyes merry with laughter. "Backbone?"

He nodded. "And she sends the new Lady Westhawke a gift."

Angela groaned. "You mean you spent all that time with her and you didn't manage to convince her we weren't married?"

Looking at her, Nicholas decided not to admit that he hadn't even really tried . . . or that he didn't know why he hadn't. He merely shrugged and proffered the velvet box. "If you don't open it, I will," he said with a teasing smile. "I'm curious."

She snatched the box out of his hand playfully and opened it. "Oh, my word!" she gasped.

He leaned closer and peered down. Leave it to Lady Anne to know just exactly which jewels would best suit Angela, even if she'd never seen her, he thought. The necklace was of squarely cut rubies surrounded by emerald brilliants.

"Here," he said softly, without thinking. "Let me put it on you."

"No!" She laid the box on the counter. "We shouldn't have something that—er—expensive in the house, even. Much less on my neck. We've got to return it immediately."

And this was the woman he'd thought was a fortune hunter? "But they suit you," he found himself protesting. He definitely wanted to see how they'd look against her skin, even though they weren't really married and she wouldn't be keeping them.

"No," she said flatly.

"Well, then," he said, his voice low and husky again. "I'll put them in the safe while you change."

"Change for what?" she asked.

He shot her a playful grin and shrugged. "I don't know, but I'd suggest jeans and a jacket." He lifted the necklace from its box and held it to the light. It really was an exquisite piece. He headed for the door, then glanced at Angela again. "Meet you out front in ten minutes."

"Not until you tell me where we're going," she said. But her eyes were all lit up in anticipation of a surprise.

"Be there or be square," he teased over his shoulder. Then, becoming suddenly serious, he said, "We do have a few things to discuss."

"Like what?"

"Like my daughter," he said, just as the phone rang. He lifted the kitchen extension. "Hello?"

It was Sylvia Sinclair's mother. She sounded nearly hysterical, and Nicholas turned his back to Angela, as if to close her out of the conversation. "Yes," he said after a long moment. "That would be fine, I'm sure."

"Who was that?" Angela asked, when he hung up and turned to face her. Her eyes were searching his face, as if for clues. She'd clearly picked up on the fact that it wasn't a social call.

"Ten minutes," he repeated. And then he headed for the safe.

ANGELA LEANED AGAINST a tall wrought-iron lamppost in the driveway and shooed away the summer insects that were gathering around the light, wondering who had called and just what he'd meant by his parting remark about Rosemunde. "Can't we just take a car?"

The man merely revved the engine of his motorcycle and held out a helmet. He looked pretty dashing, too. He'd changed from his slacks and sport coat back into jeans and was already straddling the bike. His long white blond ponytail tumbled from beneath his helmet and trailed between his shoulder blades, over a jean jacket. He crooked a finger at her, as if luring her toward the bike.

"Well," she said playfully, as she walked toward him, "seeing as I don't get out much and that I'm being held captive in your castle, I suppose I'll take transport of any kind."

"Just don't try to escape," he returned as he handed her the helmet.

"Why?" she asked lightly, plopping it on her head. "Because you'll lock me in the tower and feed me nothing but gruel?"

He threw his head back and laughed. As she began to fumble with the strap, both his hands caught hers. "No, luv," he said, buckling it under her chin for her. "I'll ravish you, take your maidenhead and then hunt you for blood sport."

"Lovely," she managed to say dryly, feeling how his fingers lingered briefly along her jaw.

"For me, anyway," he quipped. He nodded behind him. "Get on, luv."

She grabbed his shoulders, hoisted herself onto the bike, then realized just how close she was to him. She surreptitiously tried to scoot back on the seat, but he reached behind him, grabbed her wrists and wrapped them snugly under his jacket and against his waist.

"Hold on tight or else," he teased over his shoulder.

"Or else what?" She nearly gasped. The large bike seat was vibrating beneath her and her legs were straddled on either side of his thighs.

"The tower, gruel, you name it," he said. And then he gunned the engine again and they flew down the drive.

"Who called?" she yelled, telling herself she had no choice but to hug his waist and squeeze her thighs against his. *It's nothing personal,* she thought, *I'm just holding on for dear life.*

He didn't respond, but one of his hands left the handlebars and closed over both of hers. "You need to steer!"

He merely glanced over his shoulder and shot her a grin. Clearly, he had no intention of slowing down. Or of putting both hands on the handlebars. In fact, his fingers were now twining through hers. "Just hang on, luv," he yelled, as they shot through the open gates of Westhawke Hall and onto a cobblestone road.

"I am hanging on," Angela returned, but the sound of her voice was carried away by the rushing wind.

"Give yourself over to the feeling!" he called out. "Don't fight it."

At the tremulous sound of his excited voice, a thrill raced through her body. And she gave in. She found herself smiling as the wind whipped around her. Tendrils of her hair blew wildly, then lay plastered against her face. Her whole body felt cold, except where she held him . . . except where his powerful thighs touched and warmed hers, and where his large, warm hand covered both her own.

And then her whole body started to warm. She'd worn a jacket, as he'd asked, but she'd forgotten to button it, and either side of it flapped in the wind. Because the tight bodice of her wedding gown was so confining, she'd changed into a loose-fitting stretch-lace bra—the kind she was really too large to wear—and now her breasts were crushed hard against his jacket, with nothing but thin cotton between her and the rough denim. Her skin was beginning to tingle with awareness.

"Who called?" she yelled again, hoping to deflect what his physical nearness was doing to her.

"Who what?" he yelled.

She fought back another gasp, wanting to tell him to stop. Their bodies vibrated with the bike, and she was thrown against him with every bump and pothole in the old cobblestone road.

"Called!" she nearly screamed. As soon as the word was out, she found herself leaning her cheek against his jacket, then rubbing her cool skin against the rough denim.

Give yourself over to the feeling, she thought. She'd nearly done so by the time he answered her.

"Sylvia's mother," he yelled. "The police want to talk to you tomorrow."

She stiffened against him, wondering why she suddenly felt she'd done something wrong. *But you have, haven't you?* she thought. After all, she'd come here to call off Sylvia's wedding and now she was wondering if a man like Nicholas Westhawke could ever become *her* husband!

Chapter Eight

The Woodsprite was abuzz with festive talk; waiters in plumed hats and waitresses wearing green aprons ducked beneath elbows and circled around their chatty patrons. "Evening, Lady Westhawke!" one young waiter called breathlessly as he raced past.

Angela waved cheerfully, then flushed and glanced toward Nicholas. Had he caught her acting as if she were his wife?

No. Good, she thought, assuring herself that she'd only responded that way for convenience's sake. Nicholas hadn't noticed but was turning from the bar, carrying two pewter goblets. He moved even more expertly through the crowd than the staff, so lithely he almost seemed to float.

He stopped more than once in the small, cozy pub talking to friends and nodding in her direction. Across the narrow, twisting cobbled street, the Skull and Crossbones, which had a pirate theme, looked just as busy. Tiny tourist shops, full of wool sweaters and British flags, curved in a semicircle. The street was lit by wrought-iron lamps.

When she glanced at Nicholas again, he was smiling. He almost seemed to be talking about her! But what was he saying? He finally ambled over to her, then unceremoniously slid beside her in the booth, rather than across from her. She scooted toward the wall, but not before she'd felt his thigh and shoulder press against hers. He leaned over, placing a goblet in front of her.

"So you're willing to talk to the police?" he asked.

With her sharp intake of breath, she caught another dizzying whiff of his woodsy-smelling skin. "Of course," she said. "I have nothing to hide."

He gazed at her, as if he didn't believe her, then suddenly smiled. "So, what do you think, luv?" He glanced around the room. In the flames from the candlelit oak tables, his eyes seemed to flicker with sparks of purple.

"I love it here," she said spontaneously. The Woodsprite pub had a small sign on the door saying it had been established in 1645, and its decor paid tribute to Cornwall's reputation for housing gnomes, goblins and elves.

"Given Lady Anne's appearance, dinner wasn't much," he said. "Would you care for something more? Fish and chips? Shepherd's pie?"

"No, thanks." What she really wanted was for her heart to quit thumping so wildly. As soon as he'd sat next to her, she felt she was riding recklessly on the wind again, with her arms wrapped tightly around him. She could still feel the muscles of his stomach flexing against her hands.

"Ever been to England before?"

Her magical English lord turned Evil Knievel was trying to talk to her and her mind was in the gutter! She managed a chuckle. "I'd never even been on a plane before."

She glanced sideways. His head was turned toward her and his shockingly violet eyes were narrowing. Suddenly, he smiled that quirky, sexy smile again. "Well, that settles it," he said, his voice lowering and becoming tantalizingly seductive.

"Settles what?"

"You must attend the Seymour engagement party." He winked. "And drink your pint of warm ale. You can't leave England without it."

"What's the fact that I've never been here before have to do with the Seymours and ale?" she asked lightly. *He's not trying to find out where Sylvia is. He's definitely attracted to me,* she thought. She hadn't loved Frankie passionately, but she had hoped theirs would be a companionable marriage. Could what she was feeling for Nicholas turn into passion?

"Luv," he finally said, leaning close. "Ale and parties are both part of your British experience."

Everything in his eyes said he was part of that experience, too. Feeling his breath against her cheek, she tried to shift back from him, but there was nowhere to go. He casually stretched and leaned his arm along the back of the booth, so that his fingers trailed downward and nearly touched her shoulder.

Feeling suddenly hemmed in, she leaned forward, lifted her goblet and took a gulp of the ale. Then she realized she'd feel claustrophobic if the two of them were alone in Madison Square Garden. So she leaned back.

He took it as an invitation; his arm dropped promptly onto her shoulder. She glanced at him again and smiled weakly, thinking it would feel so wonderful just to relax in his embrace. Not that she could. The man hadn't bothered to tell his aunt they weren't married. Besides, he didn't trust her. And furthermore, his wealth and status made her feel a bit uncomfortable, as if he were way out of her league.

"I can't go to a party as your wife," she finally said.

"Why not?"

Had disappointment really crossed his features? She glanced around the crowded room. "Well, because we're not—"

"I know that." He looked at her as if she were a little daft. "But it would be rather fun. Think of it as a lark."

Her mouth dropped. He made it sound as if she lacked a sporting nature! She knew how to have a good time, but pretending you were married when you weren't seemed dishonest, plain and simple.

"And you would see a side of England that tourists never see," he continued. "The upper crust in home environs."

"I do believe I've already seen that," she said wryly. Still, she had to admit he had a point. Just thinking about going made her feel like Cinderella. When she'd opened the envelope, she'd found a beautiful invitation. The paper was of heavy cream stock, the words were embossed in scripted gold lettering and the party was a formal high-society ball.

"So just say yes," he was saying. With every word, his voice dropped an alluring notch.

"I—I can't," she managed to protest.

"But you can, of course," he said in a singsong, clearly meant to lead her on.

His wheedling was working. His husky voice was an invitation in itself. Beneath his suddenly hooded gaze, his deep violet eyes smoldered. What was his real motive in wanting to play out this charade? she wondered. Why would a man of his stature introduce her into society as his wife? It was more than a lark. It had to be...

"I just—" How could she explain that things had already gotten out of control? That she was a lower-middle-class kid from New York. And that tending his garden—something she'd initially done for him—now made her begin wishing all those lovely roses were her own. As much as she didn't want to admit it, those cream silk sheets on her antique bed were beginning to feel way too good, too.

She was beginning to dread the day when she no longer woke to the breathtaking view of cliffs beyond diamond-paned windows and when she woke to face yet another brick building. She loved New York, but Westhawke Hall was astounding. *And so is Nicholas.*

"Are you still with me, luv?" He relaxed his arm around her shoulder, but kept her close.

"It's just that I'm not your wife," she said again, leaning into his embrace. *Don't worry,* she thought. *As soon as Sylvia calls, I'll be heading home. And he'll want me to go.* "Besides," she added, somehow feeling that her refusal was a blow she needed to soften, "Lady Anne will eventually find out and—"

"And I'll be the one in trouble, not you."

"But I'm not your—"

"For not being my wife, you sure took it upon yourself to plan my daughter's birthday," he suddenly said, sounding gruff.

Blowing hot and cold again. "Now, did you seriously remember?" she chided.

"Absolutely."

She merely smirked, since she knew he was lying, and took another sip of ale. She wasn't much of a drinker and couldn't touch hard alcohol without choking, but the ale was surprisingly good.

"Just who did you invite to this party, anyway?"

She gulped, then rushed into the explanation, feeling somewhat proud of herself. "Well, I called the nearest school, where I figured Rosemunde would go next year, and got a list of names for the incoming students."

"They just gave you the names?"

"Well—" She flushed guiltily. "I did tell them I was Lady Westhawke." Sheepishly, she added, "The name clearly carries some weight." As near as she could tell, it was akin to saying you were a Rockefeller.

He looked utterly speechless.

"What?" she finally prompted.

"Rosemunde's going elsewhere to school," he finally said. "Near London." He flashed her a quick smile. "A few of her future classmates will be coming tomorrow, for *my* party."

She gasped. Had he been telling the truth? "Your party?"

He nodded, looking a little grim. "I don't know where you got it in your head that I'm such a lousy father."

"Could have been that no one's bothered to cut or comb her hair," she mumbled a little defensively.

"She'll never let me do it," Nicholas returned. "I—" He cleared his throat. "I don't think she trusted me to find someone who would do a good job, but when she saw you . . . well, I think she means to model herself after you a bit."

Angela found herself smiling. Every day it became clearer that Rosemunde was taking to her. They'd done some baking together, and though Nicholas was none the wiser, Mrs. O'Reilly had given Angela a ride into Saint Ives this morning, to pick out a real party dress for his little girl.

"Sorry about the party," she finally said softly. "And I didn't realize you were moving so that Rosemunde could go to school. . . ." Oh, how could he stand to leave Westhawke Hall? She'd been here a mere week and she couldn't bear the thought of leaving. *But I am leaving, of course.*

"I'm not going anywhere," he said levelly.

"You're sending Rosemunde away?" she asked, suddenly realizing what he was saying.

"Of course."

"That's just awful!" she exclaimed. This time she did lean away from him, toward the wall. His palm only tightened possessively around her shoulder.

"I went to prep school," he returned coolly.

"And look how you turned out," she huffed. She glanced around the pub, as if seeking escape.

"What's wrong with me?"

She glanced at him, taking in his muscular torso, the white blond hair that fell over his taut shirt and his calm dark blue eyes. Suddenly she couldn't think of a thing. Finally she said, "Well, you don't seem to like people much."

He glanced around the room, as if to remind her that he'd talked to every soul in it before seating himself. "I admit I don't like stuffy parties," he conceded.

"And yet you want to force me to go to one," she returned, as if that settled matters.

"Don't change the subject," he said. "Prep schools are fine. So are boarding schools. They teach one how to get on with others. How not to make a fuss."

"That's the strangest excuse I've ever heard for ditching one's five-year-old."

"I'm not, as you say, ditching—"

"Where are your parents?" she asked.

He looked a little uncomfortable and shrugged. "Right now? Bali, I think."

"You most certainly are ditching," she said huffily, staring down into her drink. "Perhaps if you'd spent more time with your parents, you'd keep in closer contact now." She couldn't help but feel sorry for Rosemunde. Angela's own mother had died long ago, and she knew what it was like to be a young girl without a mother. She couldn't imagine how she would have felt being sent away, too.

She turned on Nicholas with a glare. "Do you know how many parents would kill to be in your position? How many have to work—sometimes two jobs—just to make a no-frills living? How many want nothing more than to spend that time with their kids?"

"And here I am," he said, his voice sounding lethal as he followed through with her line of argument, "rich as sin, with nothing to do, and I don't even want to take care of my own daughter."

"Right, buster," she snapped. And then it finally hit her. He had intended to marry Sylvia so she'd take care of Rosemunde. Why else would someone wealthy and drop-dead gorgeous go for a correspondence bride?

"I admit Rosemunde and I might not seem close, in the way you're used to," he said gruffly.

He sounded as pompous as his great-aunt! She was sure he was imagining her with some lusty, boisterous, clichéd Italian family. "And just how many ways are there to be close?" she challenged.

His glance pierced her very soul. "Oh, luv," he said softly. "There are many."

"And so you decided to marry a woman you didn't even know, in order to get a nanny for Rosemunde?" she shot back, ignoring the innuendo.

For a moment he looked as if he didn't have the slightest idea what she was talking about, and instead of getting angrier, he only drew her closer. "Sylvia?"

She nodded.

He smiled, though the smile didn't reach his eyes. "Jealous?"

Maybe. She arched her brow in his direction. "Of course not!"

"Just wondering," he said. "Because that would be an interesting development."

Before she could respond, a gong sounded. She glanced up, suddenly wondering what she was doing here. Was she really jealous of Sylvia Sinclair? And was she really discussing Rosemunde's upbringing with Nicholas? She thought over how Rosemunde tagged along with her during the day, before Nicholas awakened. There was no doubt about the fact that they were becoming friends.

"Hear, hear," one of the waiters began to yell. "Hear, hear."

All around them, patrons picked up silverware and tapped the sides of their mugs, until clattering, tinkling sounds filled the room.

Angela shot Nicholas another glance before turning her attention to the waiter. As mad as he'd made her, she was glad to have something else to hold her attention. And yet, she found herself wanting to make excuses for him, as the noise began to die down.

After all, he really hadn't forgotten his daughter's birthday, and in other ways he was thoughtful. Sending kids away to school was probably as commonplace to him as breathing. Rosemunde would build monied social connections that she'd have all her life. Still, it seemed horrible to Angela. If she had a daughter, she'd want her at home.

"Hear, hear," the waiter yelled loudly, forcing Angela to snap to attention again.

"Hear, hear," patrons called.

The waiter raised a pewter mug in the air. It was so full of frothy ale that some sloshed over his hand and onto his apron. He slung his arm around one of the waitresses. Both were wearing wedding bands. Perhaps they were announcing the birth of a child, Angela thought with sudden pleasure. The woman was clearly not drinking.

"We would like to announce the new, most esteemed—"

Angela's smile widened as she listened to his voice. He sounded like he was about to introduce the Queen of England.

"Most revered!" a voice called out.

"A lady," the waiter continued, "who deigns to reside in the hinterlands of her beloved Cornwall. A patroness we agree to serve, no less than if we remained her feudal subjects...."

Angela listened to all his high-toned language and chuckled. What in the world was the man talking about?

He raised his goblet even higher.

Shouts rose all around her. "Toast!"

"Good health, lady," she heard from somewhere.

And then the waiter boomed, "To Lady Westhawke!"

In a heartbeat, the room fell so silent you could hear a pin drop. Every goblet in the place seemed to reach the ceiling.

Then, simultaneously, they lowered, as every patron turned, stared directly at her and took a healthy draft.

She managed to pull her clenched teeth into a smile. She just hoped with all her heart that they all didn't start yelling "Speech! Speech!"

What happened was worse. The whole place burst into a heartfelt rendition of "For He's a Jolly Good Fellow."

At least, she thought, with a sinking heart, if they'd called for a speech, she could have explained she wasn't Lady Westhawke. Or could she have? she wondered, looking around at all the well-wishing faces. She also realized the misunderstanding was partially her fault. In her fervor to whip Westhawke Hall into shape and to plan Rosemunde's party, she'd made liberal use of the name. *But I didn't mean for this to happen,* she tried to assure herself, suddenly doubting her own motives.

In the backslapping melee that ensued after the song ended, she heard Nicholas yell, "A round for the house on your favorite lord and lady!"

THE ONLY WAY to get her home without argument had been to propel her into every store they'd passed. Every time she'd tried to open her mouth, he'd bought something else, including two goldfish for the fountain. On the back of his bike, she'd been so intent on clutching both him and the packages that she hadn't said a word.

Now he plopped the plastic bags that held the fish into the fountain water, so they'd reach the same temperature. "Sorry about the scene at the pub," he said lightly. He grasped her hand, then pulled her next to him, so that they both sat on the rim of the fountain.

"Nicholas, why didn't you tell those people and your great-aunt that we're not married?" she asked huffily. "You told everybody at the Woodsprite we were married, didn't you?" she continued in an accusing tone. "Didn't you? You lied to them!"

"I only allowed them to continue thinking what they already thought," he said, hoping he sounded less disturbed about the matter than he actually felt. What *was* he doing? Earlier in the evening, he'd told himself it was a lark. But was he confusing some semblance of real passion for his simple desire for her?

"But why?"

She looked completely exasperated. And beautiful. And he wanted to make her cling to him again, the way she had on his motorcycle. The night was a bit chilly, and he couldn't help but notice how her breasts reacted to the cold. He considered zipping her jacket for her but didn't.

Finally, he shrugged. "I really don't know why I did it." All he knew was that he wanted to feel her in his arms. "To save your reputation?" he suggested after a long, tense moment. He shot her a grin. "After all, you're living with a reclusive and rather good-looking rich man."

"And an egotist," she added. His smile deepened at the fact that she hadn't disputed that he was good-looking.

"The kind of man who always gets what he wants?" he teased, taking in how her dark hair glistened in the fountain's floodlights. The soft sound of gurgling water was all around them. It trickled slowly from tier to tier. Glancing up, he saw that Rosemunde's light was out, which meant Mrs. O'Reilly had tucked her into bed.

"Probably," she finally said. As if to end the conversation, she leaned over and studied the two goldfish, still held captive in their bags.

"Absolutely," he said softly, catching her warm fingers in his and savoring the touch of her silky soft skin. He slowly lifted her hand, turned it and kissed her palm.

When he glanced into her eyes, she looked a bit startled. *What's happening to me? For all I know, this woman really has done something to Sylvia.* "Come here, luv."

She didn't come, but she didn't resist. He tugged her hand gently, pulling her against him. She was so delicate, yet he knew there was a raw, untamed passion beating within her.... A passion she might not even suspect she had, but that burned to be released. Or was he fooling himself about that, just as he might be overlooking her involvement in Sylvia's disappearance?

He pressed her hand against his chest, then lifted his free hand, brushing a lock of her dark, shining hair from her forehead. He slowly traced the line of her jaw, before pressing his mouth against hers.

It was nothing more than the most chaste kiss, but a lightning-hot stream of arousal coursed through his veins. Without thinking, he cupped the perfect rounded column of her neck with both hands and leaned her head back to better drink in all her flavor. She tasted of toothpaste and ale, and he was sure it was the sweetest thing he'd ever tasted.

When her arms tentatively snaked around his waist, any semblance of the chastity he'd attempted vanished; his tongue plunged deeply between her lips. His hands lost themselves in her hair, then fell to her shoulders and then dropped lower still, roving over her back.

She was letting him explore her and kissing him back. The warm spear of her tongue tussled with his, plunged forward and retreated, only to find his yet again. More than anything, he wanted to lie down with her now, but they were outside, sitting side by side. He shifted his weight, turned swiftly and drew her over his lap, deepening the kiss as he did, in case she attempted any protest.

In a second, she was sitting between his legs, tucked snugly, tightly between his thighs. He trailed kisses down her neck and savored her salty skin while he ran his arms beneath hers and wrapped them tightly around her waist. Unable to stop himself, he let his hands rove upward, almost of their own accord, over the soft, full mounds of her breasts. He tried to tell himself his desire for her had nothing to do with his emotions, and that taking her to the Seymours' party was nothing more than he'd initially thought...a lark.

After a moment, he heard a low, throaty gasp escape from her. All the muscles in his body exploded with burning fire and then went rigid. He realized there was simply no more give where his thin denim jeans stretched across his lap. And no real barrier between where her tailbone crushed against him.

His lips sought hers. Again and again, his palms roved over her breasts. Through the soft cotton of her top, he could feel the comparative roughness of thin lace and how her nipples grew hard against his palms.

The only thing that kept his mouth from being utterly dry was the soft wetness of hers. He drew in a quick, sharp breath against her lips as he caught the taut tips of her breasts between his thumbs and fingers.

"It's been so long for me," he whispered against her lips. "Oh, Angel, I want you."

"Stop," she whispered, her arm dropping from around his neck, down to her lap.

Her voice sounded weak, tremulous and a little panicked. He slid his hands from her breasts and rested them against her waist, trailing fiery kisses against her throat again.

Just briefly, she rested her palms on either of his thighs. When he felt them, two warm, trembling hand spots so close to the most intimate part of him, he held his breath and shifted uncomfortably. He could have moaned out loud when she leaned back in his arms and snuggled, as if trying to get comfortable. Didn't the woman realize how close they were to making love?

"I—I'm just not ready for this," she whispered.

Both the words and the softness of her voice left him in sheer agony, but he would hardly demand that she come to bed with him, as much as he wanted her. "I'm not sure I am, either," he managed to say. "I haven't been with anyone since my wife died."

He didn't know whether it was because of sympathy or desire, but she reached up and touched his face. "We don't really know each other at all," she said softly. "And—and anyway," she continued with a lightness that utterly failed, "I'm just your captive until Sylvia calls. Then, of course, I've just got to head home."

He blew out a long sigh, then ran his hand through her hair again. It was so thick and dark and soft that his fingers were still tangled in it when he turned her face toward his. "Angel?" he said softly.

She leaned even farther back in his embrace, her hair looking lovely, spread out over his arm. Locks of it curled downward, toward the sparkling blue water, and for a moment, she almost looked as if she were floating. Her swollen lips glistened with the kisses they'd shared. When she slowly raised her heavy-looking, sensuous eyelids, her dark eyes were nothing more than bewitching, seductive slits.

"Yes?" she finally whispered.

"I want you to know something, luv."

"A secret?" she teased softly.

He nodded, wishing for all the world that she'd been ready to make love to him.

"So what is it?" she asked huskily.

"I'm not sure if I care whether or not Sylvia shows up," he whispered back. "Ever."

SYLVIA LAUGHED OVER the sound of the blaring TV. "Royal flush." She glanced at Frankie's adorably perplexed face, thinking that she'd tell him where Angela was after the very next hand. At first, she'd suspected he was flirting with her, to seduce information out of her. Now, she wasn't so sure. And the only way to find out was to see if he chased after Angela or not.

As sorry as she was about not living up to her obligation to Angela, she *had* to find out, she thought, trying to soothe her guilty conscience. She'd begun to have all kinds of fantasies about the man.... Like the one where he kept asking her to marry him. Of course, she kept reminding herself, they'd have to date first.

"Royal what?" Frankie finally murmured, still staring at his cards.

She laughed again and fanned her cards on the carpet. "You heard me."

"Beginner's luck," he groused, catching her gaze and holding it.

For a second, she thought he might kiss her again. He'd done so exactly three times now. "You wish," she said lightly.

"Oh, right," he said, smiling.

Her laughter tempered to a grin and then a sigh. She could hardly believe how relaxed she felt...and free. And all because of a muscle-bound hulk of a guy who'd taught her how to wield lock picks and play five-card stud. What would her academic friends think if they could see her now?

When she reached for the cards, Frankie's hands covered hers for the briefest of moments. She shot him a flirtatious glance, then snatched the deck.

"If you were losing, you wouldn't be so hot to play," he teased. "Now, would you?"

She shuffled, half imagining herself with some academic beau. He'd have a starched white shirt, tweed sport coat with elbow patches and be chatting away about some extremely esoteric topic. And she'd be bored stiff. She just hoped when she told Frankie of Angela's whereabouts that he didn't go chasing after her. Would he?

She dealt the cards while Frankie toyed with the remote control, switching rapidly through the television stations. She frowned, thinking that constant channel-changing was one bad habit of which she'd have to cure him. "Are you going to look at your cards or not?" she prompted.

He narrowed his eyes in mock anger, then picked up his hand. "Why don't you let me win?" he returned. "Just once. This is destroying my masculine pride."

"It could be worse," she shot back. "We could be playing strip poker."

He grinned. "Now there's an idea." Suddenly, he wrenched around and stared at the TV.

She watched his expression shift from flirtatious to concerned in less than a second. What was wrong? She glanced at the TV. It was just the news.

Reporters were gathering around Sal Mancini, who'd just been indicted on racketeering charges. Sylvia frowned. In all honesty, she was almost sorry to hear it. Before she'd moved to Connecticut, she'd lived in New York, and she'd once lived on a block that housed a number of Mancini's businesses. It had been the safest block in the city.

Not that she condoned crime, she thought as she watched Mancini make his statement, but he'd seemingly kept her pretty darn safe. She sighed again, thinking it was one of those things only city dwellers would understand.

"No," Frankie was protesting in a heartfelt voice. "Oh, no."

She glanced at him. Why was he so emotionally involved in the Mancini case?

Mancini! She gasped out loud and glanced quickly at Frankie. He was scrutinizing her features.

"My father," he said slowly. His gaze held steady, as if he expected some twitch or shudder to indicate her reaction.

"As in ... godfather?" she managed to ask.

"As in biological," he said wryly.

She gulped. "Oh."

"He's honestly gone legitimate," he said, sighing. "So I just don't get it."

Legitimate? Wouldn't any son of a mobster say that? Sylvia gulped. Was she in danger? Her jaw dropped. It was even more probable that *Angela* was in danger, which was what she'd initially thought!

She stared down at her cards, avoiding Frankie's gaze. Then she somehow managed to slowly fold her hand, even though her mind was racing. If Frankie had meant to hurt her he would surely have done so by now. But Frankie couldn't hurt a flea! Except, perhaps, Angela. Could Frankie really be involved with a criminal? Was it a case of "like father, like son"? Or was Sal Mancini innocent, as Frankie claimed?

One thing was certain. She could never divulge Angela's whereabouts. Not now. Not ever.

But how else could she determine whether or not Frankie had feelings for her? And if he did, she thought with rising hysteria, was she going to wind up married to the mob?

"THIS IS IMPOSSIBLE," Angela groaned, flinging back her covers and heading for the window. She pulled the robe to her peignoir set tightly around herself, then stared toward the cliffs. *No brides.* Four in the morning had come and gone, and Nicholas hadn't yet appeared on the lawn. Where were those three ladies who kept him so occupied during the wee hours?

"I can't believe I've actually begun to watch for them," she muttered. And yet, they were such a strange, magical sight. She loved seeing them float along the cliffs, even if she still wondered what exactly Nicholas was up to. And what was he doing tonight, if he wasn't making those brides appear?

"What he's doing is driving me crazy," she whispered, turning from the window. It was no use telling herself she couldn't sleep because of Rosemunde's party tomorrow. She was wide-awake because she could still feel his kiss and the intimate way he had touched her.

Kisses aren't everything, she thought as she plopped back in her wonderful Empire bed and pulled the covers to her chin. "But he's nice, too," she murmured, shutting her eyes. In a hazy half sleep, she wondered if their kiss had anything to do with the fact that Nicholas was elsewhere tonight, and that his misty, transparent brides hadn't appeared. Had she—a flesh-and-blood woman—suddenly become more interesting? Was that why he hadn't worked harder to deny their marriage?

Chapter Nine

"How did I ever get into the habit of sleeping so late?" Nicholas muttered, glaring through the window. He buttoned his denim shirt and shoved the tails into his jeans while he watched the bobbies leaving. He'd even set his alarm this morning, hoping to be present while they talked to Angela. Well, he thought, he had to get up anyway, to ensure preparations for Rosemunde's party were under control. Still, he'd been dying to know how Angela handled the interview with them. And now he'd blown it.

He suddenly smiled. He meant to take Angela into Saint Ives this morning, too, and he couldn't help but wonder how she'd react to his surprise trip. But what had she said to the police? Had she divulged information he should be aware of?

He sat on his chaise lounge and glanced down at today's array of newspapers. Headlines on the *New York Times* caught his attention, and he read as he donned his belt. "'Salvatore Mancini arrested on racketeering charges,'" he murmured, scanning the photo and story.

He buckled his belt, then buttoned his cuffs. "New York," he said, shaking his head. Somehow, he hated imagining Angela living in such a dangerous place, where men like this Salvatore Mancini character were on the loose.

Suddenly, he squinted, feeling something tug at the furthest reaches of his mind. He felt as if he'd been searching for a word and that it was now on the tip of his tongue. But he hadn't been trying to think of a word, had he? And yet, suddenly that name, Salvatore Mancini, seemed significant, as if it had something to do with Angela.

After a long moment, he chuckled. It was probably because nowadays *everything* seemed like it had to do with Angela Lancini.

"Dad?"

He glanced away from the paper. "Happy birthday, sweetheart." Rosemunde bounded across the room and into his arms.

"Did you get me a present?" she asked with a sly grin.

"Of course," he said. "And both Angela and I planned parties for you, too."

Her eyes narrowed. "I bet you didn't get me what I most wanted," she challenged.

"What's that?" he asked.

"Angela to be my mum," she said and grinned.

"You really like her?" he asked, drawing her closer.

"I really do," she returned.

"THERE, THERE, DEAR, don't make a fuss," one of the caterers said, forcefully nudging Angela toward the kitchen door.

"Aren't English people concerned with anything other than 'not making a fuss'?" she muttered under her breath, trying to hold her ground.

"We're also overly concerned with the weather," the caterer offered, his superficially helpful voice laced with irony. "Now out, Lady Westhawke."

"But the hot dogs!" she protested, more concerned with the party than with the fact that he was calling her Lady Westhawke. "Rosemunde has to have hot dogs for her birthday. And my cake! And—and someone's got to meet the magician I hired!''

The balding caterer ran his hand over his scalp, catching wispy strands of his few remaining hairs in his fingers. He was a bit overweight, and her exact height, so his gray eyes met hers dead on.

''I'm sure I can manage a hot dog,'' he said wryly, shoving her past his trays of neatly arranged crepes, canapés, crustless sandwiches and salmon. Against her will, he managed to propel her right out the door... and into the very arms she'd been avoiding. Thinking about Nicholas's kisses after she'd gone to bed was one thing, but seeing him so early in the morning when her defenses were down was another thing entirely.

''Is the lady of the house giving you a hard time?'' Nicholas asked, wrapping his arms around her waist.

''Just a bit, sir,'' the caterer said. He pushed her against Nicholas one more time, as if for extra measure, then rushed back into the kitchen.

They're destroying my kitchen! she thought illogically, twisting her body around and trying to follow the caterer. Before she knew what was happening, Nicholas had caught her wrist, whirled her around yet again and delivered a wet, playful kiss.

She gasped, wrenching away, but he was already tugging her toward the front entrance hall. The sheer forcefulness of his movements sent her careening down a flight of stone stairs and past a row of portraits hung in a long hallway. In seconds, he was no longer in front of her, but beside her, with one of his wide, warm hands pressing against the small of her back.

''Nicholas, Rosemunde's party is in less than three hours,'' she protested. And yet, she knew the time frame wasn't what she was really protesting, but rather the claims he kept making on her with his lips. Didn't he know how confused she'd felt when he walked her from the fountain to her room the previous night, leaving her with such a sweet, chaste kiss? *Not that anything preceding that had been the least bit chaste.*

"Did you have difficulties with the police?" he asked.

"Other than the fact that they took up so much time, no," she said huffily. "I have to get in there and prepare—"

"That's why we hired caterers," he said lightly. The soft, warm pressure of his hand increased, as he continued to propel her forward.

"*We* didn't hire caterers," she managed to say.

Outside, Mr. Magnuson was behind the wheel of the limo, facing away from them. She whirled around on the threshold and gazed at Nicholas, her eyes flashing. It would have been so simple to make love to him the previous night. She'd nearly suggested it, even though she felt more than a bit nervous at the prospect.

"Nicholas?" Just looking at him, her confusion, which was masking itself as anger, abated. *I'm starting to blow as hot and cold as he does,* she thought, reaching up and brushing a lock of his hair from his forehead gently. Actually, she thought with a sudden surge of panic, these days he was merely blowing hot and hot. Another fear flashed through her mind: was all this a farce? Was he still toying with her so that she'd tell him where Sylvia was?

He merely leaned against the doorjamb, pulling her against him. Somehow she managed to keep a decent half foot between them. "Hmm?"

"Where—" She didn't exactly know how to put it. The world was headed for the twenty-first century, and it seemed awfully old-fashioned to ask a man about his intentions. Still, he had to realize that he was beginning to make her dream of a relationship with him. Every day in this place was an adventure for her. She couldn't help wondering what it might be like to share a bed with him, or be held by his strong arms through a long, chilly English night. "Where are we going?" she asked softly, still gazing into his eyes, and feeling sure her meaning was clear from her intonation.

He lightly licked his slightly parted lips and cocked his head, as if to get a better look at her through those devastating eyes. After a long moment, he shrugged. "Just to town, luv."

He'd known exactly what she'd meant. "I figured that," she said, biting back another sudden rush of temper. "But I mean—" *You and me.*

"What, luv?" he asked huskily, leaning and nuzzling his cheek against hers.

"Do you still believe I—I'm a criminal?" she asked, instead of answering him.

"In all honesty—" He leaned back again, his glance drifting from her eyes to her lips. "I really have no way of knowing."

It was true, but the admission still stung. More so, because Frankie sort of was—or at least Sal Mancini used to be. And she felt somehow implicated. *Quit thinking about this man. As soon as Sylvia calls, I'm going to rub my ruby slippers together and head straight for home.*

"How can you—" Her lips parted and her mouth went dry when her gaze rested on his mouth. She shook her head to clear it of confusion. "Come onto me when you don't trust me in the least," she quickly forced herself to continue.

"Luv," he whispered softly, "can I tell you a secret?"

Oh, no. Another secret. Like the one where he doesn't care if Sylvia Sinclair ever turns up. "What's that?" she asked warily. She couldn't help but relax in his embrace, even if she hoped he'd perceive her movement merely as one of resignation.

"I'm beginning to believe," he whispered, "that trust is a highly overrated commodity."

"SOMETHING SLEEK, something fine, something utterly devastating," Nicholas said, thinking it would have to be. Otherwise, the Seymour women would try to eat her alive. Not that they'd succeed. Angela would give them a run for their money in a potato sack.

Celeste Dupre ignored him and paced past rows of rolled cloth. Every time she paused to snatch a swath from the top of a fabric bolt, his frown deepened. "Not beige, navy, black..." he murmured. "Angela's made for vibrant colors—emeralds, wines, violets—"

"Always nice to meet a man who has a sense of color," Mrs. Dupre interrupted, shooting him a wry glance.

The woman, he thought, was nearly as formidable as his aunt. And he'd been lucky to get her, he reminded himself. She'd become famous in London circles after designing for a royal duchess, but then she had retired to Cornwall. That she'd readily allowed them to visit her in the workshop beside her home had more than surprised him.

"What are you all doing out there?" Angela called.

He turned toward the voice, felt his lips part and his mouth go dry. Mrs. Dupre had left the door to her makeshift changing room partially open. Through the crack, Nicholas could see Angela obeying Mrs. Dupre's orders. Which meant she was stripping.

Undoubtedly, Mrs. Dupre—as both a resident of Cornwall and one who kept her finger on the pulse of London—thought they were married and hadn't worried overly much about the door. Or else it was an accident. Either way, he was left to feast his eyes on Angela's back as she hastily, and a little angrily, he thought, undid her buttons and shrugged out of her blouse.

Through the crack, the visible sliver of her skin encompassed her very fine backbone. He was close enough that he could hear her zipper, too. She quickly stepped out of her jeans, letting them fall to the floor, then crossed her arms over her chest. "Do you mind telling me what this is about?"

From where he was, her skin looked soft, silky and well toned. Her knickers were the high-waisted kind and of white lace. "Your dress for the Seymour party," he managed to return, still watching her.

As near as he could tell, the proximity of his voice startled her into action. When she whirled around, he caught a flash of lace bra and cleavage, not to mention a lethal stare, right before she slammed the door shut in his face.

"She's even more temperamental than the duchess," Mrs. Dupre remarked with seeming approval. She spun around and hurried toward the door with a black sheath dress and a number of fabric samples over her arm.

As she passed, Nicholas waylaid her with a light touch. "I'm just curious," he said. "Why did you agree to design for her?"

"She's a completely unconnected American, is that so?"

Nicholas nodded. At least, as far as he knew, she wasn't connected to any well-known circles in New York. Of course, given that he still knew precious little about her, it was possible. He could only hope, if she were, that they weren't circles of ill repute.

"And she's to attend the Seymour ball?"

Nicholas nodded again, still wondering about his motives in taking her. He assured himself he was merely showing a New York woman the London scene, in the grandest style.

Mrs. Dupre smiled wickedly. "There's nothing we English love more than seeing such a woman put the peerage to shame. Besides, I owe Lady Anne a favor."

With that, she whisked into the dressing room, leaving him to stare at the closed door, wondering just what exact state of undress Angela happened to be in at the moment.

"Very nice," he murmured, when Mrs. Dupre pushed Angela back into the room.

"Nice!" Mrs. Dupre exclaimed, turning to frown at him. "Turn and walk, dear, and move about in the light," she continued, turning her full attention back to Angela, who was blushing like the devil.

"Well, the dress isn't so nice," he said, shooting Angela a quick smile. He now realized it was nothing more than the seamstress's prop. Mrs. Dupre wanted an idea of how cloth moved against Angela's body.

And it moved just fine. He was so intent on watching Angela stride across the room, whirl gracefully and return that he barely noticed when Mrs. Dupre did begin holding swaths of brightly colored material by her chin.

"Over to the light, please, Lady Westhawke," the woman said, directing Angela toward the far end of her workroom and toward a window.

"I'm not—"

"Quiet, please!" Mrs Dupre exclaimed, interrupting Angela. "I am trying to think, dear." The seamstress stared from one piece of fabric to another, then to Angela's face and back again.

With the light behind Angela, the sheath became nearly transparent. And for the briefest moment, he really thought he'd die if he didn't hold her in his arms again soon. Where was their relationship heading? He knew very well that was what she'd been trying to ask. But how was a man supposed to answer something like that? He had to know so much more about her before he could even begin to answer.

Her voice was low, and from across the room, he could only hear snatches of her and Mrs. Dupre's conversation.

Suddenly, he smiled, realizing Angela was clearly taking the upper hand in the matter of the gown. "Don't want...what I want...better if..."

He shook his head, in amusement, his gaze drawn to the swath of emerald that now lay over her shoulder. She really was a natural. A born princess. And that color against her skin was dazzling.

"That sounds perfect!" she suddenly exclaimed, her voice rising in excitement.

"You can change now," Mrs. Dupre said.

"What's the final word?" he asked, watching Angela walk toward him.

She merely glared and elbowed him when she passed. Hard. It was clearly meant to punish him for spying on her through the door. Could he help it if she was parading around in a see-through black sheath? "I'll take that as a love tap," he called after her retreating back.

In mere moments, she was dressed and ready to go. She breezed past him and shook Mrs. Dupre's hand. He placed his hands on his hips in mock chagrin. "Do I need to remind you ladies that I'm paying for this? Aren't you even going to tell me what this dream dress looks like?"

Angela shot him a challenging smile. "No."

"Doesn't mince words, does she?" Mrs. Dupre said, laughing. "It's pretty clear which of you visited the well at Saint Keyne."

At that, Nicholas threw his head back and laughed. "I do believe you're right," he said.

"So what's the well at Saint Keyne?" Angela demanded once they were on the street again.

She was merely playing at being standoffish. He was sure of it. The longer she'd stayed at Mrs. Dupre's, the more her eyes had flashed with excitement over the gown. He was fairly certain that the magic of shopping had made her forget all about the hot dogs and the magician she'd hired for Rosemunde.

"What's the well at Saint Keyne?" she asked again, this time more insistently.

"What's your gown look like?" he returned in a singsong voice, looping his arm around her, and feeling the perfect fit of his palm as it cupped her shoulder.

"I asked first," she teased.

He felt her arm snake around his waist, and shot her a quick glance. "Is that a bribe?"

Her hand squeezed his side tightly. "Take it how you will," she said.

"You sure know the way to my secrets," he said playfully. *If I only knew the way to yours,* he thought, pulling her even closer and feeling how evenly their strides fell. Physically, they were perfect for each other. "Well..."

"That's exactly what I was asking about," she said archly.

He smiled at the play on words. "Well, luv," he continued, "rumor has it that the well at Saint Keyne holds waters with magical properties." He glanced down, watching the sunlight shine in her dark hair. "And that the first person to drink from it—a husband or wife—will always have the upper hand in the marriage."

She stopped dead in her tracks, next to a wrought-iron lamppost. He turned to face her, and when he saw her expression, he said, "What's your problem? Mrs. Dupre clearly meant *you* have the upper hand."

"The problem!" she burst out. "The problem!" She placed both hands on his waist, as if to somehow steady herself. She suddenly looked a little stricken. "We are not," she said, placing emphasis on each word, "I repeat, not, married!"

He turned and leaned back against the lamppost, drawing her against his chest. "And what would be so bad about it?" he teased, wondering what in the world he was saying, even as he said it.

She merely stared at him. Her skin went deathly pale. Her mouth fell open, snapped tightly shut, then dropped wide open again.

"Aren't you having fun?" he asked.

"What's fun got to do with anything?" Her muscles were becoming more rigid against him by the moment. She felt frozen, and just as unyielding as a block of ice.

Yes, what would be so bad about it? he wondered. Unless there really was something terrible in her past. "I'm dangerously attracted to you. Rosemunde seems to like you. You may speak wretchedly about the house, but I know you secretly adore it...."

"You are crazy," she said levelly.

Getting crazier by the minute about you. "Maybe," he conceded with a smile. "But just think, the neighborhood school, where you think Rosemunde should go, needs a teacher...."

"It does?" The second the question was out of her mouth, her eyes narrowed in horror. Somehow, he hoped she was just trying not to look too interested. "But Rosemunde's not going there!" she suddenly exclaimed, as if somehow the words were saving her life.

"I might have to reconsider," he said with a smile.

"That's low," she said. "Using your daughter so I'll stay here. You know, I think it's awful that you're sending her away."

He couldn't help but tease her. "I don't recall actually asking you to stay, luv." He was instantly sorry he'd said it. She whirled out of his arms and stalked toward where Mr. Magnuson sat with the limo, her arms swinging wildly. She didn't even bother to look back. Which was probably for the best, he thought. He'd been a fool to initiate the conversation, and he was merely under the illusion that he might fall in love with her. She was the first woman he'd so much as looked at since his wife's death.

He wasn't going to run after her, either. Besides, Mr. Magnuson was hardly going to leave without him. But what *had* he been asking? For her to stay permanently? Wasn't that what he'd been driving at? Surely, it had just slipped out because he was teasing her. He watched her fling open the limo door, get in the car and slam the door shut.

Can't live with them, he thought, shoving his hands in his pockets. Can't live without them. "Who are you, woman?" he whispered aloud.

ANGELA HEADED FOR Rosemunde's room, more glad than ever for the diversion the little girl might offer. Unfortunately, she found her lying on her bed crying. The covers were strewn with clothing.

"Rosemunde?" She rushed forward, dropping her birthday package on the floor. "Rosemunde?"

"What?" Nicholas's daughter said meanly. She rolled over, pulling fistfuls of various wrinkled outfits with her. She was wearing a particularly horrid pair of torn jeans and a T-shirt. "I don't even have anything to wear to my own party!" she exclaimed. Her tears dried up instantly, and her tone was confrontational.

"Oh, but you do," Angela said. She reached beneath her and plopped the box on the bed.

You blow as hot and cold as your father, she thought, watching Rosemunde instantly tear off the bow. If someone had told her that Rosemunde had just been crying, Angela would never have believed them. The wrapping paper crinkled as she tore it off, handing it to Angela, which Angela supposed meant she was to throw it away.

For long moments, Rosemunde merely stared down into the open box. "Is it okay?" Angela finally asked.

"It's a real party dress," Rosemunde said. "Daddy said I didn't need dresses until I go to school."

"Well," Angela said, as she lifted the lace confection from the box. "Your father isn't always right."

Rosemunde grinned, this time her trademark wicked grin, and then she hopped off the bed and gave Angela a shy hug. Holding her, however briefly, Angela wondered what it would be like to be her mother.

"Let's get you dressed," she said, trying to shake off the thought. Still, as she helped Rosemunde dress, the question still lingered in her mind, causing flashes of inward temper. If Nicholas wasn't leading her on, she would never be thinking about such things.

"ANGELA?" HE GLANCED around the kitchen at the members of the catering staff. They were all attending to him, even if she wasn't. She'd refused to look at him in the limo, and had then fled into the house to change herself and Rosemunde for the party. His breath caught in his throat as he thought about how lovely Angela had made his daughter look. Now she continued to rearrange sandwiches on a platter, as if he didn't exist.

"Everyone may leave," he said softly, watching how her sundress fit snugly to her hips, then dropped to flouncy floral ruffles that swept the backs of her knees.

"Of course, Lord Westhawke," the head caterer said.

Already, scurrying sounds emanated from all quarters of the room. Platters clattered, jars grated against the refrigerator racks as they were slid inside, counter doors were slamming. The caterers began grunting, shouldering trays and filing past Nicholas in such a flurry that he would have laughed, if it hadn't been for Angela. The damnably impossible woman had wedged herself between two men and was trying to escape. He caught her upper arm and hauled her out of the serving line.

"You sure know how to clear a room," she said, sounding a little astonished in spite of herself.

"They were paid to take my orders," he said simply.

"And when Lord Nicholas says jump," she returned, her voice turning low and throaty with contained anger, "we know *everyone* asks how high."

Her black eyes were dancing with sudden temper, and her pursed heart-shaped mouth held a challenge. "That's right, luv," he said, feeling his heart skip a beat.

"Let me assure you," she said, "it's not everyone." She shrugged out of his grasp.

Nicholas stared pointedly around the silent, empty room and then back into her eyes. "Oh, no?"

"Perhaps everyone," she said, "except for me." She leaned against a counter and crossed her arms tightly over her chest.

Her silky sundress had a scooped neck, and her movement served to lift her breasts, accentuating the visible cleavage. His lips parted and without thinking, he licked against their dryness. "Oh, how I'd love to have you at my beck and call," he said softly.

"I'm sure you would," she said testily.

"I just admitted it," he returned, forcing himself to keep his tone gentle. "Why are you so skittish?" *You're the way I used to be.* He wished with every breath that she, too, was one of those people he could tell to jump . . . and how high. Of course, jumping wasn't exactly what he'd have her do, he thought, his gaze dropping over her full breasts, slender waist and lush hips.

"I am not skittish," she finally protested, even though the emotion in her eyes said she knew it was true.

Since she'd backed herself against the counter, he took two swift steps toward her and placed his hands on either side of her, trapping her. "What are you afraid of, Angel?"

For a moment, he thought she was going to tell him everything. She'd admit her attraction to him and tell him something more about her ex-fiancé, thus solving the mystery of herself for him, once and for all. "You can tell me anything."

Warring emotions continued to dance in her dark gaze. "There's nothing to tell," she said, sounding almost exasperated. "Why do you keep insisting there's more to me than meets the eye?"

Because I know you're attracted to me and keep fighting it. Because you arrived here under such unusual circumstances. "It's just something I sense," he said persuasively. And then it hit him. "Frankie," he said, his hands moving from the counter to her shoulders. He gripped them tightly.

"What?" she asked warily.

"What did he do to you?" he demanded, as a million nightmare scenarios flashed through his mind. "You were running away from him... he must have—"

Her face became an impenetrable mask. "You believe I'm not falling willingly into your arms at every second because of Frankie?" She arched her dark brows. "Certainly, extreme abuse would be the only reason a woman wouldn't fall in love with you in a week," she said venomously.

"You've been here longer than that," he said levelly. She was so close that he could rest his face against her breasts in a heartbeat. "And if he did harm you..." His eyes narrowed.

"You'll what?"

"I'll send him to jail," he said flatly.

A small smile tugged at the corners of her mouth. "Honestly, Nicholas, Frankie didn't do anything to me."

He didn't believe a word of it. "I have money, connections. If you're in some kind of trouble..."

At that, her luscious lips parted and he had to fight not to kiss her. "I'm not in trouble," she said adamantly, as if what he was suggesting were ludicrous. She tried to back away from him, but there was nowhere for her to go.

He leaned hard against her and sighed, not believing that, either. He wasn't quite sure it was wise to offer to help her, not without knowing more about her. But one look into her bewitching eyes and he'd suddenly felt he'd risk it all, just to know her better. His title, his social position, Westhawke Hall. Everything.

"Rosemunde's party's underway," he said, unable to believe what was happening in his life. Was he really living for those brief moments when she gave into her clearly growing feelings for him? When she relaxed against him, as if she were ready to pursue their relationship? "Can't we just try and have a jolly time, luv?"

"And not make a fuss?" she added in a soft voice, tinged with irony.

"For Rosemunde's sake," he said, though what he meant was for his own.

A guilty flush crept into her cheeks, as if she'd forgotten completely about the party. "For Rosemunde's sake," she echoed contritely.

"IT'S NOT SO DIFFICULT to have a good time, now is it, luv?" Nicholas whispered, as she leaned back in the crook of his arm, watching Rosemunde open her packages.

"A bike," Angela said softly when the little girl opened the one from him.

"Isn't that what you said we should get her, dear?" he teased. "Instead of a crawling hand. Playmates, too," he added, glancing around at the forty or so kids who were present, as if to say there were plenty.

"Sorry," she said. "You really are a good father."

His gaze caught hers and held. "Thanks."

Twenty minutes later, he headed off to referee the kids' cricket match on the lawn. His clown circulated through the party goers, while her magician set up his props. "Keep having a good time," he called over his shoulder, with a teasing wink.

That's exactly the problem, she thought. It was impossible not to have a good time, and just as impossible not to fall for him. One day soon, he was going to say jump. And she really was going to ask, how high.

She circulated awhile, then sat in the shade, under the tent Nicholas had ordered, and somehow she managed to rip her eyes from him and turn back to the women who'd crowded around her.

"How'd you manage to snag 'im, luv?" Angela glanced at the woman whose name was Maggie Pottage, then at the others seated around her. Suddenly she understood why Nicholas had had reservations about the mix of people. She'd invited regular folks; he'd invited the crème de la crème.

"I really don't know," she finally said noncommittally, wondering if she was, in fact, snagging him. The things he said sure made it sound that way.

Lady Elizabeth Wooster laughed, with a voice that tinkled like bells, and ribbed Maggie's side in a lusty gesture. "He is quite the charmer," she said.

"The only one of 'em around 'ere, to be sure," a woman named Erin White said, tossing her head of red curls.

"Quite!" agreed another of Nicholas's guests.

"But 'ow is he in the bedroom, luv?" Maggie continued.

"He looks rather—er . . ." Lady Elizabeth paused for effect. "Equipped."

Angela felt her flush deepening by the second. Without looking, she knew her face was crimson. She found herself almost wishing that the classes didn't mix together quite so well, but they did, she thought looking around. Everybody was having fun.

"Well, darling?" Lady Elizabeth prodded.

"'Ere's nothing like new brides determined not to kiss and tell, that's what I say," Maggie said, smiling. She turned to Lady Elizabeth and told a rather rollicking story about her own husband.

Angela couldn't help but listen with fascination as Lady Elizabeth began to tell a tale of her own. Then Erin said she'd been sure her husband was having an affair, only to find out he'd taken a second job so he could buy her a special birthday gift.

After some time, every face turned back to Angela. She realized with horror that they'd been divulging these confidences in order to hear about hers!

"The honeymoon night must have truly been something," Lady Elizabeth said, her eyes lit up with imagined romance.

Their honeymoon night! She certainly couldn't say she didn't have a clue. Not only didn't she know how Nicholas might have been . . . she didn't know that about *anybody*. "I—I—I think he's very nice," she managed to say.

Everyone at the table hooted with laughter and made her feel doubly embarrassed for sounding so naive. There was nothing she hated more than being the object of laughter.

"Well, he's very romantic," she added a little haughtily, in the hope that would appease them.

"Yes, luv?" Maggie said.

Angela couldn't fight her smile. "I thought English people were supposed to be reserved," she chided.

"An old wives' tale, darling," Lady Elizabeth said.

"And here we are," Erin put in, laughing and glancing at the others. "Old wives!"

"In the company of a new wife," Lady Elizabeth said, "who doesn't want to help us relive our glory days."

Angela sighed. They just weren't going to quit. She cleared her throat. "Well, our honeymoon night was wonderful," she said smiling. She suddenly giggled, and everyone leaned closer.

"Yes?"

She realized there were a few facts she could divulge, without outright lying. She glanced around the table.

"Aw, look," Maggie said softly. "Her eyes are mistin' up."

Angela wasn't about to tell them they were seeing tears of unshed laughter. "He looked at me," Angela began, unable to help the grin that was overtaking her features, "as if he'd never even seen me before."

"I remember when Stevie looked at me that way," Maggie said, her eyes softening. "Still does sometimes," she added.

"And..." As Angela felt herself drawn further into the small circle of women, she almost felt as if she really were married. "And he carried me through all the hallways—we were married downstairs in the chapel—all the way upstairs."

Lady Elizabeth emitted a soft sigh and leaned closer, pressing both hands over her heart. "How fabulous! Don't you just love it when a man carries you?"

Angela nodded, biting back her smile. "He carried me cradled in his arms...." Suddenly, her mouth went dry and she swallowed, remembering how stunned she'd been by his looks and how her body had molded against his. "And he turned on the light...."

Maggie gasped. "Dear heaven, I made Stevie turn it off, I surely did."

"Well—" Angela nearly laughed aloud, thinking back to the moment when Nicholas had turned on the light and how unromantic it had actually been. "Nicholas generally gets his way."

"He does look rather 'take charge,'" Lady Elizabeth said.

Angela nodded. "And when we made love—" *What am I saying?* Suddenly her voice faltered, thinking of the times she'd wondered what it would be like. And what if it happened? Worse—what if it *never* happened? She was sure it would be... "It was the most magical, wonderful night of my life," she found herself finishing softly.

"Well, darling," Lady Elizabeth said, "a woman as beautiful as you surely had scads of beaus before Nicholas."

"Actually," Angela found herself saying, "that night, Nicholas became my first, true love."

"Your first?" Maggie asked.

"Very first."

"And I'm sure he'll remain that way always," Lady Elizabeth said, leaning over and squeezing Angela's hand. "You love him very much, don't you?"

Caught up in the moment, Angela suddenly felt true tears well in her eyes. Why was she such a sap? she wondered. But her heart suddenly ached for her dreams of love to come true.

"I love him with all my heart," she murmured.

"You do?" Behind her, Nicholas's voice was so low it was almost rough with huskiness.

"Absolutely," she managed to say weakly, still looking at the group of misty-eyed women. "With all my heart."

"THIS IS CERTAINLY news, luv," he teased, casually laying an arm across her shoulder and walking toward where the magician had set up his props. The kids were already gathered in a semicircle on the ground. "I'd like to explore your undying love for me further, but I'm afraid the magician has asked for you."

"Oh, he's ready?" she asked, as if relieved not to further discuss her little chat with the ladies.

"Yes," he said, with a playful smile, "and since he intends to do you bodily harm, I think we should savor these last moments together."

"I was hoping the cricket game might have worn you out too much to tease me," she said a little huffily.

"Nothing wears me out, luv," he said lightly. In fact, he felt great. It had been a long time since he'd refereed a big group of kids. He'd supervised cricket and cookie handouts, not to mention petty squabbles.

"They wanted to know about our honeymoon night!" she suddenly exclaimed, as if it had been the most horribly embarrassing moment of her life. And as if it were all his fault.

He glanced down, his eyes lingering briefly on her chest. "I think you told the story well," he returned. "I particularly liked that it was the most magical night of your life."

"What was I supposed to say?" she nearly wailed.

He smiled, watching two almost round spots of color appear on her cheeks, then glanced toward where the magician was pulling scarves from a hat. Suddenly, he laughed out loud. "Well, you could have used more words like vital, virile, overwhelming..."

She stared up at him, but her attempt to look angry was failing miserably. Her narrow eyes twinkled, her pursed lips lifted at the corners and her shoulders were starting to shake with merriment.

"Vital?" she finally echoed, giggling.

He wiggled his brows. "You should hear what I've been saying about you."

"Believe me," she said wryly. "I don't want to know."

He emitted a long, playful sigh. "I guess there's only one thing to do with you," he said.

"What's that?" she asked lightly, glancing around at the children. She waved at Rosemunde, who was so engrossed with two other girls that she barely nodded in return.

"Saw you in half," he said.

"Ah! Our victim!" The magician called out, waving at her with his wand.

Angela stepped from Nicholas's grasp and headed for the long, narrow box. She was definitely the best-looking magician's assistant he'd ever seen. He couldn't take his eyes off the way her sundress moved against her body. *Delightful,* he thought with her every movement.

His smile deepened, as the kids fell silent. Their eyes were wide and their lips curved into awed circles. Glancing from Angela, over those excited faces, he wished for the first time in a long time that he'd have more children some day.

And, then, suddenly he chuckled. The magician was pacing to and fro, giving the trick the ultimate buildup, as he helped Angela into the box. When he picked up the saw, Nicholas's brows crinkled. Sawing Angela in half was a trick, of course, but there was something oddly disconcerting about seeing the woman he...well, desired...cut into two separate parts. He nearly flinched when the saw went through the box, feeling as awed as the kids. The magician rolled the two halves away from each other.

"She's at your mercy, now, Lord Westhawke," the magician boomed.

"She certainly is," Nicholas returned. Angela's feet stuck out of one box and her head out of the other.

"Kiss her, Daddy!" Rosemunde squealed.

"Well, it is your birthday, dear," he teased, striding toward the magician. When he walked between the two boxes, the kids hooted and hollered. He glanced from her protruding feet, to her head, then back again. "I always was her better half," he remarked dryly, making a few of the adults laugh.

Angela, who'd played the dashing magician's assistant with flying colors, now looked a little panicked. "I hired you," she called to the magician. "How could you do this to me?"

"Daddy, hurry up and kiss her!" Rosemunde yelled again, then burst into a hysterical fit of giggles. "Do it before that man puts her back together!"

Tufts of her hair were stuffed around the box's small head hole. He towered over her for a moment, then began to slowly swoop down.

"Don't you dare kiss me," she said.

He merely bent closer.

"The kids," she protested.

"Have seen this at weddings," he said, bending another notch. "Besides, I'm only doing this at Rosemunde's insistence."

"You are incorrigible!"

"And you're how I like you best."

"How?" she murmured, her voice becoming suddenly low.

"Utterly defenseless," he whispered.

And then he kissed her, just thoroughly enough that when he lifted his face, her mouth was glistening wet and her eyes half closed. Everybody started to applaud.

"She's rather easy to manage now," he teased, when the laughter and hand clapping died down. "Do you think I should leave her this way?"

Chapter Ten

Rosemunde snuggled sleepily against her father's shoulder while he carried her upstairs and down the long corridor, not stopping until he reached her room. "Daddy, you'll read the Castle of Light story, won't you?"

"I'll see you both tomorrow," Angela murmured. She leaned in the bedroom doorway, wondering whether or not she should talk to Nicholas about the decor. It was a cozy room, full of old mahogany furniture, but hardly ideal for a little girl. Given the pleasure with which she'd worn her new party dress, Rosemunde probably wanted a pastel room, with a canopy bed and flouncy dust ruffles. It was what Angela, herself, had dreamed of at Rosemunde's age, though her father had never really understood.

When Angela leaned over, to smooth the lacy bottom edge of Rosemunde's dress, her hand brushed Nicholas's arm. His gaze flitted across her features as the awareness of that light, harmless touch coursed between them.

"Happy birthday, Rosemunde," she said. "And good night."

"You have to come, too," Rosemunde protested in a sleepy voice.

"It's her birthday," Nicholas said with a playful smile. "How could you refuse?" When he nodded in the direction of the bed, his chin just touched his daughter's hair. He planted a quick, absent kiss on her forehead.

For a moment, Angela stood uncertainly in the dim corridor. No matter how much Nicholas could irritate and confuse her, there was a certain domestic peace in this moment that bothered her even more. He hadn't become the least bit angry when she'd divulged the particulars of their supposed honeymoon. Instead, his eyes held a certain knowing light, as if to say it were all true...and that a night with him could lead to something more.

"Now, Angel," Nicholas teased, "don't you need a bedtime story?"

She smiled, thinking she'd now read Rosemunde's favorite story more times than she could count. "Oh, I suppose so," she found herself saying softly.

As soon as Nicholas had deposited his daughter on the bed, she sat up, her tawny wheat-colored hair falling in a disheveled mass around her shoulders. "Now, Daddy, you have to leave for a minute, so Mum can help me undress."

Angela fought back a smile, sure it was the first time Rosemunde had ever demanded that her father leave a room. For a moment, he merely stood there, his eyebrows raised in slight surprise. Then he turned on his heel and strode back into the corridor.

"I'll get the zipper for you," Angela said.

"I wish you really were my mum," Rosemunde said, obediently turning around.

So she does understand that I'm really not, Angela thought. "Yes, well . . ." She cleared her throat, not knowing what to say.

"And thank you for getting the dress for me," Rosemunde continued, sounding about as worn out by the party as Angela felt. "But I wish I had a nightgown like your white one." Angela headed for the closet and hung up the dress.

"And I want pierced ears, too," Rosemunde added sleepily, as Angela returned with a nightshirt. "And when I get pierced ears, I want—"

"Do you realize how many of your sentences are beginning with the word *want* lately?" Angela chided as she helped Rosemunde pull the nightshirt over her head.

Rosemunde merely rolled her eyes and punched the insides of the shirt, fighting to get her arms in the sleeves. When she'd accomplished the feat, she turned and looked at Angela for a long moment. There was so much of her father in her. Rosemunde didn't have his eyes or hair, but she had his face, with its high cheekbones and firm, square jaw.

"But I *do* want earrings like your long, dangly pearl ones," Rosemunde protested.

That gave Angela pause. The earrings, which matched her wedding dress, were hidden in a zippered side pocket of her suitcase. She pulled back the covers, urged Rosemunde beneath them, then sat beside her. "Have you been going through my personal belongings?" she asked, trying to keep her voice level.

"Just to look!" Rosemunde's eyes grew wide, as if she knew she was about to get in trouble.

"That's okay," Angela quickly assured. "But if you want to look at my things, all you have to do is ask."

"I will," Rosemunde said promptly, as if acting otherwise had never once crossed her mind. She snuggled back against her pillows.

A lecture about not snooping in other people's private property was still on the tip of Angela's tongue, but the child had had a long day. She was simply curious and hadn't had a woman's influence in so long.

"May I come in now?"

Angela glanced toward the door, half tempted not to respond, just so she could hear him again. How could such a gruff bass voice sound so melodious? She was still wondering when Rosemunde called, "Yes, Daddy."

"We want to hear all about the princess," Angela echoed. She shifted on the bed, meaning to head for an armchair.

"You need not get up, luv," Nicholas said, as he reentered the room. He switched off the overhead light in favor of a bedside lamp, lithely circled the foot of the bed, then sprawled in the chair nearest her—the one she'd been about to claim.

She managed to shrug, as if sitting on a bed when he was in the room didn't phase her in the least, and then nestled back next to Rosemunde. The little girl curled against her in the dim room, so sleepy and relaxed that it was easy for Angela to imagine that she was really the child's stepmother.

"You ladies want the princess story, right?" Nicholas asked softly, riffling through a stack of thin gilt-edged books.

Angela turned her head on the pillow and smiled. "Where it's all rags to riches?" she asked as he opened one of the books.

She was sorry she'd said it. An unmistakable dark shadow fell over his features, and his eyes seemed full of questions again. He didn't still think she was a fortune hunter, did he? Even now? *And who is he?* she thought. Had she really seen the brides on the lawn for the last time? And why had he had her fitted for a gown that she would wear while being introduced as his wife? *You're not the only one who'd like some answers.*

"Rags to riches," he finally said in a playful tone. "And where everything turns out right in the end."

"But this time when you read it," Rosemunde put in, "the princess has to wear a lacy summer dress just like my new one. All right, Daddy?"

"Why, of course, Rosebud," he said, chuckling.

Rosebud? Angela glanced at Nicholas, realizing, as she had throughout the day, that he indulged Rosemunde more than she'd previously thought.

His gaze caught hers and held. "But only if this princess, who we know to be currently blond, can have long, black, beautiful curling hair and eyes as dark as a starless night," he said.

Angela fought against the strange, lazily romantic heat that suddenly infused her limbs. She had a sudden urge to turn the overhead light on again and then flee to her room. "Now," she chided, "this princess has honey tresses. I've read the story."

"Not any more," Nicholas said, his gaze never leaving hers.

Rosemunde yawned. "Well, okay," she finally said in a puzzled voice, clearly wondering why her father had suddenly decided to change how her princess looked.

"Do you ladies have your eyes shut?" he asked, though he was staring right into Angela's.

"Yes, Dad."

Angela obediently shut her eyes and sucked in a deep breath. She couldn't see, but felt his gaze flit across her cheeks and forehead and then linger on her lips.

"Once upon a time..." Nicholas began, his voice lulling her into the fantastical, yet predictable world of a little girl's favorite book. In this story, an evil knight held the beautiful Griselda captive in his castle, until she was rescued by her dashing prince. His name was Hans and he lived in a castle in the Kingdom of Light, which he also ruled. It was a place so full of gold that it gleamed brightly for miles, even in the darkest night.

Nicholas's voice was pure magic, full of long, polished vowels and British cadences that rose and fell like music. And yet there was something beneath those cultured sounds that defied them. In his voice, Angela fancied she could hear a wealth of battling emotions. Darker, more passionate sentiments surfaced above gentler ones, then submerged again, as if the warrior aristocrat of bygone days were forever fighting tenuously with the contemporary man. Yes, the strains of his voice seemed to be engaged in a duel. And that duel reminded her of his kisses...so gentle at times, so impassioned at others.

In fact, everything about Nicholas seemed as magical and fantastic as the wonderful story he was reading aloud. After some time, Angela blinked, sure she'd dozed, and then her eyes drifted shut again. His voice, as mesmerizing as his eyes, had slowly conjured a world far more real than that of Rosemunde's room. Sleepily, she wondered, yet again, if he was really a flesh-and-blood man at all.

The magical kingdom had leapt to life so surely that she could smell the forests and dewy grass. The sparkling Castle of Light beckoned her, until *she* was Griselda, locked away in the castle tower, held captive because of her radiant beauty.

In the distance, she could see Westhawke Hall, shining against the night sky. Rays of light poured through its diamond-paned windows, so boldly bright that eerie night—so full of beasts and shadows and evil knights—no longer existed.

Just as Griselda was lifted onto the back of Hans's stallion, Angela was lifted, too. She was Griselda, riding through the forest. Nicholas had locked the evil knight in the very tower where she had lived. And she was flying toward Westhawke Hall, her arms clinging around his waist. Silver beams streamed through the forest trees; the wedding goers waited. She was to marry now and lie in the arms of her prince....

Rousing from the image, she blinked but saw nothing. Then she realized that Nicholas was carrying her. "Where are we going?"

"The Castle of Light," he said softly. She smiled in the darkness and relaxed, no less amazed at his strength than she had been the very first night he'd cradled her in his arms and moved smoothly down the long, dark corridors. He walked through the threshold of her room, and she couldn't protest, not even when he leaned and pulled back the covers of her bed.

"The Castle of Light?" she murmured softly, peering up at him in the darkness.

He didn't respond but only lifted her feet, one by one, and took off her sandals. His touch lingered, his hands cupping the arches of her feet. Then, he tucked her feet beneath the covers and drew them to her shoulders.

In the haze of her half sleep, she could sense him somewhere near. Perhaps, she thought, he really could see in the darkness, and he was watching over her while she drifted into deeper sleep.

She only hoped she wasn't dreaming, because sometime later she was sure she felt him lean down, kiss her lips and whisper, "Good night, my princess."

SYLVIA WHIRLED AROUND in front of a showcase of ancient tribal masks and faced Frankie. She'd been looking forward to this exhibit for a long time, but she wished she hadn't come with him. And why hadn't she fled back to Connecticut when she'd realized who Frankie was? It was simply beyond her.

She blew out a long sigh. "It's not that I don't want to tell you where she is," she huffed. "But you're going to do something terrible to her!"

"To Angela?"

Sylvia turned back around and glared inside the case. Painted masks stared back at her. Some were made of coconuts, some of clay. The warriors had bared teeth and mouths drawn downward, in terrifying frowns. Others smiled gayly. *Was Frankie wearing a mask?*

"Yes," she said over her shoulder. "To Angela."

He caught her wrist and turned her around forcibly. "I don't care about Angela," he said softly. Everything in his eyes seemed to say that he was falling in love with the woman he was with now.

"Who *do* you care about, then?" she snapped, hating herself for still wanting him to like her, under these circumstances.

"You."

"So, why are you still so intent on finding *her*?" she asked, glancing at the masks again, as if they might tell her whether or not he was telling the truth. "I swear she's safe."

He sighed. Then he stepped forward and drew her close, pressing her against the museum display. He seemed completely oblivious to the fact that a number of patrons were now looking at them, instead of at the masks. "She's like a sister to me," he said.

I want to believe you. "You promise you don't mean to do anything harmful to her?"

"I swear on my life," he said softly, in a voice she wished wasn't quite so persuasive. He nuzzled his cheek against hers. "And I swear on our future."

Our future. The past—the time before she'd met Frankie—suddenly seemed very far away. And the future seemed to have arrived, with what might happen once Angela and Frankie made a clean break.

It seemed years since she'd been a shy woman, one who quaked every time a man came near. She'd shrugged off the burden of the terrible shyness that had kept her from loving. It was not worth seeing Angela Lancini hurt.... But it sure came close. How could she live without this hope of love again?

"You can't tell me you don't have anything to do with your father," she said, protesting her own thoughts more than anything he'd said.

"I've told you he's legitimate," Frankie returned, his voice lowering with self-contained anger. Just as quickly, it softened again. "I just wish you'd believe me, Sylvia."

His embrace tightened around her in a bear hug, and he held her as if he never meant to let her go. "And you do swear you mean Angela no harm?" she asked insistently.

"Right," he murmured, dipping his head to kiss her earlobe.

She was tired of thinking, tired of wondering. She had to know who this man really was and what he was made of. The words had been on the tip of her tongue for so long that they slipped out before she could catch them. "She's in England."

Frankie let go of her so quickly that she had to grab the display case to steady herself. "England?" he echoed.

"Cornwall," she clarified in a shaky voice.

HE REMAINED IN the dark for a long time, just watching how the faint moonlight from the window danced across her shoulders, and how the thin straps of her sundress dropped to her lush, full breasts. She truly was Griselda, the dark-eyed, dark-haired beauty who could hold men captive with a mere glance.

And he'd told her that she was his captive. What a joke, he thought now. It was he who was truly captivated. Just watching her, he felt a whimsical desire to kidnap her and somehow take her to the fictional Castle of Light . . . where anything was possible and all dreams came true.

In sleep, her expression was as relaxed and untroubled as his daughter's. While he'd read, she had been smiling, too...swept away into a magical, mystical world where true love reigned and where everyone seemed to live forever. Perhaps that was the most difficult part of wanting her, he thought. Knowing that such things might not last.

He blew out a soft sigh. He knew he had to work. He should put on his hospital greens and lock himself in the lab. After all, he was falling dangerously behind schedule. He should let Baskerville out for a final run, too, and maybe check on Rosemunde again. He'd done no more than merely glance at the newspaper this morning, scanning another story about that horrid mobster. Oh, there were so many things he should do. But he couldn't move.

He knew so much about her now. How she looked when she slept. That she was uninitiated in the art of lovemaking, and a great cook. That she was a teacher, who loved kids, and that she had been engaged to a man named Frankie.... He ran through his mental checklist of facts about Angela, suddenly smiling when he recalled hearing her dishonest speech about their supposed honeymoon night.

And yet, watching her sleep, he knew that all his facts could never explain the mystery of her. Who was Frankie? Why was she running from him? And where had she been running to? Had it really been to Westhawke Hall and into his arms? Was fate somehow at work?

He sighed, wondering if he really was Hans to her Griselda. And wondering if Frankie—whoever he was—had hurt her. He suddenly realized he'd lied about one thing. If Frankie ever got near Angela again, he wouldn't have him jailed. He'd kill him.

"Yes?" Angela called, turning toward the door and wishing she were dressed in something other than a robe. After all, she knew Nicholas well enough to recognize his knock. Three soft lazy-sounding raps.

"May I come in, luv?"

She quickly gathered the lacy lingerie she'd laid out on her
bed and placed it in a drawer. "Just a minute," she called,
trying to sound casual, even though she didn't feel it. Ever
since he'd carried her to bed, something in Nicholas had
seemed to gentle yet another notch. *Is he falling in love with
me?*

"You can come in," she called, glancing down once
again. When she'd complained about not having a comfortable robe, he'd left her one of his. She'd found it carefully laid out on her bed. It was white and of thick, heavenly
terry cloth. She tightened the belt as the door swung open.

The first thing she saw was the giant box in his arms. And
then him. He hadn't showered yet for the Seymours' party;
his denim work shirt had a gaping hole in the shoulder and
the knees of his jeans were ragged. She smiled. Why would
someone so rich insist on wearing such threadbare clothes?

"Your gown, luv," he said, plopping it on the bed. The
box was so large, it covered half the mattress.

"Did you peek?" she managed to tease, even though she
felt suddenly uncomfortably aware of her own body. He was
leaning against a post that formed the canopy of her Empire bed, and the post somehow seemed to draw her eye
down the full length of him.

He shook his head slowly, gazing into her eyes. "I like a
surprise, every now and then," he said.

"Oh, you do?" she returned lightly, even though her
every sensation seemed intensified. She could feel the dry-
ing strands of her damp hair curling against her neck and
had to fight not to fidget with the robe's collar. The way he
was looking at her made her suddenly sure she wasn't quite
covered up.

"Absolutely," he finally said, his voice lowering another
seductive notch as he swung around the post. One of his
long fingers reached for her, then trailed across her lower

back. His hand dropped, grazing over her backside so lightly it could have been an accident but wasn't. Just as his hand dropped again, Rosemunde bounded into the room, and Angela released a soft, somewhat relieved sigh.

"Hi," she said as Rosemunde jumped on the bed and put her hands on top of the box. *Like father, like daughter,* she thought, taking in Rosemunde's ratty T-shirt and jeans. "At least, take off those filthy sneakers," Angela continued pointedly.

Rosemunde obediently kicked off her shoes. They fell to the floor with two thuds. "Dad, you have to leave," she said, "so Angela can open her present. And then we have to get dressed."

Nicholas chuckled. "We do, huh?"

Angela's brow shot up at the use of her proper name. The closer she got to Rosemunde, the more the child seemed ready to admit she wasn't really her mother. After a moment, Angela realized Nicholas was watching her closely. "Hmm?"

"Look dashing for me," he said softly. And then he was gone.

She stared at the door for a long moment, wondering what was happening between them. Was she a fool to let him pursue her? *Surely, he doesn't mean for something to come of this. He just can't, not when his world is so very different from my own.* And yet, she was beginning to have the time of her life, at least when she allowed herself. He seemed so perfect and the world he inhabited so magical. But if she let herself love him, she'd surely wind up with a broken heart. After all, the box on the bed, which held all the romance and promise in the world to her, represented nothing more than a lark to him.

"Come on," Rosemunde said in a demanding voice. "Open it!"

Within seconds, Angela shoved her thoughts of Nicholas aside, feeling every bit as excited as Rosemunde. She ran her nails beneath the handle and envelope-style flaps, opened the lid, then fought through the layers of tissue. "I don't believe this!"

Rosemunde was staring at it critically. "Well, we'll have to see how it looks on you," she said as if she'd seen a million such confections and was reserving judgment.

"You just got your first real dress. How can you not be wowed by this one?" Angela asked in astonishment.

"Well," said Rosemunde in a practical voice. "This one is for a London party, and that's quite different."

"It's beautiful!" Angela couldn't take her eyes off either the gown or the matching cape beneath it. Her only reservation was that the gown itself was strapless and cut so low she was sure she'd fall right out of it. And that the slippers in the bottom of the box were of ruby silk, which made her think of Dorothy... and of going home.

"It must have cost a fortune," she whispered, staring into the sea of fabric and gently lifting it from the box. It was dazzling, covered with black, emerald and wine beads.

She gasped when Rosemunde matter-of-factly named a figure. When she whirled around, Rosemunde shrugged. "I heard Daddy talking to Mrs. Dupre on the phone," she said. "Now, hurry up, because we've got to do makeup and everything."

"Fully backless, too," Angela suddenly murmured, realizing that Mrs. Dupre had taken a few liberties.

After another long moment, she managed to lay the dress aside and seat herself at the vanity. She stared at her face in the mirror, just as critically as Rosemunde had viewed the dress. When she glanced up, she could see Rosemunde behind her, bouncing excitedly on the bed.

"Ready to knock him dead?" Angela teased.

Rosemunde giggled and her head bobbed up and down. Angela turned her attention back to the mirror, suddenly wishing her brows weren't quite so thick and that her lips weren't quite so small. She set to work, applying her makeup with a deft, light hand, drawing out what she thought were her best features.

As she worked, she tried not to think too much about how sensational she wanted to look for Nicholas. *Don't worry. This is like living in a fairy tale. I'm just enjoying it while I can, without illusions. Because, come ruby-slipper time, I am going home.*

"And you'll have to wear your hair all piled up on your head, like a lady," Rosemunde said, after she'd finished her makeup.

"I hadn't considered that," Angela said absently, pulling some strands upward. "But I think you're right, kid."

It took a full hour, with Rosemunde standing on a stool and handing her pins or holding stray hanks of her unwieldy hair, but when she was done, she knew it was the right move.

"And now for the gown," she said triumphantly to Rosemunde.

"Mrs. Dupre knows what she's doing," Rosemunde said breathlessly, and in such a tone that it was clear she'd spent more time around adults than kids. "Still, I do hope it fits."

"Me, too, honey," Angela returned with a sigh, thinking about that neckline again. "Me, too."

Chapter Eleven

Where the bloody hell is she? Nicholas's glance swept over the ornate ceiling molding in the entrance hall, the chandelier, then dropped to his Rolex. He shifted his weight in the overstuffed chair again, this time to get a better look at the long stone-railed corridor above him and the wide staircase.

Ten more excruciating minutes passed before Rosemunde shot into view, bounding down the corridor. She came to an abrupt halt at the top of the stairs, then excitedly thumped her hands on the head of a stone gargoyle that served as a newel post. It was merely a face with wings behind it, and she looked like she was smoothing its hair.

"Is she coming or not?" He tried not to sound too impatient, but Mr. Magnuson was already waiting in the car outside and the pilot was at the airstrip. Rosemunde didn't respond but merely patted the gargoyle's head again, then twined her arms through the railing, glancing from him, down the corridor and back again.

And then he wasn't sure, but could have sworn he actually heard a faint rustling and smelled a wafting trail of luscious perfume. Above him, Rosemunde suddenly seemed to be holding her breath. The air stilled, as if a bell had just rung or as if someone had been announced. He sensed her coming with the strange, uncanny awareness one might experience during a mystical premonition.

Then, Angela did float down the corridor above him. His heart stilled like the air and his mouth went dry. Her mass of curls was piled regally on her head and a long, black beaded cape glittered in between the stone banisters. When she reached the landing, she turned gracefully. The magnificent overgarment swirled around her ankles and she merely stood there, as if waiting for his reaction.

He rose to his feet instinctively and strode to the foot of the stairs. The cape was simple and elegant. It clasped at her slender throat with no adornment. The plunging neckline of the black beaded gown beneath it was heart shaped, and a black silk stocking-clad leg peeked dangerously through a long slit in her skirt. Clusters of emerald, ruby and pearl beads formed a piping that wound around the neckline.

He didn't wait for her to descend the stairs. Instead, he walked upward slowly, until he reached her. He leaned and took both her hands in his. "We're not going anywhere," he said huskily.

"Don't I look all right?" She was attempting to tease, but her voice fell flat, as if she was a bit unsure of herself.

"Incredible," he said. And she smelled like heaven. He lightly pulled her down the corridor, in the direction from which she'd come.

"I thought we were leaving," she protested. "What do you mean, we're not going anywhere?" She really sounded panicked this time.

"What I meant—" He glanced over his shoulder, realized Rosemunde was close on their heels and shot her a pointed look. His daughter promptly seated herself in one of the many chairs that lined the corridor, looking no less excited than she had at the prospect of following them.

"What's wrong with the gown?" Angela nearly wailed. One of her hands shot to the top of her head and touched the knot of curls. "I mean, I can take my hair down, you know."

He came to an astonished standstill and turned to face her. "Angela," he found himself murmuring. "You look—" He couldn't think of a word to say. Finally, he settled on "devastating."

"But you've decided not to take me," she said, sounding thoroughly unsettled.

"Maybe I have," he teased. They were late, but he couldn't stop himself from touching her waist. He held her at arm's length, wanting to look at her even as he touched her. Against his fingertips, the beads were hard and cool, making him long for her skin and its smooth warmth.

"When I saw you," he said huskily, "I admit I did consider staying home." He gazed into her eyes for a long moment, then pulled her down the corridor again, not stopping until he'd reached his room.

He'd known how being in a bedroom with him made her feel. It had happened exactly three times now. As much as she tried to hide it, her eyes would involuntarily flit from him, to the bed and back to him again.

This time, the bed seemed the least of her concerns. She fled straight for a mirror, put her hands on her hips and looked herself over, from head to toe. She had to have known what he'd meant by his comments about not taking her to London, he thought, heading straight for a painting that hid his wall safe. He pulled it outward on its hinges, opened the safe then stared inside. He began slowly sifting through the tangled jewelry he'd tossed there, at one time or another.

He glanced over his shoulder. "Take off the cape, luv."

"I think I look fine," she snapped.

"And you do," he returned, biting back a smile and trying to disengage a bracelet from an infernal fistful of knotted jewels. He glanced over his shoulder at her again and

watched her unclasp the cape. *Fine is an understatement.*
She had the most remarkable neck he'd ever seen. Long,
slender, with such creamy skin he felt he could lap it up like
a cat. Reminding himself they were late, he forced himself
to turn back to the safe again.

When he'd seen her, he hadn't merely wanted to stay
home. He'd wanted to undress her slowly, taking off every
blessed bead she was wearing, one by one. Yes, when he'd
seen her, his many questions about her had suddenly become extremely basic. He just wanted to know what the
back of her gown looked like. And whether her stockings
were panty hose or held up by garters.

"Such are the great mysteries of life for a man," he murmured wryly. Then he sighed, staring down into the handful of gems he'd collected and turned around. Before he
even fully registered what he was seeing, the muscles of his
lower body tightened involuntarily. Desire held him mo-
tionless and his lips parted. "Unbelievable," he said, enun-
ciating each syllable.

She didn't turn around but continued her critical self-
appraisal. "I know, it is a little revealing," she said in a
distressed voice.

"Quite," he agreed, his voice catching in his throat. The
gown was utterly backless, and he didn't have a clue in the
world as to how it stayed on her body. Because she was still
standing in the mirror, he could see the front, too. Graceful
lines framed her full breasts. The beaded black sheath
tightened beneath them, showing off a waistline that suddenly looked inches smaller than he'd imagined.

But her back took his breath away. Her tiny, delicate
bones and smooth skin were outlined by the clusters of piping. The dress molded over her hips and the beads became
larger, forming clusters that reminded him of grapes. It was
a design meant to re-create the old-fashioned bustle effect.

"No wonder Mrs. Dupre's famous," he found himself murmuring. The woman had managed to accentuate every curve of what Nicholas was sure was an already perfect body. Generally, he couldn't care less about clothes, but now he found himself wondering whether or not Mrs. Dupre might agree to design all of Angela's.

What am I thinking? He tried to assure himself that as much as he liked and desired Angela, he wasn't serious about her. After all, she was the first woman he'd spent time with since his wife's death. He was merely showing her a good time, since she'd agreed to stay until Sylvia called. *Or are you just holding back because you fear losing another wife?* With one deep sigh, he forced such thoughts from his mind, crossed the room and stood behind her.

"I was looking forward to this party," she pouted, meeting his gaze in the mirror.

His mouth was still so dry that he had to clear his throat before speaking. "Luv," he said softly. "We're going to the party."

"Well, I don't want to go, if I don't look like..."

"Like you'll fit in?" he asked, leaning back and letting his gaze rove over her bare back.

She looked a little embarrassed, but nodded. "And I hate the way you're looking at me. Scrutinizing me, and then just staring with that expressionless look!"

"It's not expressionless. It's..." *Desire.* He licked his lips and ran a finger down her spine.

"It's what?" she asked, her anger barely contained.

"Just shut your eyes," he said.

The resigned way she shut her eyes brought a smile to his lips. He dug in his pocket, found the ruby-and-emerald necklace his great-aunt had brought for her, placed it around her neck and clasped it. "Don't open your eyes," he threatened softly.

"You're putting jewelry on me," she said. "I can't wear..."

"You can and will," he said, just hoping her fingers were the right sizes. Two of the three rings he'd chosen did fit, though not on the fingers he'd intended. Which was just as well, he thought. The diamond-and-emerald band wound up on her ring finger, where it might pass for a wedding ring. Somehow, he felt a moment's guilt over the fact that he wasn't wearing one. A round ruby fit her index finger perfectly.

"And we'll top you off with a ruby earring-and-bracelet set, luv," he said, glad to hear some hint of playfulness had returned to his voice.

"Rubies?" she echoed.

"You may now open your eyes," he said.

Her eyes snapped open and kept opening, until he wondered just how wide they could get. And then she gasped out loud.

"Don't worry," he teased. "They're insured."

"Oh," she said breathlessly, "I certainly hope so."

A relieved smile twitched at his lips as his arms circled her waist. He'd been sure she'd refuse to wear them. He nuzzled his chin against her bare shoulder. "We look rather dashing together, don't you think?" he asked, taking in his own tux.

"So, I really look all right?"

He leaned closer, turning her gently to face him, and kissed her lightly, licking her bottom, then her upper lip. "I wouldn't keep you from this party for the world. When I said we were staying home," he whispered, "I meant that I wanted to take you to bed."

Just as she said "Oh," his lips claimed hers again, in another gentle kiss. He was about to deepen it, thinking maybe they really would stay home, but she leaned back.

"My lipstick," she protested shakily.

He leaned back, sighed, shook his head and then merely said "Women."

SHE'D MEANT TO ASK him what was in the wicker basket over his arm. She'd thought they were going to a ball, not a picnic. Instead, she gasped and said, "You have your own plane?"

A small jet was on the airstrip, with its engine running. Nicholas didn't bother to respond but merely shot a quick, wry glance in her direction, as if to say *of course*. Then he placed his hand beneath her elbow, as if to steady her, and nodded, indicating that she should precede him up the stairs.

Glancing over her shoulder, she noted the pilot's appreciative glance. He was an oddly mismatched sight, in an orange flight suit and tweed cap. His sneakered feet were surrounded by more cigarette butts than she could count, as if in testament to the fact that he'd been waiting a very long time. "Sorry, we're so late," she called, as she entered the plane.

Nicholas reached around her, unclasped the cape at her throat, then gently laid it on one of the four seats. "I'm sure he feels as I do," he said softly, as she seated herself.

"How?" she asked, smiling.

"Like it was worth the wait," he said.

Her gaze fell from his face, over his tux as he seated himself next to her. She'd never known a man who owned his own tuxedo, but Nicholas apparently had at least two. This one was simpler in cut than the one he'd worn the night they met, with a wider cummerbund, and he wore a thick, short black tie, held with a pearl pin. He looked so amiable and elegant that she forced herself to remember that she was going home soon. *Think of this as a last fairy-tale moment. The night of the ball, before your coach becomes a pumpkin.*

"Even though the plane's private," he finally said, catching her gaze and holding it, "you do have to wear your seat belt, luv."

Wondering just how long she'd been staring at him, she fumbled for the belt, but his hands found both ends first. He buckled it over her waist, then tightened it, his fingers lingering against her stomach. Only when he was done did she realize she'd been holding her breath.

"Thank you," she managed to say weakly. *Even though I'm mixing fairy tales—and it was in* The Wizard of Oz *not* Cinderella, *I'll soon be clicking the heels of my ruby slippers. The good witch will tap my head with her sparkling wand, and I'll find myself hiking from school to school with my résumé.*

"You're most welcome," he finally said, in a tone that was as playful as it was thoughtful. He leaned close, looking past her and out the window as the plane began to taxi. Feeling a flush rise to her cheeks, she turned her gaze to the countryside, too.

"Hmm," she murmured as they took off.

"Hmm?" he returned.

"This place doesn't look like New Jersey anymore," she said, remembering her initial impression of the landscape near Heathrow airport.

He chuckled. "Did it ever, luv?"

"Sort of." She shrugged, hearing him move around next to her. She started to turn, to see what he was up to, but the landscape held her attention. They flew over the forest, the cliffs and then above the ocean.

"And what's it look like now?" he asked.

Home. She nearly gasped, wondering where that thought had come from. Worse, she'd nearly said the word *home* out loud. "I don't know," she managed to say. "Just not like New Jersey."

But it did look and feel like home. She liked how the salty air stung her nostrils, how the gulls cawed when they circled overhead and how the waves crashed against the cliffs. She thought afternoon tea was a civilized custom, and that Rosemunde seemed happy to have a companion with whom to share those small crustless sandwiches. She loved the way the fountain looked, all lit up, too. And how many stars were visible over the ocean late at night.

And how Nicholas looks in the morning. He'd risen much earlier today, and his brides no longer haunted the cliffs. She really would have to leave soon, she thought. She had to send out her résumés. The meager few hundred dollars she had was in Frankie's account. Besides, Nicholas had clearly been joking when he'd said that he didn't care about Sylvia. Briefly, worry tugged at her consciousness. What if something had happened to the woman? Somehow, it didn't feel as if it had, but then Angela was hardly given to premonitions.

Suddenly, she noticed the hint of her reflection in the window. It caught her by surprise. *No wonder he was so taken aback.* She did look beautiful, she thought without a trace of vanity. Of course, she'd scrutinized herself half the day, but seeing her reflection when she hadn't been looking for it forced her to see herself objectively. She felt as if she'd been walking along a sidewalk and had accidentally seen herself in a storefront. She felt almost as if she were looking at a stranger.

Yes, she looked more beautiful than she ever had. More than she ever would again, she suddenly thought a little sadly. Living in Nicholas's world was truly like living in a storybook. The characters lived happily ever after, but she was carried off, tucked in, and the book was closed. She was left by herself, to merely dream of love. Would she ever find her own happily ever after? She blew out a long, heartfelt sigh.

"Something wrong, luv?" He was so close, his breath whispered by her ear. "You've gotten rather quiet."

She shrugged, still lost in thought. "It's all so... so very perfect."

He chuckled. Then, she heard a soft popping and the bubbling, sighing sound of a bottle opening. "Maybe this will cheer you up," he said.

Champagne, of course, she thought. *He really is a class act.* She turned around and found herself smiling. While he poured her champagne, her eyes roved over the table he'd released in front of their seats. It was covered with white linen. A platter of ripe, juicy fruit sat in the center. A separate crystal bowl of strawberries and a matching crystal container of sugar were next to it.

Knowing full well he was watching her expression carefully, she squinted, then lifted a sterling lid from a warmer dish.

"Oysters," he said, lifting the lid from a smaller dish. "And cocktail sauce."

"And that?" she asked pointing.

"I believe those are the avocados," he said, lifting yet another lid. "And olives." He held out a long crystal flute, which she took. "Champagne," he continued, turning back to the table and pouring his own.

"Real champagne, from Champagne, France, undoubtedly," she said with a hint of wryness.

"California, actually," he said, his smile deepening. "And, more correctly, sparkling wine. But a good year."

When he raised his gaze, looking deeply into her eyes again, she felt another flush threaten to rise to her cheeks. How could one man be so incredibly romantic? "Quite a spread," she managed to say.

He continued to chuckle softly, his smile spreading into a full-fledged and very sexy grin. He shrugged playfully.

"Well, in my efforts to romance you, I brought every aphrodisiac I could think of, Angel."

Is he serious? Is he honestly romancing me? Whether he was or not, it was sure working. Her cheeks warmed and she found herself laughing as she lifted her glass.

"Are you proposing a toast?"

"Yes," she said.

"To?"

"To the classiest guy I know," she said softly.

"Since I rarely drink to myself," he returned, "I propose..."

His eyes narrowed, and for the very briefest moment, he seemed lost in thought. Her mind couldn't help but supply the missing word "marriage." She swallowed quickly, assuring herself it was a matter of word association, pure and simple. After all, "marriage" did usually follow "propose." She cleared her throat. "Yes?" she prompted a little shakily.

"A toast..." he said, his expression clearing.

"To?"

"To my most heavenly angel," he said.

"Cheers," she said, more throatily than she'd intended.

"Cheers," he said, his voice sounding equally husky.

The glasses rang when they touched, sounding almost like bells. Over the rim of her glass, she found herself staring into his incredible eyes again. They captured her attention so fully, that she poured more champagne down her throat than she could swallow. She sat forward quickly, leaning so the dribble wouldn't fall on her gown.

"Leave it to me to ruin a mood," she managed to say, in what she hoped was a lighthearted tone. *This is the second time I've drooled on myself! How long would I have to know this man, before I could gracefully sip a beverage when he's in the room?*

He merely chuckled and said, "Your lipstick, luv." In less than a second, he was dabbing at her lips with a linen napkin. "Perfect," he pronounced, tossing the napkin aside and reaching for a strawberry.

She set her flute on the table, watching him dip one of the ripe red berries in sugar. He turned, leaned toward her again, then lifted the berry toward her lips. When she reached for it, he laughed. "We've established that you have difficulty feeding yourself, luv," he teased. "And given the elegance of your gown, I'd just hate to see it ruined." He dangled the berry in front of her lips, clearly unwilling to relinquish it.

I am going to melt. He was handsome. He was rich. He was thoughtful and kind and loved his daughter and Baskerville. The only thing she could remotely construe as unpleasant was his occasional bad attitude. And she had to admit she even liked that.

"Maybe I should have started with the oysters," he said, with a playful sigh.

She flashed him what she hoped was a saucy smile. "Maybe."

"Open up, Angel," he singsonged.

Angel. I really like his nickname for me. All at once, her throat constricted and she felt a little dizzy. Her mouth went so dry she knew it was useless to even try to swallow. She sucked in a sharp breath as her lips parted. How could something so simple as a man in a tuxedo feeding her a strawberry make her feel as if she was about to faint?

Time seemed to be standing still. She simultaneously parted her lips wider, caught the berry between her teeth and raised her glance. His mesmerizing violet eyes met her dark gaze, dead on. Slowly, she bit into the berry.

The luscious, sugary juices wet her mouth, and as she began to chew, she recalled meeting him on the cliffs the night she'd tried to leave. He'd told her she'd know when she fell in love. And now, she knew.

For the briefest instant, she decided she'd do whatever it took to stay with him. She would capture, ensnare, chase and pursue. She would act catty, if she really had to. She might even make love outside of wedlock. But she didn't want to go home!

She swallowed, forcing all those thoughts away. *When it's over, it's over. I'm clicking my ruby heels together, right back to Little Italy and Mott Street.*

"That was some strawberry," she finally managed to say.

"Then, you should certainly have another," he said promptly, reaching toward the delicate crystal dish.

"REPORTERS?" SHE ASKED, staring out the window of the limousine. "And the hotel's called the Bromley?"

"My great-aunt's acquisition," he said. "I don't know why, but it was her life dream to own a hotel. It's got the largest ballroom in the city. Lady Anne stays in the penthouse when she's in town. Come along, luv," he said as the door swung open.

She felt herself jostled between Nicholas and the driver who'd met them at Heathrow. They ran for the door. Lights flashed around them and people yelled from all directions. They were nearly inside before she realized the reporters were yelling rapid-fire questions about her.

They reverberated in her mind. Where did you meet Lady Westhawke? Who insisted on the secret marriage? Will you talk publicly about the ceremony? Is it true it took place at midnight? How did the Honorable Rosemunde handle the news?

The Honorable Rosemunde? The title hardly jived with the messy-haired child. All thoughts of Nicholas's presence beside her fled. As soon as she was inside, she leaned breathlessly against the wall, near one of the many palms that lined the walls of the main lobby and the plush corridors.

"Are you all right, Angela?" Nicholas was peering into her face.

She couldn't even nod. "What am I doing here?" she found herself saying.

"You mean you don't like pretending you're rich and famous?" he asked with a wry smile.

She managed to shake her head. It wasn't only that but that the deceptions ran deeper. She kept forgetting that people thought they were married. Worse—she knew she was forgetting because she *wanted* to forget. She'd been enamored of his many beautiful—if dusty—belongings and the coast where he lived, but she'd also begun to know Rosemunde and him. Moments such as these made it impossible to pretend he was a regular guy. *And if he's not a regular guy, I can't fall for him. Oh, he's going to break my heart! Remember those ruby slippers....*

He was still watching her closely. "It's why I never come to London," he said. "I don't like pretending, either."

"But you're not pretending," she protested.

His soft chuckle held a hint of bitterness. "Oh, but I am," he said. "We're no more interesting than anyone else, luv. We're just people."

At that, she burst out laughing. "Just people?" she echoed.

He nodded. "What else could we be?" he asked, smiling.

"Well," she said, feeling her mood suddenly soar, just from looking into his eyes, "now that I've experienced it, I can definitely say it's kind of exciting to be whisked from a limo and past a bunch of cameramen."

He laughed. "That's the spirit. And if you liked that, you'll just love being announced."

"Announced?" she repeated, thinking she was truly beginning to sound like a parrot.

"Yes, luv," he said as they walked up a flight of stairs.

Within moments, they were in a long, lushly carpeted corridor. She gulped, catching glimpses of others who were arriving, while Nicholas introduced himself to a uniformed young man.

As if he needs an introduction, she thought, still reeling from the crowd outside, and still feeling a dual tug of self-consciousness and unmitigated excitement.

Nicholas returned to her side and crooked his arm. She placed hers through it. "When we reach the stairs, someone will step forward and remove your cape," he said.

She was so intent on glancing around that she barely heard him. Beautiful women in heavenly fabrics swirled past the leafy palms that lined the hallway. All were squired on the arms of tuxedo-clad men who looked powerful and exuded confidence. *People really live this way,* she thought illogically, as some cast curious glances her way. And yet, in spite of all the grandeur, she found herself wishing Nicholas really were from a more ordinary world.

Heaven knew, in his everyday clothes, on the back of his motorcycle, he could almost pass for an average citizen. If he only were, then she could better analyze her feelings. How much of her reaction to him was bound with the fact that his world was so dazzling?

None of it, she suddenly thought. *I'm just trying to mask my attraction to him by pretending I'm falling in love with everything that goes with him, instead of him, for himself alone. I keep thinking I'm falling in love with the castle or the cliffs or the gulls...but it's really just with him. Oh, boy, have I been lying to myself.*

She tightened her hold on his arm. He leaned and kissed her nose. She managed a confused expression that she hoped could pass for a smile. If the people she saw in the corridor were any indication of what was to come, she wasn't sure she could rise to the occasion. Her hands were growing damp with perspiration and her heart was thudding dangerously. Then the soft hum of speech seemed to die down and everything grew unnervingly quiet.

After a moment, Nicholas whispered. "I knew the place would become utterly silent."

"Why?" she whispered back. *Why are you introducing me as your wife?* Suddenly, she felt a tiny flash of temper. She was a regular girl! How could he toy with her this way...making her wish and dream?

"Because no one's ever seen you before," he said softly, just as the young uniformed man gestured toward them.

"Lord and Lady Westhawke of Cornwall," a loud voice boomed.

If she'd ever felt she was living a fantasy, she surely felt so now. Time had stopped again, and yet she was somehow moving forward over the thick, lush carpet. The only thing that held her steady was Nicholas's arm. Everything else seemed to shimmer and waver, as if it were all an illusion.

When she reached the staircase and turned, she froze. Above her, a great prismed chandelier twinkled. Below her, a sea of glittering gowns seemed to toss rays of light in all directions. Illogically, she thought of Hans and Griselda and the Kingdom of Light. But she wasn't on the back of a stallion with the man of her dreams. She was on a stair landing, and every eye in the ballroom below was riveted on her. No one said a word.

Don't blow it, Angela, she thought.

She squared her shoulders and told herself she really was Lady Westhawke—wife to Nicholas, stepmother to Rosemunde, Countess of Cornwall. *At least for this one moment.* Suddenly, almost magically, the last semblance of self-consciousness seemed to fall from her shoulders. *I am*

Lady Westhawke, an American beauty, presented to London society for the very first time.

Her glance into Nicholas's eyes assured her she was as stunning as any woman in the room, if not more so. Gazing downward, she instinctively cast a barely perceptive nod in the direction of the crowd.

"Your cape, darling," Nicholas said softly. She didn't fidget or fumble, but slowly reached for her throat and gracefully unclasped the cape. Behind her, an attendant's hands lifted it from her shoulders in a swirl.

As she and Nicholas began to descend, a soft hum of conversation began to build in the ballroom again. By the time they'd reached the bottom, a swarm of people greeted them. Some quickly squeezed her hand or clapped Nicholas's back, with a quick, "Good to see you, old boy." Without exception, they congratulated them on their marriage.

"Of course, we're quite happy together," she found herself telling one woman. To another, she said, "We didn't take a honeymoon, but we've planned a holiday in the future." There was no time to even wonder about what she was saying, or to contemplate the soft light that seemed to enter Nicholas's eyes every time she lied.

At the first lull in conversation, she nearly collapsed against him. "I've got to find the ladies' room," she said breathlessly.

"Fine, I'll walk with you to—"

"Please, find us some drinks or something," she said quickly, even though waiters were circling the room.

"Are you all right?"

"I just want a moment alone," she said softly. *To process this magical night.* Without a backward glance, she weaved between party goers, smiling at all of them. She found herself heading toward an archway at the far side of the room, which led back toward the lobby. She wasn't sure, but she thought she'd seen a ladies' room near the palm-flanked bank of elevators.

Do I really love him? she wondered as she headed that way. Could people really fall in love so quickly? She blew out a quick, breathless sigh. Spotting the ladies' room, she paused to let some guests pass her. She was in no hurry. She merely wanted to let it all sink in.

This night is really happening to me, Angela, from New York. And it was all because of Nicholas. Surely, he had growing feelings for her. He had to. What man's eyes would light up when he looked at her the way Nicholas's did if he weren't falling in love?

Her throat constricted and she swallowed. Could she become the real Lady Westhawke? *Impossible. Don't kid yourself. Think about those ruby slippers. Remember that the clock always strikes at midnight and that the carriage is a pumpkin.* She shook her head as if to shake off her thoughts and continued toward the ladies' room. Suddenly, she stopped in her tracks. American voices?

"They're more trouble than they're worth," a voice that sounded incredibly familiar said.

Who was it? Was she going out of her mind, or did it really sound like Paulie inside that elevator? She stepped back, but there was nowhere to go. She was trapped against a wall! She attempted to ease herself behind a palm tree nearest the open elevator door.

About a million people seemed to be slowly exiting the fool thing. Where was the speaker of that voice? She whirled around, faced the wall and slumped her shoulders, so she'd be shorter than the palm. Then she cocked her head and strained to hear.

"What's the trouble?" The second voice was definitely American. Worse—the speaker was New York born and bred. She'd recognize the sound anywhere and could swear it was Eddie.

"Broads're the trouble. She wants some special kind of face cream."

Angela didn't have time to wonder who the "she" was. Because, this time, there was no doubt about the identity of the speaker. Frankie waltzed out of the elevator and stepped into view.

So did his father. "When you kids get old like me," Sal Mancini said, as Angela grabbed a palm frond and drew it in front of her face, "you'll understand that those women— who you keep calling broads—are a man's only key to happiness."

Chapter Twelve

"Angela?" She was weaving almost drunkenly along the corridor, hugging the wall as if she needed to steady herself. Nicholas shoved his hands in his tux pockets and followed. "Angel?"

When she glanced over her shoulder, she saw him but didn't stop. As he closed the distance between them, he could hear the clusters of beads at her hips; they were tinkling together in a way that sounded almost musical.

He caught her near an arch by the ballroom. She was sitting on a sofa, her back unnaturally erect, looking white as a ghost. She didn't so much as nod when he sat down next to her, but only stared down at her hands. They were folded in her lap so tightly that her knuckles had turned pink.

"It didn't seem likely that the crowd overwhelmed you, but you left so abruptly that I got a bit worried. Are you all right?"

"Fine," she said in a faint voice. After a long moment, she raised her gaze and looked into his eyes. "Nicholas..." she began. "I—I have to..."

"Are you ill, luv?" He scooted closer and covered her hands with his own. They felt like ice. Color had drained from her face, making it look starkly pale against her dark hair; her rouged lips trembled. If anyone was overwhelmed, he thought, it was him. Her perfume was so soft, alluring and feminine that he leaned even closer, until their cheeks nearly touched. "Do you want to tell me something?"

When he looked into her eyes again, a thousand warring emotions flickered in her gaze. "What's wrong, Angela?"

"I—" She blew out a sigh so short and breathy that his gaze dipped to her bare shoulders. He was trying to listen, but it was terribly difficult. Her sheer, charming femininity—how she looked and moved and smelled and felt—was assaulting all his senses at once. Had the night overwhelmed her so much that she was going to admit she had feelings for him?

"I—I want to say some things," she suddenly continued. "Because there's somebody here who—"

She's going to say she cares for me. "As far as I'm concerned," he interrupted softly, "there's only one person here."

"Who?" she asked, sounding almost irritated.

"You." He smiled.

She didn't. Instead, she disentangled her hands from his. "Please," she said, a little huffily. "Would you just listen?"

If her strange shift in mood was giving him pause, the look in her eyes stopped him cold. Those bewitching, dark twin pools were begging him to listen...and saying he wasn't going to like what she said. *Is she leaving England?* He felt something inside him snap as tightly shut as a suitcase.

"Remember when I told you about Frankie?" she began.

"Frankie?" he echoed, feeling a little numb. Had he really hoped she might say she loved him? He peered into her face and sighed. He'd been living for this moment, he thought, when she'd tell him more about her past relationship, hadn't he? What had the man done to her, if anything? Right now, answers were about to tumble from the tip of her tongue. Without thinking, he lifted his finger quickly and pressed it to her lips.

"I don't care," he said softly.

"Care about what?" she asked, her voice suddenly sounding hoarse, the way it did when she felt stressed.

"About your past, certainly not about your relationship with your ex-fiancé," he said. "What I care about is..."

"Please," she said, the word catching in her throat. "It's nothing really terrible or anything, it's just that—"

Before she could finish, he pressed his lips to hers in a quick, hard kiss. "Don't you want to know what I care about?" he asked, mustering a tone of playfulness as he whispered the words against her lips.

"Oh," she said quickly, her mouth not an inch away. "I do."

He swallowed, reached for her hands again and warmed them between his. "I care about how you've made me feel," he said. "About how much you've made me want to live again...how much Rosemunde seems to like you. And I care about tonight. Because it's ours."

"But Nicholas—"

He kissed her again, with the speed and intensity of a bolt of lightning.

"That's better," he said, when she made no other effort to speak. He glanced over his shoulder toward the ballroom. "Luv, I want this night to fulfill your fantasies." *And I want this night to make you want to stay. For how long, I don't know, but for a while.*

"Oh," she murmured softly. "It has been. Nicholas, everything's so..."

"Perfect?" he finished, remembering what she'd said in the plane.

"Yes," she said, her own voice growing husky.

He ran a long finger from her temple over her cheek, then cupped her chin. Looking at her, he realized that it had been a very long time since he'd thought about his past and his life before Angela. "So, tonight, let's forget about the past," he finally said. "And . . ."

"And?" she prompted breathlessly.

"And keep on creating our future, Angel."

"NICHOLAS," she said laughing, "I really don't want to dance." She hadn't exactly forgotten that Frankie was in the hotel, but Nicholas was sure making the memory fade. Throughout the evening, Frankie had become more and more like a wavery mirage from a barely remembered dream. Yes, Nicholas could make her believe that there was no other man in the world except him.

They'd circulated among the other guests all night, and when he wasn't at her side, he exhibited an uncanny knack for reappearing just when she wanted him. He'd fed her dainty party food and plied her with another flute of champagne.

Lady Anne had found them and had kissed Angela heartily on the cheek, as if no bad words had ever passed between them. Then, during the engagement announcement for Catherine Seymour, Angela had caught Nicholas looking at her with such passionate intensity that she was sure he wanted to propose to *her*. But he'd never done more than hint at his growing feelings for her. Could a girl from Mott Street really expect to marry such a man, and marry into a world such as this one?

Now, his chin lowered and he stared at her pointedly. "You can't go to a ball and not dance," he said levelly.

"Please," she said. "I'll look like an idiot!"

In spite of her protests, she let herself be pulled forward, into the thick of the crowd in front of the orchestra. The music was dramatic, saucy and Latin. Nicholas drew her in his arms, saying, "You could never look like an idiot, luv."

When he laid a hand on her waist, her exposed lower back went white-hot where skin met skin. He caught one of her hands in his free one, clasped it tightly, twined his fingers through hers, then lifted their arms high in the air.

In a quick, practiced move, he bent her so far backward she was sure she would fall, but his strong arms steadied her. "Tell me this is not a—" she said breathlessly, as he brought her upright.

"Sorry, luv," he said, his lips dangerously close to her own. "But it really is a tango. Just move with me." He laughed. "Actually, you have no choice."

"I'm trying," she managed to say. She couldn't think, much less dance. The rhythm of the drums and violins was enough to make her heart skip a beat. Frankie was out there somewhere, and yet, it didn't seem to mean a thing. She'd searched for years, knowing there was only one man in the world for her. And she'd given up, only to find him.

"I can't believe I'm actually tangoing," she said, laughing. Or at least she was, until he whirled around and pulled her flush against him. Her thighs were suddenly wedged between his. Their stomachs touched. Her skirt was slit to mid-thigh, and she could now feel the elegant, finely woven fabric of his trousers graze against her stockings. As he picked up the music's rhythm, his hips undulated across her lower half in a way she could only think of as scandalous.

"I thought you said tango, not limbo!" she exclaimed as she leaned, her back supported by his arm.

He chuckled. "Are you saying you'd *prefer* to limbo?"

She gasped, as he helped her to her feet. He strutted a few paces, with his cheek pressed to hers. "Look," she said, trying to sound playful. "I got the initial moves, but what are you doing now?" *Besides driving me crazy, when you hold me so tight.*

"Upping the ante," he said, as he spun her around again.

"But you can't up the ante, when there was no bet," she returned.

"Oh, but there was," he said, whirling her around for yet another one of those backward dips. This time, she reclined in his arms, inch by excruciating inch, until her head nearly touched the floor.

"I don't recall making one," she said, swallowing air in quick gulps and hoping she wouldn't drop to a dead faint. She felt breathless, overheated and dizzy. And it had nothing to do with the exertion of dancing.

He was towering over her. Instead of pulling her up, he was slowly leaning over the whole length of her body. "It was my own personal bet, luv," he said softly.

"Which was?" she managed to ask, as he leaned far enough over that his lips finally grazed her own.

"That I'd make love to you, tonight," he said.

"IT'S REALLY ALL OVER, isn't it?" she asked softly, watching Nicholas remove his jacket. "And we're really back home."

He felt his heart skip a beat, while the word "home" echoed in his mind. She gracefully laid back on the drawing-room sofa cushions and rested her head on the armrest, looking as fresh and beautiful as she had when they'd left.

"Yes," he said softly, seating himself on the sofa and placing her feet in his lap. "Your footmen are all mice now." He chuckled softly. "And there's no way for you to get anywhere, except in your pumpkin...."

"My fairy godmother's deserted me," she whispered, shutting her eyes and picking up the thread of his thoughts, which were so close to her own. "And soon, I'll be sweeping cinders, once again." *And tapping my ruby slippers together and heading home.*

"Think positively, Angel," he said. "Because there's one good thing." His finger trailed from her knee to her ankle, then dipped into the instep of one of her high-heeled, ruby silk slippers; he slowly pulled off the shoe and placed it on the floor.

"What's that?" she asked. As he slipped off her other slipper, his finger traced swirls on her stocking, making her skin tingle beneath.

"The good thing?" he asked gently, his gaze moving from her feet, over her slender legs, her breasts and then her face.

"Yeah," she said, opening her eyes.

"Well, the good thing is..."

She smiled, feeling him inch up the length of her body, with more of his weight covering her each time he moved. A languid heat infused her limbs. She didn't feel sleepy, at all—just dreamily relaxed.

"The good thing—" his breath now whispered against her cheek "—is that a prince has roamed the earth for you...."

He smiled, watching her eyes narrow in dark, sexy slits. She looked as languid and sinuously sexy as a torch singer. He held up one of her high heels. The shoe was so soft, delicate and shapely that it might have been one of her feet.

"A prince?" Her half chuckle sounded more like a throaty gasp.

He nodded. "And this poor prince has absolutely nothing with which to identify you, except this magical slipper."

"Perhaps it's not really *my* slipper," she said huskily.

"Ah," he said, relaxing against her. "But since I just removed it, I know it's a perfect fit."

It was unspoken, but she knew he meant *they* were the perfect fit. She swallowed against the lump that suddenly formed in her throat. "Well, I'd hate to see such a charming prince lose a bet tonight," she finally said softly.

"Especially—" his eyes roved over her face "—when the stakes are so very high."

Her parted lips went suddenly dry. "Nicholas," she whispered. "I'm the kind of woman who's waited . . . and who wants the whole kingdom." *Marriage*.

"Like I said," he whispered. "The stakes are high." Lithely, he rose from the sofa, holding out his hand to her. "Come with me, Angel."

He felt as if he'd stood there with his arm outstretched for an eternity. And then she placed her hand in his. Her body followed, as if by magic.

She didn't know what she expected. For him to carry her again, perhaps. Maybe she thought he would stop and ask her if she was sure. But he didn't say a word.

They merely walked silently, side by side, through the long corridors toward his room. He held her hand, and with his free one, he carried her two ruby slippers. In the darkness, she could just make out the outer salon of his suite. They passed through a number of other rooms and when they reached his bedroom, he left her. She heard one of her shoes drop to the floor. A moment later, the heavy curtains swept back and the room was bathed in moonlight.

"Is this all right, Angela?"

She nodded slowly, taking in her surroundings. The floor was covered with a plush oriental rug. In front of her ran a long gilded rail. And beyond the rail, in a cozy alcove, was a stately canopy bed hung with green velvet. From somewhere beside her, Nicholas tossed her remaining slipper. It landed soundlessly on the bed, as if to say he were her Prince Charming.

Without looking at him, she knew he was a handsome silhouette by the window, and that moonlight showered over his shoulders, making his white shirt gleam. She knew he was watching her, giving her time. That she could change her mind and leave and he would accept it.

She turned toward him slowly. "No matter what happens, I won't regret this," she said softly.

He silently crossed the room, stopped in front of her, then kissed her. It was such a soft, sweet, loving kiss that she arched against him, her softness meeting his harder strength.

After a moment, he leaned back and looked into her eyes. "I'll do everything in my power to ensure that regret is the last thing on your mind." Slowly, he began to take the pins from her hair. One by one, he let them drop to the floor.

"Have you really never been with anyone?" he asked, when all the pins had fallen. He ran his fingers through the mussed curls that framed her face.

She shook her head. "No, Nicholas," she whispered. "You're the only one."

He merely nodded, leaned and kissed her again. His hands cupped her chin while he drank from her lips, as if from an overfilled cup. He very slowly increased the pressure, as if afraid one drop of her sweetness might spill.

He explored her with his hands, thinking her skin was smoother than the finest silk. In their travels, his long fingers almost lazily discovered mysteriously placed zippers and buttons and hooks and eyes. One by one, he began to release them, too.

"Oh, Nicholas," she murmured, unable to believe the desire building within her. When he slowly lowered the bodice of her dress, she sighed sweetly. And when he held her breasts in his hands, she moaned softly. He showered her neck with kisses that fell lower still, until they fell all over her, like a sprinkling of stars over a magical night sky, or like a light, warm rain on a summer's afternoon. "Oh, Nicholas."

"Hmm?" His hands circled her waist possessively.

"Just, oh, Nicholas."

His lips claimed hers again, with such passion that she barely noticed when his shirtfront opened and she was pressed against his chest, or when her gown fell away, eddying in a dazzling, glittering pool at her feet.

When she was wearing only her panties, she realized she felt no self-consciousness, at all. She wanted to tell him she was ready, that he needn't draw out their lovemaking for her sake now. Instead, she reached for his broad, strong shoulders and gently pulled off his evening shirt.

As it dropped to the floor, he lifted her into his arms and carried her to the bed. Once he'd removed her shoe, he laid her gently across the bed. When he covered her body with his own, she realized the spread beneath her was as soft and smooth as his skin. Desire and a tremor of fear coursed through her, as the aroused intimate part of him nestled in the juncture of her thighs, with nothing between them but his slacks and her underclothes.

"You're so beautiful," he whispered, resting on his elbows and gazing into her eyes. "I've imagined your hair like this—all spread out on a pillow. And such a mystery. No questions I could ask would ever tell me what I want to know about you."

"I'll tell you anything," she said raspily.

He shook his head. "The answers I want to find, I won't find in words—just in loving you."

She was breathless, and yet her body felt amazingly warm and sexily soft. She was so very close to making love for the first time, and yet she hadn't expected this mysterious feeling of simultaneous relaxation and excitement. "I—" Her voice caught in her throat. "I can't think of how many times I wondered who..."

"Who your first lover would be?" he whispered.

She nodded, as her hands roved over his broad back, slowly exploring it.

"Did he look like me, by chance?" Almost involuntarily, he shifted his weight on top of her, knowing that without their remaining clothes, he really would be inside her.

He sighed. She was just so beautiful, and he wanted to be slow for her, because he wanted her so much.

"He never had a face," she said.

Nicholas smiled gently. "He does now, Angel."

When he kissed her again, she knew he wouldn't stop. They moved rhythmically against each other, the rest of their clothes leaving them, as if by magic. During that one long, unbroken, loving kiss, he urged her hands toward special places she reached for, but couldn't quite bring herself to touch.

"Oh, Angela." The sound of his voice, as he explored her intimately, was so masculine and full of need that she clung to him, feeling as if she'd never let him go.

"Sweet—" His breath came in a ragged sigh. "You're so sweet." Her skin was like fire to the touch now, and he wondered how it was that a woman so passionately responsive had never made love. He raised his gaze, carefully watching her face, aware he was about to take something from her that could never be restored. She was breathless, her hair wild, her lips swollen.

"I'm not scared," she whispered. "I want you, Nicholas."

His own body ached for her. He approached her as slowly as he could, saying, "I don't ever want to hurt you, Angela." When he sank into her, he felt the barrier and when he broke through, her body tensed. For a long moment, he stayed inside her, forcing himself not to move, keeping his lips pressed to hers, until she leaned away from the kiss.

"That's it?" she asked, sounding more breathless than frightened.

He chuckled softly. "No, that was just the beginning, luv." He moved ever so slowly, building her pleasure again, until she began to love him back, arching against him, claiming him with her hands and her lips and her heart. When his own desire overtook him, driving him forward with a strength and intensity he had never known before, she was with him.

"Was that something like you thought it would be?" he asked breathlessly, when they began to relax.

"Better," she whispered. Their bodies were still twined. Their limbs curled like vines that had grown together so long they might be one. "Thank you."

His low, throaty chuckle was barely audible. "No," he said, "thank *you*."

She laughed softly. "Did you find out what you wanted to know?"

"Not really," he said, sighing and nuzzling his cheek against hers. "Every time I'm with you, I feel some fundamental question's just been answered. Then, a thousand new questions arise." He pressed his lips to hers. "But now I know how you look when you want me. Or, at least, how you looked on this particular night."

"But I might be so different, some other night?" Her voice was low and still sounded tremulous with discovery.

"Hmm," he murmured. "And that's your mystery."

"So are you going to tell me about those brides now?" she whispered.

"Oh," he teased, "I like to leave a little mystery in *my* wake."

"They seemed a little weird, if sometimes beautiful to watch," she finally said. "They're not—er—anything bad, are they?"

He laughed. "No," he said. "Nothing bad." After a moment, he disentangled his arm just enough that he could run his fingers through her hair. "Angela?"

"Hmm?"

"I want you to stay here."

They rolled together, lying on their sides, touching each others' cheeks. He faced the window and his eyes caught the moonlight. Looking into his gaze, she simply couldn't imagine life without him, yet she wished she knew what he intended. Would he ever offer the whole kingdom? Would he really offer marriage?

He was watching her closely. "Will you consider it?"

"We haven't known each other very long," she said softly.

"Long enough that I know what I want," he said.

"For me to live with you?" she ventured.

He nodded.

It had taken her years to make love out of wedlock. She didn't know how to tell him that being wed out of wedlock was yet another huge step. Still, she knew she would probably do it for him. "I'll have to sleep on it, Nicholas," she whispered thoughtfully.

He smiled. "So long as you sleep on it in *my* bed, Angel."

"WHAT'S HAPPENING?" Angela bolted upright, pulling the bedspread to her chest. Nicholas was already out of bed and tugging on a dark-colored robe. "What's wrong?" She flung back the covers and threw her legs over the side of the mattress while her hand fumbled for the floor, seeking something she could wear. She found his now-wrinkled evening shirt.

"I think someone's breaking in," he said gruffly, already heading for the door. "Just stay in bed."

She wasn't about to. She trotted after him, shrugging into the shirt. She was in the corridor before she realized she was barely covered. Since the shirt had been held together by pearl studs, it lacked buttons, and she had no underwear. Fortunately, he was much taller, and the shirt did cover her to her knees.

"Nicholas?" She sped her steps, wrapping the shirttails tightly around herself, then folding her arms across her chest to hold them in place. "Where are you going?" She rounded a corner. "Nicho—" She stopped dead in her tracks.

The door to his padlocked room was banging on its hinges, and the lock swayed, clanking against the door. She followed more tentatively. The first room was dark, though a light in the next now snapped on.

"Nicholas?" The large, nearly empty room lacked the grandeur of the rest of the castle. It felt like an unused warehouse and the tiled floor chilled her bare feet, making her shiver. Suddenly, she wanted to be back in bed, all well loved and cozy, with Nicholas holding her.

As her eyes adjusted, she could make out the long rough-hewn worktables that lined the walls. "Oh, no," she gasped. "No." Her body, so warm just moments before, went icy cold. A human hand was lying on one of them! And a woman in a bridal gown was staring at her! Angela screamed.

"I told you to stay in bed!" Nicholas yelled from the adjoining room.

She barely heard him, but realized the woman hadn't so much as blinked. She crept forward, toward both the woman and the connecting room. When she was just a breath away, she determined that the woman was a mannequin. She heaved a sigh of relief... until she realized it was one of the brides that haunted the cliffs. The hand, she discovered was a mannequin part, made of plastic.

Her heart felt suddenly heavy. She didn't care if someone was breaking in the darn castle. What mattered most was that she'd fallen for someone very strange. Why would Nicholas have these odd, truly morbid things? How could a man so loving and gentle do whatever it was he was doing? Their lovemaking had convinced her that she'd want him always, but she had to know what this was about....

She took a deep breath, squared her shoulders and stomped into the other room, meaning to get to the bottom of this. But when she reached the lit room, she came to a complete standstill again.

"Video monitors?" Her jaw dropped. To her left, was a solid wall of television screens. To her right, were computer screens, running screen savers. In the middle was one very large screen. Nicholas's gaze was riveted on the TVs on the left. He punched a remote device, as if he were changing program channels, and various rooms in the castle appeared on the screens.

One room completely captured her attention. "That's *my* room!"

"No one's in there," he said calmly. "I think they're still outside." He punched the remote again. Now, the screens filled with exterior views of Westhawke Hall, seen from different angles.

"There," he said softly, clicking a button and squinting at one particular image. A shadowy figure was running up the front drive. She thought it was a person, though it was too dark to tell. It could have been Baskerville. Had they left the dog outside? After a moment, some other figures—seemingly men—followed the first. Nicholas glanced quickly over his shoulder at her. "Come work these levers."

She stared back, slack jawed, unable to believe that he was now grinning. She marched over and positioned herself next to him.

"These?" she finally asked, venomously. Had Nicholas actually been spying on her? *What kind of man am I falling in love with?* She jerked one of the levers downward, hoping it would make his whole infernal castle explode. Instead, hidden floodlights bathed the back of the castle and the cliffs.

"Not yet!" he exclaimed, quickly leaning and dimming the lights. "See the next lever, luv? Shove it up."

For some reason, she found herself actually doing as he asked. When she did, those three misty brides appeared on the front driveway. On one of the video monitors, Angela could see their faces, close up. And the mystery was solved. They were—without a doubt—the brides of Dracula. They had long pointy fangs and puncture dots on their necks. Not to mention hopelessly out-of-date hairdos, Angela thought with irony.

Nicholas leaned near her, reaching for a roller ball that was inset in the panel. When he rolled it with his fingertips, the brides dutifully moved forward, back or to the sides.

"Mind doing the brides, luv?" He placed her palm on the roller device.

"I take it we're terrorizing our burglars?" she asked, taking her anger at Nicholas out on the roller ball. As she made the brides advance, one of the shadowy figures leapt behind a tree. Others slowed their steps. She squinted, wondering if she were seeing men or the trees now...and yet the intruders were only one of many things on her mind. Had she and Nicholas really been making love, like normal people, just hours before? Was it really this strange man who had fully awakened her body? Had he been spying on her or not?

Oblivious to her racing thoughts, Nicholas burst out laughing and hit another switch. "I hope we're scaring them senseless," he said jovially, just as a low, menacing, howling sound played in the room.

"Sound effects, too?" she managed to ask.

"Absolutely."

Outside, the howling was slowly rising, gaining eerie momentum. In spite of how angry she was, Angela couldn't help but obediently toy with the roller. Negotiating the brides along the driveway was akin to playing a video game. When the shadowy figures tried to advance again, she sent the brides flying forward. The intruders stopped in their tracks. She didn't even feel all that guilty about scaring them. After all, they *were* burglars. But was Nicholas just as bad? *Please tell me he didn't spy on me with all this state-of-the-art security equipment.*

"Now," he said softly, almost to himself, "before we make them turn tail and run, I want to see their faces."

She glanced between the monitor that showed the brides and the larger middle screen, where Nicholas was zeroing in on the shadowy figures. "I think there're four of them," she said.

"And it looks like one has a gun," he said grimly.

She gasped and glanced back at the monitor again. Nicholas was readying a number of levers on the panel. After a moment, he rolled another ball-style device. This one picked up sounds from outside.

"Should have come a week ago," she thought she heard someone say. Another snatch of conversation followed. "Had to get passports. Everything by the book, because of..." She cocked her head, sure she'd heard the name Sylvia. Impossible. No, she'd surely misunderstood. The words were garbled, mixed with birdcalls, rustling wind and the still rising howl.

"Hit the floodlights, Angela," Nicholas said. "Once you do, we'll get a good look at them, then give them every scare tactic in the book."

She put her hand on the lever, feeling curious but not afraid. There was no way these guys would get past Nicholas. In fact, if she weren't so sure Nicholas had spied on her, she'd have a good time helping him get rid of the thugs.

"Now!"

She shoved up the lever. The screen turned bright white with light. Four men leapt back and drew their arms over their faces.

I know every one of them! Frankie had a gun and Eddie was wielding a tire iron. Sal clutched his chest, as if he were about to have a heart attack—which she certainly hoped he didn't, because it would be his second. Paulie's teeth were chattering.

"That's Sal Mancini," Nicholas said.

Angela forced herself to turn away from the screen and look at Nicholas. "You *know* Sal?"

He stared at her, without responding. Then, he turned slowly back to the panel. His face had become a mask of self-contained fury.

"What are you so mad about?" she asked, not really expecting a response. How did he know the Mancinis? Nicholas was working one lever after another with the speed of light, and—judging from the screens—all thunder was breaking loose outside.

She started to tell Nicholas she'd get dressed and find out why Frankie was here. Instead, she found herself murmuring, "My word." Whole legions of transparent ghostly frogs leapt through the grass. The brides floated slowly toward the men. The men backed down the drive, with their hands held out to their sides, as if afraid to turn and run. Wolves seemed to appear in the trees and other scary sounds were added to the wind's howling.

And then, suddenly, Frankie, Eddie, Paulie and Sal whirled around simultaneously and fled down the drive, as if the hounds of hell were on their heels.

When she turned toward Nicholas, his gaze was unnervingly steady. "Remember all those nice things I've said to you, Angela?"

She returned his stare, trying not to look cowed, and nodded. "Yeah."

"Well, luv," he said dryly. "Forget you ever heard them."

Chapter Thirteen

"You know Sal Mancini?" she ventured after a long moment.

He shook his head. "No, but he was recently indicted on racketeering charges, and his picture made all the papers."

"Sal's in trouble?" She gasped, looking worried.

He stared at her, wishing her long, slender legs didn't look quite so appealing peeking out from beneath his rumpled shirt. "Well, you clearly know him," he continued, wondering just exactly how much about herself she hadn't revealed. "Would you mind telling me how?"

She turned, squared her shoulders and leaned against the panel of levers. Her arched eyebrows and the haughty tilt of her chin indicated that she found it necessary to be on the defensive. Did that mean she was guilty of something?

When she didn't respond, he said, "I also wouldn't mind knowing why you failed to mention that those guys were in the Bromley tonight."

Her face colored and her eyes flashed. "How do you know that?"

"I heard them mention both Sylvia and the Bromley over the speakers, didn't you?" he asked, feeling exasperated.

"No."

"You simply weren't going to mention a word of this, were you, Angela? And what do Frankie and Salvatore

Mancini have to do with Sylvia's disappearance?'' Was the woman he was falling for accustomed to getting herself into untoward situations?

"I tried to tell you," she said, sounding self-contained. "Even if I really don't know where Sylvia is. But you didn't want to know anything more about me, did you, Nicholas? You want me to remain some mysterious stranger.... Because if you don't really know me, you can so easily ditch me! After all, I wouldn't be suitable for your world, now would I? Except for a lark."

Where had that come from? It was so far from the truth, that he felt his temper flare. She hugged her arms across her chest, making her shirttails go askew and exposing more cleavage than he wanted to see at this particular moment.

"So, how do you happen to know a New York gangster?" he asked softly, feeling angered by her myriad accusations.

"Well—" She smiled sweetly. "First, he's my godfather."

"Don't tell me," he said, matching her irony. "You kiss his ring, hide lethal weapons for him, and he occasionally gives you dresses that have been stolen from the backs of trucks—just like in the movies." That would get her to tell him the truth.

Her eyes narrowed and her mouth pursed into a tiny red dot. "My godfather," she repeated. "As in when I was baptized as a baby."

"Ah, luv," Nicholas said, politely, feeling more sure than ever she was lying about having no knowledge of Sylvia Sinclair's whereabouts. "So the two of you go way, way back."

"Yes," she snapped. "And I did tell you about Frankie."

Frankie. Their names rhymed! Lancini and Mancini! That had been the word on the tip of his tongue, the day he'd read about the charges leveled at Salvatore Mancini! "Frankie Mancini? He's related to Salvatore Mancini?"

His curiosity over whether or not she was deceiving him was surprisingly replaced by jealousy. *Will she leave me, the way she left him?* He watched Angela's lips stretch thin. What did she have to be mad about? He'd never played stand-in groom, or left a woman at the altar.

"Frankie's his son," she said in a clipped tone.

"Well, gee," he muttered, suddenly illogically supposing she might still have feelings for the man. "Perhaps we should have invited them in. It would have been such a treat to meet your almost-in-laws."

"I didn't marry Frankie!"

"Probably wise," he returned. Looking at her, he remembered their lovemaking and swallowed around a lump in his throat. "As I said, Sal's under indictment. Isn't he breaking some kind of law just by being here? Isn't that a bond violation?" Nicholas's smile didn't reach his eyes. "But, then, laws are made to be broken, now, aren't they?" *Has Angela broken any? If she has, it will break my heart.*

"At least Frankie never stooped so low as to suggest that I live with him out of wedlock," Angela said primly. "And he doesn't keep a room full of morbid items. Why don't you explain that?"

The comparison of him to Frankie rankled, but he chuckled, anyway. Not that it defused her temper. "I may have a morbid streak, and I may be a little gun-shy when it comes to proposing to a woman without fully knowing her. But, Angela—" His voice lowered. "Wouldn't you rather have a gun-shy fellow than one who shows up with his gun in hand? They were wielding Lugers and tire irons, luv."

"Pistol, not Lugers," she snapped.

"Well, thank heavens," he said. "I'd hate to think I slept with a woman who doesn't know her guns."

"And there was only one," she added. "Not Lugers, as in plural."

He arched his brows. "And how could I possibly get upset about one little itty-bitty gun?"

"Who knows?" she said quickly. "Because you sure didn't think twice about spying on me with all your high-tech *security* paraphernalia."

The way she said "security" made it clear she thought that was the last thing on his mind. He turned and backed her up against the control panel. "When I look at a woman," he said sweetly, "I like her to know I'm looking."

She tried to move away, but there was nowhere for her to go. "You never watched me?"

His low, throaty chuckle was meant to indicate that such a thing had never crossed his mind. It had, but he'd kept his impulses in check. "Believe me, Angela," he finally said. "I've got better things to do with my time."

Looking into her beautiful eyes, he wondered why they'd begun arguing. He was surprised that she knew the Mancinis, of course. He was shocked that the Mancinis knew of Sylvia's whereabouts, which meant Angela might have known all along, too. He was upset that the men had shown up on his doorstep with a gun. But it was more than that. The love they'd shared had considerably upped the stakes of their relationship, and just when they'd discovered it, it was clear they didn't trust each other, at all. Did Angela really believe he'd spied on her?

"You swear?" she finally asked.

"Since I have to consider that you might be as devious as you are beautiful, I probably *should* have watched you," he returned, wishing she'd given him the benefit of the doubt. *Not that he was giving it to her.* "Mind telling me exactly what you're involved in?"

"Oh, but I thought you liked to keep the mystery in our relationship at an all-time high."

"I've just changed my mind," he almost singsonged.

"It's you who owes me an explanation." Her gaze dropped from his and flitted all around the room. "This is a pretty weird setup, if you ask me."

"But I didn't ask you," he couldn't help but say.

"Well—" her breath so close he could feel it on his face "—what about some answers?"

"I'm an FX man," he said, his gaze never leaving her face. "I'm working on special effects for a *Brides of Dracula* made-for-TV remake. Before my wife died and I got so *morbid,* as you like to call it, I used to work on 'Masterpiece Theatre.'" He blew out a quick sigh, not about to tell her that her appearance in his life had made him want to do that kind of work again. "I'm gainfully employed by the BBC. Free lance."

"The BBC?" she echoed.

"British Broadcasting Corporation," he crooned. "Don't try to change the subject."

"Which was?"

"That you're such good friends with the Mancinis, and they seem to know where Sylvia Sinclair is."

"I doubt Sal and Frankie know anything about Sylvia. And they *are* great people," she returned.

His eyes narrowed. If they were so wonderful, why had she been running away from the altar? "Did they coerce you into becoming engaged to Frankie?"

"Oh!" She gasped. "That would make everything all right, wouldn't it? Well, I'm sorry to inform you that no one coerced me. In fact, when my father got sick and I was saddled with more medical bills than I could pay, Sal sent Frankie over to offer to help out. He was sweet and kind. He seemed like the most perfect man in the world."

The most perfect man in the world? "Well, he'll clearly sink to all kinds of lawbreaking to get you back, at any rate," he said, before he could stop himself. "Or were they after goods," he continued, "rather than your person? Perhaps you were just casing the joint, Angela." He hardly assumed it was true, but he didn't know what else to think. "I simply can't believe your presence caused those guys to attempt a break-in."

"I'm sorry."

"Me, too, luv." He wished for all the world that none of this had happened. The two of them would be back in bed, wrapped in each others' arms. "If it were just me...," he began.

"If it were just you, what?"

Her lovely, lively eyes made all his better instincts flee. He wanted her. He was never going to stop wanting her. "We could deal with this."

"Deal with what? That I happen to know the Mancini family? I'm sorry people such as us aren't suitable for your fancy London friends."

"I don't care about the London people," he said softly. "Never have, never will."

"Right."

It was true, even if she didn't believe him. "But I do care about Rosemunde. Those men had a gun, Angela."

"They could have broken in," she conceded. "And there could have been—" she cleared her throat and swallowed "—an accident."

At least she'd admitted that much. "Now, where's Sylvia Sinclair?" he asked.

"I really don't know," she snapped. "If you choose never to believe me, that's your problem. Now, may I please get by you?" She stared at him pointedly.

He stepped back. She didn't even look at him but simply headed for the door.

"Where are you going, Angela?"

"It's about four in the morning. I know *you're* used to strange, late nights, but *I'm* not. So, I'm going to bed. My bed," she said without turning. "But don't worry, I'll vanish at first light."

"Vanish?"

"You slept with me," she said, stopping and glancing over her shoulder. "And now you're going to use any excuse you can to make sure there's no commitment involved. Face it, Nicholas, you were looking for a fight. So, now I'm disappearing, just like one of your infernal brides."

His mouth dropped open in astonishment, as she turned and headed for the door again. "Maybe it's just as well," he said gruffly. He watched how the long, rumpled shirt swept against the backs of her knees and tried to tell himself it really was for the best. Hell, maybe she was right. Maybe he had been looking for a fight. When she'd nearly reached the door, she shrugged right out of the shirt in midstride. As it floated to the floor, she continued walking toward the corridor, in all her naked glory.

How am I going to live without her? Easily, he hoped. She was the type of woman who embroiled herself in odd, little intrigues, like showing up as a stand-in bride. And as far as he was concerned, known gangsters made strange bedfellows. He took in how she managed that sassy stride without even the tiniest hint of self-consciousness.

"I'd have that shirt laundered by professionals before you wear it into London again, dear," she called over her shoulder. "After all, Angela Lancini, that down-and-dirty gun moll, was last seen wearing it."

HE SAT IN THE DARK in his bathrobe for what felt like eternity, with only Baskerville for comfort. "Lovely," he finally muttered, looking at the dog. "Just bloody lovely." What was he going to do?

Her jeweled necklace was on his nightstand. Next to it, the little pile of her earrings, rings and bracelets gleamed dully in the moonlight. An edge of her wispy-looking panties peeked out from beneath his trousers, which lay crumpled on the floor.

He stood and crossed the room, stepping over his cummerbund, then kicking aside one of his dress shoes. "Ouch!" He glared down, then realized he'd stepped on one of the pearl studs from his shirt. The floor was equally littered with hairpins, and Baskerville was now sniffing her gown, with a pleased expression on his face.

With a sweeping arc of his arm, Nicholas leaned and caught her dress. "It looked a whole lot better when you were in it, luv," he said wryly. He held it up for a moment, then turned to toss it on the bed. He stopped in midgesture. The sheets were so tangled that only true lovers could have mussed them.

He circled the gilded rail, gently placed the dress on the bed, then laid down. When he shut his eyes and took a deep breath, he realized that everything in the room was positively permeated with her sweet scent, no less than the way every facet of his life had been touched by her.

Suddenly, Baskerville's paws landed squarely on his chest and his tail thumped once on the mattress. After a moment, he whimpered pathetically.

"Oh, what do you want?" Nicholas opened his eyes and a wry chuckle escaped his lips. Baskerville was proudly exhibiting his big catch. One of Angela's ruby slippers was in his mouth.

"Well, Prince Charming, you always were good at finding shoes," Nicholas said, prying the slipper from Baskerville's mouth. He rested it on his chest. Baskerville bounded off the bed, clearly in search of other such prizes.

Nicholas stared at the slipper. Had he really thrown it onto the bed when they'd first entered the room? Had he really been her Prince Charming tonight?

"Guess your fairy godmother did desert you, luv," he said, tapping the shoe against his chest. He smiled. Had he really been reduced to rolling around in bed with a shoe?

He raised up on an elbow, steadied his aim, then threw the slipper as far as he could. It flew through the doorway, before Baskerville trotted after it. Then, something in the next room crashed to the floor and shattered. Baskerville quickly reappeared, sitting guiltily on his haunches as if he were about to be accused of wrongdoing.

Nicholas winced. "Hope it wasn't that Victorian vase," he muttered.

"Oh, hell," he added, after another long moment. He rolled off the bed, found his trousers and stepped into them. Fishing under the bed, he found a pair of sneakers, that didn't exactly do his tux pants justice, and a hair band. On his way out, he stopped at the closet, grabbed a T-shirt and pulled it over his head.

As he walked down the corridor, he pulled his hair back into a tight queue and wondered just what he was going to say to her. Maybe there was some way he could talk to Frankie and get to the bottom of the matter. Still, Frankie had to be a hot-blooded, jealous, scorned boyfriend. Why else would he come after her this way? And would he tell Nicholas where Sylvia was? Her mother was terribly worried.

"Come on, boy," Nicholas said, realizing Baskerville was on his heels. "Though I can't imagine why you'd want to," he added.

After all, what more was there to say? He didn't feel like fighting. And he hadn't proposed to her, now, had he? If he wasn't thinking along those lines, then it really didn't make sense to try and make peace with Frankie.

He was so lost in thought that he barely paid attention the first time Baskerville growled. When the throaty sound became more menacing, he glanced down. The second he did, Baskerville lunged through the air.

"What the—" Nicholas looked up. A man was carrying Angela's suitcase! The Mancinis had returned! They'd not only gotten into his house, but Angela was bound and gagged and flung over Frankie's shoulder! At least, he thought it was Frankie; the man looked like a younger version of Salvatore. Angela was kicking like the devil. Unfortunately, she and Frankie were a good forty meters down the corridor.

"What do you think you're doing?" Nicholas shouted, running full scale after Frankie. He couldn't *not* rescue Angela, though he had no clue concerning what he'd do with her when—or if—he got her back.

Another man ran right into Nicholas, pushing his chest and blocking his way. Fighting wasn't exactly his style, but Nicholas sidestepped, then threw a lightning-quick punch at the man's jaw. The man reeled away, his shoes scuffing across the floor. Nicholas heaved a sigh of relief over the fact that he hadn't had to belt Sal Mancini . . . yet. He took off running again.

"Put her down!" With a sixth sense, Nicholas managed to duck when a wild punch came at his head in the darkness. It was the man with the suitcase. Once again, it had been bound by Angela's veil. Beneath the second thug's swing, he could see Baskerville bare his teeth, catch Frankie's pant leg and tug viciously. "Jolly good, Baskerville," Nicholas called, as he lithely ducked another punch. He elbowed man number two's belly, then bolted after Angela and Frankie again.

Still a good thirty meters away. The two men had really slowed him down. *Twenty meters, ten meters,* he thought as he ran. Suddenly, the second man he'd waylaid tackled him from behind. As they rolled over each other, the first man ran past with the suitcase. Nicholas got his footing, then ran five paces, only to be tackled again.

He was close this time, so close he could hear Angela's muffled pleas. So near that he could see Salvatore Mancini's face. The man smiled pleasantly, then patted Baskerville on the head. The fool dog wagged his tail!

Nicholas wrenched, turned and pinned his attacker to the floor, then sprinted toward Salvatore. The thug was only ten paces away. "You're such a good boy," the oldest Mancini said as he shoved Baskerville into a room and slammed the door.

Five more paces, Nicholas thought, still coming at a dead run. He reached for Angela, nearly touching her hair, but something metal made hard contact with his midsection. A blow to his head quickly followed. At least, it was a fist, not the tire iron, he thought, as he doubled and fell.

He blinked. How long had he lain here? *Not long.* Far off, he heard his front door clang shut.

He staggered to his feet, one hand still clutching his abdomen, and headed for the door. Outside, the Mancini car was fishtailing down his drive! As he ran for the garage, he hoped at least one of the cars had keys in it.

"Where are they?" He dodged from car to car, throwing open the driver's-side doors. *None in the sports car. Motorcycle keys in the house. None in the compact.* "They would be in the limo," he said wryly as he slid into the seat. "Not exactly the car most likely to do one-eighty and turn on a dime.

"Yes, this really is quite wonderful," he continued as he turned the key in the ignition. "It's four against one, I'm injured and they're professionals, who actually enjoy this kind of thing. No big deal," he tried to assure himself, as he stomped his full weight on the gas pedal.

"AND YOU WONDER WHY I left you at the altar!" Angela shrieked, continuing the same tirade she'd begun in the car. She paced across the large, luxurious suite in the Bromley Hotel, ignoring its elegance and the many connecting doors that led from the main room.

"Sorry, Frankie," Paulie said huffily, collapsing into an armchair, "but I'm truly beginning to think we should gag her again."

"Why did you gag me at all?" she shouted.

Sal ran his hand over his balding scalp. "Angela, honey," he said, with a wan expression. "We thought you were in danger. After we saw the strange goings-on at that horrible place, we were afraid you'd inadvertently make noise."

"You stay out of it," she snapped. "You were hauled in on racketeering charges and shouldn't even be here." She glared at the elderly man, whose jaw dropped in shock.

"I was helping the Feds!" he exclaimed, grabbing a newspaper from a table and tossing it in her direction.

Without looking at it, she tossed it on top of her suitcase. "How could you jerks storm Nicholas Westhawke's house with guns? Guns!"

"Angela," Frankie groused. "It was a water pistol!" He jerked it from his waistband and pulled the trigger. Indeed, a water jet arched into the air. "See? I was just going to scare him if he gave us trouble."

"Oh, you really are a maniac!" She stalked close to him. "Maniac!" she repeated. And as such, he made the perfect target. After all, if it weren't for her long-standing, almost familial relationship with the Mancinis, she'd be with Nicholas! Right now, anger seemed the best medicine. Without it, she'd be in a puddle of tears.

"Do you remember when you said that we were perfect together because our last names rhymed?" she snarled.

Frankie gulped and nodded.

"Do you know how stupid that is?" Her head suddenly swung toward the half-open door to a connecting room. "Who is in the shower?" she thundered. "Did you bring the whole darn neighborhood?"

"Just a friend," Frankie said weakly.

"At least *you* have friends," she snapped, "because you've sure alienated all of mine!" Remembering that Nicholas was far more than a friend made her feel dangerously close to crying.

Frankie had ruined her plan to win Nicholas back. She'd hoped to rise in the morning, stay at Westhawke Hall and try to talk to him. But now, she was never going to see him or Rosemunde again. Frankie had even brought her fool suitcase! She had no excuse to return.... And it was clear Nicholas didn't want to see her again! *Maybe it's just as well that you leave.*

"I think you and I were meant to be just that, Angela— friends," Frankie was saying softly. "And you have a lot of other friends. That's why we all came to take you home."

"I don't have a home!" *My home was Westhawke Hall.* But Nicholas didn't want her there. "It's bad enough that Nicholas thinks you're a bunch of lowlife thugs, but then you show up with guns and tire irons and prove it!"

"You're on a first-name basis with this weirdo?" Frankie interjected, looking shocked.

"He's not a weirdo. And for your information, he has an excellent job with the BBC," she said, suddenly sniffing. "We're on far more than a first-name basis, too, if you must know."

Frankie's hand shot to his heart. "Angela, did this guy take advantage of you? I mean, did he . . . you know?"

"Did he sleep with me?" she nearly screamed, whirling around for emphasis. She found herself face-to-face with Nicholas, who was leaning in the doorway between the rooms.

"You son of a—" Frankie began.

"I not only slept with her," Nicholas said with a quick smile that didn't reach his eyes. "But I enjoyed it immensely."

"How did you get in here?" Paulie exclaimed.

"I'm well connected at the Bromley," Nicholas returned calmly.

As Frankie lunged for him, Angela stuck her foot out and tripped him. He sprawled across the floor. Behind Nicholas, there was a flurry of motion.

"Nicholas Westhawke?" a woman said. She wore a Bromley bathrobe with a big *B* emblazoned across the lapel, and her hair was bound in a towel, turban style.

"Sylvia?" Angela gasped.

"Sylvia?" Nicholas echoed.

"Nice to meet you, Nicholas," Sylvia said, breezing right past him and kneeling on the floor next to the dazed Frankie. "Are you all right, darling?"

"Darling!" Angela exploded. "Do you mean to tell me you two have been together this whole time?"

"How was I supposed to know this brute was taking advantage of you?" Frankie yelled, his eyes shooting Nicholas daggers. Paulie and Eddie rose stealthily and edged toward either side of Nicholas. When Frankie managed to shrug off Sylvia's arms, he lunged toward Nicholas a second time.

"Look, kids, why don't you just calm down?" a weary sounding Sal Mancini ventured from his armchair.

Angela glanced at Nicholas, but his face was impassive. "He didn't take advantage of me, Frankie!" she shouted, just in time. Frankie skidded to a halt, his fist half raised. He pivoted and stared at Angela.

"He said you slept with him," Frankie snapped.

"But I wanted to," Angela returned, feeling her cheeks color. "Okay?" She glanced at Nicholas again, but his face remained expressionless. He looked thoroughly out of place, too, with Paulie and Eddie looming on either side of him, in case he decided to fight. She glanced away, her throat constricting.

"You really slept with him?" Frankie repeated in shock.

"So what!" Angela stomped her foot and stared at Frankie. Couldn't he see that eyes were begging him to shut up? Couldn't he see that if he said one more word she was going to cry?

"Well, Angela," Frankie finally said. "If you slept with him, I guess you gotta marry him."

"We've still got rice bags all done up from your last wedding, honey," Sal said with a sigh.

"I gotta get in a tux again?" Eddie groused.

"I'm not marrying anybody," she managed to say. Unfortunately, Frankie threw his arms wildly in the air, as if she'd committed a cardinal sin. *Which I have,* she thought.

"I mean, you can't do something like that and not get *married,* Angela!" Her ex-fiancé was glaring at her as if she should be hanged, not wed.

And Nicholas hasn't said a word. She didn't dare look his way. *Isn't this where he changes his mind, steps in and proposes?*

She gathered her pride around her like a toreador's cape. "Not only am I remaining single," she declared loudly, steadfastly avoiding Nicholas's eyes. "But I intend to borrow one of these plane tickets, if you don't mind."

"We got you one, too, Angela," Sal said. "But we thought we'd be leaving from Cornwall, so these are for the Exeter airport. We were going to change to Heathrow later and—"

"This will be fine." She stomped across the room, plucked a return ticket from the table, then whirled around and met Nicholas's gaze. "Thank you ever so much for hospitably rescuing me," she crooned, feeling the skin around her eyes tighten with unshed tears. "As you can see," she continued, her voice growing suddenly raspy. "I am in no danger, and you may return home."

He didn't move. He didn't say anything. His eyes seemed to touch her everywhere. She could feel them on her face, her legs and her hair, as she gathered up her purse and suitcase. She pointedly grabbed a box of tissues from a table, figuring she'd need them and hoping the gesture gave Nicholas pause.

"Please excuse me, Lord Westhawke," she said haughtily when she reached the doorway.

"Certainly, madam," he returned.

She swept past him, ensuring that her suitcase hit him good and hard.

"I TRULY LOVE THE FACT that you're frugal, my dear," Lady Anne said. She grabbed Angela by the elbow and stared at her luggage with a shocked expression. "But certainly Nicholas wouldn't mind buying you a new suitcase!"

For some reason, Angela felt compelled to swipe away the tears that were beginning to fall and plaster a smile on her face. Lady Anne kissed her cheek and shoved her suitcase almost behind the palm tree nearest the hotel's front door.

"I saw Nicholas just a moment ago," Lady Anne continued. "He wanted access to one of the upstairs rooms for some reason, and he said you two were doing quite well. I hear you're taking a trip to the States to see your family! Such a shame he can't go because of his work...."

Angela felt her false smile giving out. *I have no family!* she wanted to scream. The mere mention of Nicholas's name was enough to reduce her to self-pity. Worse—the fool man clearly meant to pretend they were married, even after she'd gone! She was so upset, she was barely aware that Lady Anne was prattling on.

"So you need only sit and wait," her supposed relative finally said, gently pushing Angela into a chair. "My personal driver can take you to the airport. I don't need him for the rest of the day."

Angela stared glumly at her ridiculous suitcase, feeling suddenly glad for her last limo ride. Somehow, she'd managed to keep her tears in check while upstairs, but at any moment the floodgates were going to burst. *I hope I cry so much that Nicholas Westhawke drowns.*

Fumbling beside herself, she found the box of tissues and clutched them to her lap, feeling as prepared as a Girl Scout. Then her gaze caught the newspaper, which she'd inadvertently brought. The headline read: Sal "Mr. Clean" Mancini Helps Feds Clean up City! Indictment a Hoax!

Maybe I can show Nicholas the newspaper. But that wasn't the real issue, she thought, biting her lower lip. After a moment, Lady Anne reappeared and walked her out to her Rolls limousine.

As soon as they reached the curb, Angela's eyes started to fill and blur. "Thank you," she murmured to the driver who had opened the back door. She concentrated on not blinking, hoping to hold back the crying jag as long as she could.

When she was safely ensconced in the back seat and the car had pulled out of the Bromley's circular drive, and when there was no chance the damnable Nicholas Westhawke would see her in such a state, she let loose.

Glancing up, she realized the glass partition between the front seat and the mammoth back was open a few inches. "Sorry if this—if this bothers you," she called to the driver. She hiccuped, staring at the back of his head and at his chauffeur's cap. "I—I just can't help it."

And she really couldn't. She flung herself across the seat, one hand wringing a wadded tissue and the other wrapped around the box. The newspaper tumbled to the floor.

She was really leaving England. She was never going to see Nicholas or Rosemunde again. Because she couldn't imagine being held by another man, she knew she was destined to die an old maid. Realizing that she was a spinster before she was thirty was enough to send her into another breathless bout of hysterics.

She didn't know how long she lay there, curled on the seat and wallowing in grief, but it felt like an awfully long time. "Are we almost—" She drew in a wavery breath, wondering if she should find her makeup bag and try to fix her face. "But I don't—" A sob escaped her lips. "I don't care one iota about how I look," she mumbled to herself. "What's the p-p-point?"

"Almost what, ma'am?" the driver called.

"Almost there?"

"Not at all. So go ahead and cry, if you will."

He had a pronounced cockney accent, the likes of which she'd never hear again. That he was so sweet about her crying made her double over in sobs again. But every time she shut her eyes, she saw Nicholas and knew his mesmerizing gaze would haunt her for a lifetime.

She relived their every moment together—how gruff he'd been when she met him, how he used to eat at that horribly long table in the stuffy dining room and how he'd slowly changed, becoming so flirtatious and thoughtful. Once again, she felt his hands touching her neck as he clasped her necklace. Again, he took out her hairpins, one by one, and lifted her into his arms, carrying her to his bed.

But when she opened her puffy eyes, she was only staring at fistfuls of tissue. At some point, she must have clutched the newspaper, because there was ink on her fingertips. The black-and-white photo of Sal grinned at her and she snapped her eyes shut once more, wondering just how many tears she had left. Not many, she decided after a long moment. Her eyes felt so swollen she could barely open them and her throat ached.

No, whether or not Sal's a criminal was never the issue. It's not even that we're from separate countries. It's that we're from separate worlds and don't trust each other. His world is the one where everything glitters and turns to gold. Where princes rescue girls from Little Italy and they live happily ever after, in castles. It's a world where the princes have real names, like Nicholas Westhawke.

Suddenly, she bolted upright, putting her hands on her hips. "Turn around," she said raspily.

The driver stopped the car. The glass partition between them hummed as it came all the way down. The driver slowly turned his head.

"As far as I'm concerned," he said, "we've reached our destination."

She could merely stare. From the back of the long limo, he looked a million miles away.

Nicholas flashed her a grin. "I really didn't want to talk with Frankie so close by and foaming at the mouth, Angel."

"How could you let me go on crying like that, Nicholas!" she exclaimed, trying to sound mad.

"Luv," he said, "I assumed you needed to get it out of your system." When he turned back around, his eyes caught hers in the rearview. "Besides, I figured I'd have a better chance if your defenses are down."

She cleared her throat. "Better chance?"

He nodded.

She felt weak from all the crying but smiled. *This sounds promising.* She ducked her head and walked toward the seats nearest the driver's partition. When she stared through the front windshield, she realized he hadn't taken her to the airport, at all.

"Westhawke Hall," she murmured. While she was still gazing lovingly at the castle, Nicholas hopped out and opened the back door. One of his long, strong arms reached inside and he offered her his hand.

Taking it, she thought, *I feel lucky. So incredibly lucky.* In a second, she was out of the car and wrapped in his embrace. His lips sought hers in a slow, sweet kiss.

When she leaned back in his arms, he lifted his cap, and all his beautiful white blond hair tumbled over his shoulders. "Will you stay with me, Angel?"

Looking into his eyes, she wished it was more, but she knew she wouldn't last a day without him. "Yes," she said, her voice husky with both the tears she'd shed and emotion. She reached up and touched his face. "I'll stay."

He chuckled and threw his cap in the air. It spun somewhere above them, so high, she was sure it reached the clouds. His eyes twinkled. "You mean you'll live with me?" he asked, as he lifted her, pivoted and plopped her onto the hood of the limo.

As he wedged himself between her knees, she laughed. She rested her hands on his shoulders and nodded. "Yep."

He sighed and shook his head. "Just what kind of a man do you take me for, Angela Lancini?"

"The one I'm in love with," she returned promptly.

"Far be it from me to live with a woman out of wedlock," he said.

Her smile vanished. "Nicholas, don't feel you have to—"

"Marry you?" He leaned even closer and twined his hands through her hair. "Luv, I don't do things I don't want to do," he said huskily. "I'm rather bad at taking no for an answer, too. So will you marry me, Angel?"

"And become the lady of the realm?" she asked softly.

"I want to give you everything." His voice lowered and his lips came closer to her own. "Everything."

"But there's only one thing I want."

"Name it and it's yours."

"You."

"As simply as that, I'm yours forever." His lips grazed hers. "But is that a yes?"

"So many yeses we could never count them all," she returned as the soft pressure of his lips parted her own and he leaned into the kiss that would last them both a lifetime.

Epilogue

"I do," Angela said softly, then tried to listen, as the priest continued with the ceremony. But her heart was pounding and the order of whirlwind events suddenly seemed dangerously jumbled. Had she really become engaged? Had invitations been sent? Were her friends really here? And was this truly her wedding? She glanced down, suddenly wondering if she was wearing her wedding band yet. Was he?

No. She was so excited she could barely concentrate. Under any other circumstances, she might have looked around, to take in the congregation and the elegant surroundings.

After all, she thought, hers was truly a fairy-tale wedding. They were in the sweet-smelling rose garden, and in the distance large white tents billowed with the summer breeze. A new gown, lovingly hand sewn by Mrs. Dupre, graced her figure; a new gem had been set in an old Westhawke heirloom band to signify her engagement; and Nicholas was wearing a new tux.

Oh, yes, in other circumstances, she might have looked at all the well-coiffed Londoners and the many friends that Nicholas had flown from New York to England for the wedding. But today she only had eyes for him.

"I do," Nicholas said huskily, looking more serious than she'd ever seen him.

Her mouth went dry, and she could do nothing more than sigh when she felt the band of gold nestle above her engagement ring. She gazed at him, and time seemed to stop. *It always does when I look into those eyes,* she thought, feeling breathless.

How long had she merely stared into those mesmerizing blue-violet eyes? The oh-so-entrancing eyes of her prince, the man with whom she would share her life?

"I now pronounce you husband and wife."

Husband and wife. Tears sprung to her eyes. *He's my destiny.*

"You may kiss the bride."

He cupped her face gently and touched his lips to hers, in a kiss that burned bright with promise. And then he lifted her in his arms, cradling her against him, and began to carry her over the long white aisle that led through the roses. He stopped once, briefly, plucked a rose effortlessly from a bush, and held the full-bloomed flower against her cheek. She grasped the stem and smiled. He began walking again.

From somewhere, a loud organ burst into merry song. "I love you, Nicholas," she whispered, without even bothering to look at the crowd.

"I love you, too," he said gently, as he lithely stepped along the white aisle.

It felt like an eternity before Angela could catch her breath. Somehow, Nicholas had helped her change into her travel suit and led her to the alcove nearest the front door of Westhawke Hall. *My home.*

"Don't worry, we'll find Rosemunde," Sal was saying now, kissing Angela's cheek.

"I'm sure she's about," Lady Anne added, resting her hand on Sal's arm and tugging him in the direction of the doorway. "And probably as relieved as I am that you two are actually married."

As Sal and Lady Anne headed for the drive, where the wedding goers waited with rice bags, Angela heard Lady Anne say, "Did I tell you how pleased I am to have met the man who's single-handedly brought so much civic pride to New York?"

Nicholas's arm looped around Angela's shoulder. "And I thought the man was a criminal," he said.

"Told you so," she returned, smiling. Suddenly, she gasped and pointed through the window, past the many people who were waiting for them to appear. "Look at that!"

"Oh, no," Nicholas said, laughing.

Nicholas's limo pulled in front of the castle. Frankie leapt out of the driver's side and Sylvia Sinclair jumped from the passenger side. The car had the words Just Married written all over it, and streamers and balloons were tied to the back bumper. Judging from the can of shaving cream in Sylvia's hand, she and Frankie were the culprits.

Nicholas chuckled. "Sal says Sylvia and Frankie are getting married."

"It's strange how things turn out sometimes," Angela said softly. She smiled, thinking they made a cute couple, and leaned against Nicholas. She wasn't sure, but she thought he still smelled of roses. "I can't wait to really see Italy," she said. *And I can't wait for tonight, our honeymoon night.*

"Ready to make a run for it?" he asked, as the door was thrown open by an unseen party.

"I just hate to get rice all over Mrs. Dupre's travel suit," she said playfully.

"Too bad, luv," he returned, dropping his arm from around her shoulder and grabbing her hand.

"This is it?" she asked.

"This is really it, Angela."

They squeezed hands tightly, squinted their eyes and ran the gauntlet of well-wishers, while rice rained down on them from all sides. When they reached the car, Nicholas practically pushed her inside, and Angela found herself laughing so hard she was sure she'd never stop.

"But we really can't leave without saying goodbye to Rosemunde," she said breathlessly.

"Goodbye," Rosemunde said matter-of-factly.

"You're in the car!" Nicholas put his arm around Angela again and pulled her close.

"Before you leave, do you promise I can stay here and go to school, since Angela's—" she smiled shyly "—Mum's going to be a teacher?"

"Absolutely," Nicholas said. "Now give us a hug."

"But I don't want to get out of the car!" Rosemunde protested.

"The sooner you do, the sooner you may find yourself with brothers and sisters," Nicholas returned.

Rosemunde squinted at him, clearly wondering what the connection was between their leaving and her having siblings. Nonetheless, she hugged them both. "I'm really going to have brothers and sisters?"

"Oh, probably," Nicholas said, just as Lady Anne arrived and coaxed Rosemunde from the car. The two of them waved a last goodbye, then Nicholas turned to Angela. "We do have some extra rooms in the house."

She threw her head back and laughed. "Sorry, Nicholas," she said, glancing at Westhawke Hall as the car began to move down the long driveway, "but I am not having two hundred kids."

He chuckled. "Well, we don't have to fill up all the rooms."

"You'll settle for one or two?"

He smiled. "Or three or four. It's negotiable."

Her laughter tempered to a smile. "So what do we do on the way to the airport?" she teased. "Play road games?"

In a quick movement, he pulled her across his lap. "No, luv," he whispered. "I'll tell you a honeymoon story."

"Oh?" she prompted, gazing into his eyes. "Is that sort of like a bedtime story?"

He grinned. "Exactly."

"Well, be my guest," she said raspily.

"Once upon a time..." he began softly. When he nuzzled his face against hers, strands of his hair tickled her cheeks. "There was a prince named Nicholas, who loved a princess named Angela."

"But poor Angela was locked away, in a tower?" she asked, shutting her eyes.

"Only until Nicholas rescued her," he murmured.

"Nice prince, this Nicholas," she commented dreamily.

"Not nearly as nice as Angela," he returned. "After all, she'd been fed nothing but gruel for so long, in that tower, and yet she was still sweet and beautiful."

She opened her eyes and shifted in his lap. "And then this knight in shining armor took her to his kingdom...."

Nicholas nodded. "A magical kingdom, where one emotion was valued above all others."

"Which was?"

"Love, my angel."

She smiled. "Ah, that sounds perfect. What happened then?"

"They had two hundred children," he whispered, deadpan.

She giggled. "And then?"

He dipped his head and kissed her for a long moment. "Why, luv," he said huskily. "And then they lived happily ever after."

MILLION DOLLAR SWEEPSTAKES (III)

No purchase necessary. To enter, follow the directions published. Method of entry may vary. For eligibility, entries must be received no later than March 31, 1996. No liability is assumed for printing errors, lost, late or misdirected entries. Odds of winning are determined by the number of eligible entries distributed and received. Prizewinners will be determined no later than June 30, 1996.

Sweepstakes open to residents of the U.S. (except Puerto Rico), Canada, Europe and Taiwan who are 18 years of age or older. All applicable laws and regulations apply. Sweepstakes offer void wherever prohibited by law. Values of all prizes are in U.S. currency. This sweepstakes is presented by Torstar Corp., its subsidiaries and affiliates, in conjunction with book, merchandise and/or product offerings. For a copy of the Official Rules send a self-addressed, stamped envelope (WA residents need not affix return postage) to: MILLION DOLLAR SWEEPSTAKES (III) Rules, P.O. Box 4573, Blair, NE 68009, USA.

EXTRA BONUS PRIZE DRAWING

No purchase necessary. The Extra Bonus Prize will be awarded in a random drawing to be conducted no later than 5/30/96 from among all entries received. To qualify, entries must be received by 3/31/96 and comply with published directions. Drawing open to residents of the U.S. (except Puerto Rico), Canada, Europe and Taiwan who are 18 years of age or older. All applicable laws and regulations apply; offer void wherever prohibited by law. Odds of winning are dependent upon number of eligibile entries received. Prize is valued in U.S. currency. The offer is presented by Torstar Corp., its subsidiaries and affiliates in conjunction with book, merchandise and/or product offering. For a copy of the Official Rules governing this sweepstakes, send a self-addressed, stamped envelope (WA residents need not affix return postage) to: Extra Bonus Prize Drawing Rules, P.O. Box 4590, Blair, NE 68009, USA.

SWP-H794

This summer, come cruising with Harlequin Books!

PORTS OF CALL

In July, August and September, excitement, danger and, of course, romance can be found in Lynn Leslie's exciting new miniseries PORTS OF CALL. Not only can you cruise the South Pacific, the Caribbean and the Nile, your journey will also take you to Harlequin Superromance®, Harlequin Intrigue® and Harlequin American Romance®.

- ♦ In July, cruise the South Pacific with SINGAPORE FLING, a Harlequin Superromance
- ♦ NIGHT OF THE NILE from Harlequin Intrigue will heat up your August
- ♦ September is the perfect month for CRUISIN' MR. DIAMOND from Harlequin American Romance

So, cruise through the summer with LYNN LESLIE and HARLEQUIN BOOKS!

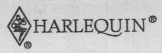

®HARLEQUIN®

Weddings, Inc.

THE WEDDING GAMBLE
Muriel Jensen

Eternity, Massachusetts, was America's wedding town. Paul Bertrand knew this better than anyone—he never should have gotten soused at his friend's rowdy bachelor party. Next morning when he woke up, he found he'd somehow managed to say "I do"—to the woman he'd once jilted! And Christina Bowman had helped launch so many honeymoons, she knew just what to do on theirs!

THE WEDDING GAMBLE, available in September from American Romance, is the fourth book in Harlequin's new cross-line series, **WEDDINGS, INC.**

Be sure to look for the fifth book, **THE VENGEFUL GROOM,** by Sara Wood (Harlequin Presents #1692), coming in October.

HARLEQUIN
AMERICAN ◆ ROMANCE®

A NEW STAR COMES OUT TO SHINE....

American Romance continues to search the heavens for the best new talent... the best new stories.

Join us next month when a new star appears in the American Romance constellation:

Kim Hansen
#548 TIME RAMBLER
August 1994

Even in the shade of a broad-rimmed Stetson, Eagle River's lanky sheriff had the bluest eyes Katie Shannon had ever seen. But why was he in the ghost town—a man who was killed in a shoot-out one hundred years ago?

Be sure to Catch a "Rising Star"!

RISING STAR

STAR2

HARLEQUIN®

Don't miss these Harlequin favorites by some of our most distinguished authors!
And now you can receive a discount by ordering two or more titles!

HT #25525	THE PERFECT HUSBAND by Kristine Rolofson	$2.99	☐
HT #25554	LOVERS' SECRETS by Glenda Sanders	$2.99	☐
HP #11577	THE STONE PRINCESS by Robyn Donald	$2.99	☐
HP #11554	SECRET ADMIRER by Susan Napier	$2.99	☐
HR #03277	THE LADY AND THE TOMCAT by Bethany Campbell	$2.99	☐
HR #03283	FOREIGN AFFAIR by Eva Rutland	$2.99	☐
HS #70529	KEEPING CHRISTMAS by Marisa Carroll	$3.39	☐
HS #70578	THE LAST BUCCANEER by Lynn Erickson	$3.50	☐
HI #22256	THRICE FAMILIAR by Caroline Burnes	$2.99	☐
HI #22238	PRESUMED GUILTY by Tess Gerritsen	$2.99	☐
HAR #16496	OH, YOU BEAUTIFUL DOLL by Judith Arnold	$3.50	☐
HAR #16510	WED AGAIN by Elda Minger	$3.50	☐
HH #28719	RACHEL by Lynda Trent	$3.99	☐
HH #28795	PIECES OF SKY by Marianne Willman	$3.99	☐

Harlequin Promotional Titles

| #97122 | LINGERING SHADOWS by Penny Jordan | $5.99 | ☐ |
| | (limited quantities available on certain titles) | | |

	AMOUNT	$
DEDUCT:	10% DISCOUNT FOR 2+ BOOKS	$
	POSTAGE & HANDLING	$
	($1.00 for one book, 50¢ for each additional)	
	APPLICABLE TAXES*	$_____
	TOTAL PAYABLE	$_____
	(check or money order—please do not send cash)	

To order, complete this form and send it, along with a check or money order for the total above, payable to Harlequin Books, to: **In the U.S.:** 3010 Walden Avenue, P.O. Box 9047, Buffalo, NY 14269-9047; **In Canada:** P.O. Box 613, Fort Erie, Ontario, L2A 5X3.

Name: _____

Address:_____ City: _____

State/Prov.: _____ Zip/Postal Code: _____

*New York residents remit applicable sales taxes.
 Canadian residents remit applicable GST and provincial taxes..

HBACK-JS